TWISTED
LIES

BOOKS BY ANGELA MARSONS

DETECTIVE KIM STONE SERIES PREQUEL
First Blood

DETECTIVE KIM STONE SERIES
Silent Scream
Evil Games
Lost Girls
Play Dead
Blood Lines
Dead Souls
Broken Bones
Dying Truth
Fatal Promise
Dead Memories
Child's Play
Killing Mind
Deadly Cry

OTHER BOOKS
Dear Mother (previously published as *The Middle Child*)
The Forgotten Woman (previously published as *My Name Is*)

Angela MARSONS

D.I. Kim Stone BOOK FOURTEEN

TWISTED LIES

Bookouture

Published by Bookouture in 2021

An imprint of Storyfire Ltd.
Carmelite House
50 Victoria Embankment
London EC4Y 0DZ

www.bookouture.com

ISBN: 978-1-83888-735-3
eBook ISBN: 978-1-83888-734-6

This book is dedicated to Norman Forrest who continues to amaze us every day with his energy, spirit and zest for life, who never lets life or loss get the best of him.

PROLOGUE

She sits in a room that is nothing more than a magnolia-coloured square box without windows. A small arc of spotty damp is forming in the corner to the left of the door.

The single metal chair digs into the back of her thighs. It is not built for comfort. The steel table is a simple square with smear marks wiped across it. She looks around, although there is nothing more to see, and her heart races even though she knows she's done nothing wrong.

How long will she be here? Who will open the locked door and come to get her?

Despite the assurances she gives herself that she is safe, her hands knit together in her lap and begin squeezing each other to release the tension building there.

Her stomach lurches as she hears footsteps and then a key in the lock. She is apprehensive but eager to know what comes next.

Two men enter the room dressed in jeans and polo shirts. She has not seen either of them before. They don't lock the door. Does that mean they are finally taking her from this room?

She looks from one to the other but doesn't speak.

Her hands are squeezing the life out of each other beneath the table.

One man approaches while the other stays close to the door. He leans against the wall and folds his arms. Is he guarding the door in case she tries to run?

'Give me your phone,' says the man who has approached the table.

Unwittingly her left leg has developed a very slight tremble.

'Is th-that really necessary?' she asks as the quiver from her leg works its way up to her tongue.

She sees the hint of a smile which he quickly hides behind his emotionless face.

He is pleased she is nervous.

He holds out his hand in response to the question.

The man at the door yawns. He is either tired or bored. How many times has he done this before?

She reaches into her back pocket and takes out her phone. She hesitates as though she is handing over a part of herself.

That one device contains many things she needs to live: contacts; photos; social media; appointments; reminders.

'Will I get it back?' she asks, trying to force confidence into her tone.

He takes the phone from her hand, removes the SIM card and tosses the phone to his colleague, who catches it.

They have done this before. They are following a script.

The man in front of her throws the SIM card to the ground and uses the heel of his shoe to grind it against the floor. Metal and plastic split open against concrete.

Her gasp is audible as she considers what he has just destroyed.

He lays his hands palm down on the table and brings his face closer to hers.

'It's time for you to understand that your life as you knew it is gone.'

CHAPTER ONE

'Sir, are you kidding me?' Kim asked, looking for any trace of humour in his expression.

The response in her head had been: *Have you been smoking crystal meth?*, and she was momentarily relieved that her mouth had translated that thought to a more suitable response to offer to her boss, DCI Woodward.

The relief didn't last long, as she found no hint of amusement anywhere on his face.

'No, I'm not kidding, Stone,' he responded.

Kim was tempted to make use of the seat he sometimes offered but she rarely took, but his last statement to her warranted it on this occasion.

She forced herself to remain standing. Her last hope was that she'd misheard.

'Surely this is some kind of joke, because I'd swear you just said you'd sanctioned Tracy Frost spending a day with us, which obviously would mean you'd gone and lost your—'

'We owe her, Stone,' he said, cutting her off just in time.

Yes, she knew that. Only a couple of weeks ago, the reporter for the *Dudley Star* had helped them make contact with a killer who had kidnapped a six-year-old boy. She understood that some kind of thanks was in order.

'Fine, I'll buy the woman a coffee, take her for lunch. You could send flowers, but allowing her unrestricted access to us for an entire day is nothing short o—'

'It's not unrestricted. She is to remain with you and Bryant at all times.'

'Yeah, that helps,' Kim said as he destroyed the cunning plan of sitting her beside Stacey while she filed police statements.

'Stone, do I need to remind you that because of her co-operation a little boy's life was spared?'

Kim tried to quell the irritation that formed in her stomach.

'To be fair, sir, I think we had a little something to do with that too.'

'It's our job; it isn't hers.'

Good point but she wasn't done yet.

'But just imagine the article she could write. It could seriously damage the image and reputation of th—'

'Stone, she can only write what she sees, so I have total trust in you to demonstrate that we are driven, compassionate and professional.'

'You do?' Kim asked, surprised. Maybe she should send Frost out with Bryant alone.

'And I've arranged with her editor to see any article before it's published.'

Of course he had. She should have known he wouldn't allow Frost total control over what got printed; in gaining that control, he had removed her last argument.

She glanced at the stress ball that sat to the side of his mouse mat. He still used it in her presence sometimes, but not as often as he used to.

'Take it,' he said, following her gaze. 'It's going to be an interesting day.'

'Why did you choose... oh, hang on, I know your game.'

'I have no game,' he said, feigning ignorance. 'It's a slow day. You have no major case on right now, so it works well for everyone.'

The bitter taste in her mouth was still hard to swallow, but it wasn't choking her quite as much.

Her first visit of the day was to the family of Trisha Morley, a 27-year-old woman murdered by her husband just over a year earlier.

Nick Morley was a barrister who fought human rights cases and won almost every case he touched, earning him the nickname of Nick Midas. Building a case against the enigmatic man had been difficult enough, despite finding body parts of Trisha on his property.

So impeccable was his image that, despite the forensic evidence, the trial had ended in a hung jury and a mistrial had been declared.

His new trial was due to begin the following week, and Kim wanted to assure the family they were confident of getting a conviction. And she wished that were true.

The man himself had employed an expensive PR firm, and barely a day went by without some kind of article appearing in the tabloids about his generosity and good work. They were peddling the public perception train for all it was worth, and although it shouldn't make a difference, it did.

Neither the police force nor the family of Trisha Morley had the means to compete, but a mention of the victim's suffering and that of her family in the local news wouldn't hurt either, she realised, glancing at the wily old fox whose expression revealed nothing. He had certainly chosen his day well.

'Okay, have it your own way, but I'm not going to be nice to her and she's not getting to sit up front.'

She headed towards the door and then turned back.

She reached over and grabbed the stress ball.

'And you can bet your ass I'm gonna need this.'

CHAPTER TWO

'We're doing what?' Bryant asked as she shared the good news back in the squad room.

'Taking a reporter for a day trip.'

'But why that particular reporter?' he asked of Tracy Frost.

'Because we owe her apparently.'

He thought for a second and then nodded either his understanding or his agreement.

Oh, there were times she wished she could be a bit more like Bryant. Her level-headed and pragmatic partner had the ability to adjust to a new situation quickly, but inside she was still seething from having Tracy Frost foisted upon them.

'And I caught that look,' she said to the other two members of her team.

Both DC Stacey Wood and DS Penn knew of the thorny relationship between herself and the reporter.

'Not sure what you're looking so smug about; you two are taking her for lunch.'

If they made it as far as lunchtime without her murdering the woman, she was pretty sure both she and Bryant would need the break.

'No probs, boss,' Stacey said, offering the bright smile that had been glued to her face since her recent nuptials.

Kim got the feeling she could throw anything at Stacey right now and it would bounce right off her. The thought reminded her of the long overdue conversation she'd been meaning to have.

'Stace, remind me later, once we get rid of Frost, that you and I need to have a quick chat.'

A soft cloud crossed the bright horizon of the officer's expression.

'Nothing wrong,' she quickly reassured her colleague. Despite her growing ability and self-confidence over the years, Stacey still worried that she'd made some kind of mistake.

'Okay, Bryant, we're up,' Kim said as a movement out the window caught her eye. Frost's white Audi TT had just pulled into a visitor's parking space.

'Already looking forward to it,' he said, grabbing his coat from the back of his chair.

She grabbed hers as they passed the spare desk.

'So how are you going to convince this family that we're going to get a conviction this time?' her colleague asked as they headed down the stairs.

'I'll let you know when the words come out my mouth,' she answered honestly.

'Even my missus said it was difficult to believe he'd done it after reading one of the latest articles.'

'Then we'd best be glad your missus isn't on the jury next week.'

But that was the problem. Jenny Bryant was one of the most objective and decent people Kim had ever come across. If even she doubted his guilt, it did not bode well for the forthcoming trial.

One problem at a time, she resolved, stepping out of the front door of the station.

Frost hastily threw a half-smoked cigarette to the ground and stamped on it, right beside the 'No Smoking' sign.

'Hey, Inspector, thought you'd keep me waiting longer than this,' Frost said, straightening her navy trouser suit.

Yeah, ten to fifteen years if it had been up to me, Kim thought.

'Frost, you should know right off the bat that—'

'You disagree with this, that I'm to do whatever you say and not get in your way at any point.'

'Yeah, there's more. Don't look at people, don't engage them, don't scribble noisily in your little notebook. Don't eat or drink in Bryant's car. Don't annoy m—'

'So, basically, pretend I'm not even here.'

'Exactly, and I have only one more rule, which is that you're not allowed to speak, at all, ever,' Kim said, Frost teetering behind them as they headed towards Bryant's Astra Estate.

'Yeah, that's not gonna happen.'

'Worth a shot,' Kim said to Bryant across the car roof as he opened the driver's door.

Frost's four-inch stiletto heel caught between two paving slabs as she eased herself into the back seat.

'Frost, why the hell do you…? Oh never mind,' she said, closing her own door.

The question died in her mouth when she remembered that Frost had one leg shorter than the other, something for which she knew Frost had been mercilessly bullied at school. Now people thought her unnatural gait was due to the high heels she wore. And that was her intention.

Frost shimmied to the centre of the back seat so she could see through the middle of them.

A high-pitched squeak sounded from behind.

'What the…?'

'Dog's toy,' Bryant answered. 'Just toss it on the floor,' he advised Frost before looking Kim's way and shrugging. 'I didn't know we were gonna have company.'

Kim sighed heavily. It was going to be a long bloody day.

'Reminds me of one of the *Lethal Weapon* films,' Frost said with humour in her voice. 'I just need to know if I'm Riggs or Murtaugh.'

'Joe Pesci,' Kim and Bryant said together.

'Oh, proper little double act, eh?' Frost said, snapping her seat belt into place.

Bryant started the car and pulled off towards the car park exit.

'May as well get down to business,' Frost said, rummaging in her Hermès bag. 'I'm going to nee—'

'Bryant,' Kim said, turning to her colleague. 'Did you just hear Frost try to tell us how this was going to work?'

She didn't bother to wait for his answer before half turning in her seat.

'Right, Frost, what you need is of little— actually, it's of no importance to us. We are under instruction to let you tag along for no more than eight hours, excluding lunch and coffee breaks, so let's call it six cos I'm feeling generous today, during which time you are to be all three wise monkeys and you shall see, hear and speak no evil. The last will be a challenge for you, but suck it up, buttercup. If for one minute you obstruct, interfere or impede anything we do, I'll happily fly-tip you out of this vehicle and leave you on the side of the road. If you say one thing that annoys, irritates—'

'Yeah, bored of the rules speech now, Stone. Just tell me where we're going first.'

Kim took the stress ball from her pocket and gave it a quick squeeze.

Having to answer any question posed by Frost was galling to her. On a normal day she had the luxury of insulting the woman and walking away.

Sensing her annoyance, Bryant offered a response.

'We're going to see the family of Trisha Morley.'

'The wife of Nick Morley whose retrial starts next week?'

'That's the one.'

'Why?' Frost asked.

Kim squeezed the ball again.

'Because we want to assure the family that we're doing everything we can to secure a conviction for the murder of Trisha.'

'Yeah, I get that given the press coverage. They must be expecting him to get a sainthood instead of a prison sentence, considering his propaganda campaign. But why you? It wasn't your case.'

'There are reasons,' Kim said.

'Which are?' she pushed.

'None of your business.'

'Okay,' Frost said as she started scribbling in her notebook.

The action made Kim nervous. They had given her nothing.

Kim turned in her chair and glared. 'What are you writing?'

Frost met her gaze. 'Look, by the end of the day I'm gonna be writing an article. Strangely, my editor expects it, and if you're not going to share anything with me, I'm going to have to make shit up.'

Kim felt the growl begin to form in her throat, but she pushed it back down.

'Okay, the family doesn't have a great deal of faith in the Brierley Hill team, but you can't use that.'

'Why have they got no faith? Is it because, despite all the evidence, the team failed to get a conviction the first time?'

Kim stole a glance at Bryant. 'You'd have to ask them that.'

Yes, that was exactly the reason, but Kim wasn't going to confirm it. The whole case around Trisha Morley had been a fiasco from start to finish, and Kim was glad her team had played no part in it. Her attendance was a favour to Brierley Hill and the press comms team. Trisha's sister had been vocal about their shortcomings.

Suddenly Frost laughed out loud. 'Ha, Detective Inspector Stone being sent on a PR exercise. Jesus, I could run with that angle alone for at least a week.'

Kim watched her knuckles turn white around the stress ball, and a muscle was jumping in Bryant's jawline.

He glanced her way and a silent conversation took place.

Kim: *Have we got this all day?*

Bryant: *Pretty much.*

Kim: *Permission to kill her?*

Bryant: *Not yet but maybe later.*

Kim stared forward and stifled her irritation at the woman's presence and knew that her colleague was trying to do the same thing.

'Okay, so what's th—?'

'Frost, shut the fuck up,' the two of them said together.

CHAPTER THREE

Bryant pulled up at the modest childhood home of Trisha Morley. Kim continued to consider the notion of herself being sent on a PR exercise; for once she was able to understand Frost's mirth.

'It's a long way from Romsley,' Frost observed, echoing all their thoughts.

They all knew the house Trisha had shared with her husband on St Kenelms Road, in the wealthiest part of Halesowen, was a property in the one million pounds plus bracket.

Just as they all knew that money had come from Nick Morley alone.

Trisha's life had jumped from one end to the other of the lifestyle spectrum. The house they now stood before was a deteriorating mid-terrace in a street about a quarter mile from Dudley Castle.

The door of which was opened by a woman Kim guessed to be Trisha's older sister.

'Penny Colgan?' Kim asked, extending her arm.

Penny nodded and shook it briefly before looking to the others.

'My colleague, DS Bryant and Tracy Frost from the *Dudley*—'

'She's not coming in.'

Kim was tempted to agree with her, but for once felt obliged to defend the woman, not least because she knew what Woody was hoping to achieve by Frost being in on the meeting.

'She's here for us not you. To my knowledge, she hasn't written anything positive about Nick Morley.'

Frost shook her head in agreement. 'I haven't.'

Penny hesitated then stepped aside for them to enter.

'Mum's getting ready to go out,' Penny said, closing the door behind them.

'How is she?' Kim asked as the three of them tried to navigate the small room littered with toys.

'Sorry,' Penny said, grabbing everything she could and throwing it into a corner. She lowered herself to the floor as the three of them took a seat on the L-shaped sofa.

It was Kim's understanding that Penny had given up her one-bed council flat to move back in with her mother when Trisha had first gone missing. Trisha and Penny's father had died not long after Trisha had married Morley.

'Will she be attending the new trial?'

'No,' Penny said. 'We can't sit through that again. It almost destroyed her the first time,' she said, raising her eyes to the floorboards above that seemed to creak on cue. 'She's found some kind of routine that helps her get through the day. She plays with Riley; goes to the park most mornings; fusses over me… and God forbid the jury reaches—'

Penny stopped speaking as her mother came into the room.

'Oh… hello…'

Kim stood. 'Mrs Colgan, we're—'

'Police officers, yes, I can tell that,' she said, although her gaze lingered on Frost.

'She's not important,' Kim said, not realising how those words were going to sound outside of her head.

Laura Colgan shrugged, as though none of it was important, as she reached for her jacket.

'Mrs Colgan, may we just trouble you for a few minutes?'

Laura shook her head. 'I'm sorry but no,' she said, circling a scarf around her neck. 'There's nothing you can say that will help me. I have to go.'

Kim could think of no reason to try and persuade her to stay when she really didn't want to.

'I'm sorry,' Penny said as her mother left the house. 'But she doesn't have trust in any of you people anymore. She's getting ready for the bastard to walk free in a few days, and there's nothing we as a family can do about it.'

Kim caught the unsaid implication that other people could have done more.

'We have every confidence that—'

'Please,' Penny said, holding up her hand. 'Don't make assurances that you're powerless to keep. No one can predict what the jury is going to do. I just wish they could have known her,' Penny said. 'I wish you could all have known her. She's been reduced to a statistic, a domestic violence victim, a poster child for every do-gooder to wave as an example of what might happen if you don't get out of an abusive relationship. Everyone speaks of the shell she became, but there was so much more to her than the punch bag he turned her into.'

Kim said nothing as the woman glanced at the photo of the two of them hanging over the fireplace.

'Look at her,' Penny said. 'She was beautiful, alive, vital.'

Kim had no argument. It was a posed photograph of the two of them, with Trisha probably late teens.

The similarity between the two of them was obvious, but it was as though the gods had taken more time arranging the features on Trisha's face. The lips were slightly fuller, the blue eyes slightly brighter and the cheekbones just a little higher. Subtle differences that made a great impact.

'No one cares that she hated spicy foods or that she always insisted on putting vinegar on chips before the salt, insisting that it made more chemical sense.'

Kim was happy to listen, as she had no idea what more she could do for this family. She had come to reassure them, but they didn't want to hear that. It was as though they had resigned themselves to the worst possible outcome, and some part of her wondered if she was doing them some kind of disservice in trying to change their minds, when they were absolutely right that she could not guarantee a conviction. She only wished she could.

'Okay, Ms Colgan, we'll intrude no more,' Kim said, rising. 'But if there's anything you need, give us a call.' She handed the woman a card from her jacket pocket and headed for the front door.

Frost scrabbled her belongings together and offered a condolence before the front door was closed behind them.

'Well, that was a waste of time, wasn't it?' Frost huffed as she waited for Bryant to unlock the car doors.

'Told you already, Frost, you're not getting any major headlines from us today.'

'Yeah, it's hardly front-page news that your perception skills in there were not the best…'

'What the hell are you talking about?' Kim snapped, reaching for the stress ball. 'You saw for yourself how they were both feeling. There was nothing more we could do to help.'

'Yes there was, but you just didn't see it. Penny Colgan just wanted to talk about her sister. She wanted you to know and for herself to remember the person Trisha had been. She wanted you to know the woman and not the victim.'

Bryant said nothing, which told her he agreed with Frost. Her exit had been prompted by the thought they were forcing themselves into other people's grief and that it was not a positive experience having them there.

'You're talking shit, Frost,' Kim said, not sure what else to offer.

'I swear, Stone, sometimes your witty repartee—'

Frost stopped speaking as Kim's phone rang.

Oh shit, not now, Keats, she thought, seeing his name on the screen.

She opened the door and got back out of the car.

'Stone,' she answered.

'Hayes T-Trading Estate, Lye,' he said and ended the call.

She stared at the phone, dumbfounded. Not because of the pathologist's lack of greeting, or his abrupt instruction, or his summoning of her presence to a location. All of those things she was completely used to.

What she'd never encountered before was the tremble she'd just heard in his voice.

CHAPTER FOUR

Kim said nothing of the call as she got back into the car.

'Hayes Lane, Lye,' she instructed her colleague while putting on her seat belt.

She'd already worked out that they would be wasting valuable time taking Frost back to the station, where her car was parked, and she could hardly do what she'd threatened and dump her on the side of the road, not in those bloody heels. And Keats's voice had contained an element she'd never heard before. What the hell was she going to find?

'So what's that famous gut of yours saying, Stone?' Frost asked, cutting into her thoughts.

For a split second, she thought Frost was talking about what they were heading towards. She shook herself back to where they'd just been.

She opened her mouth to say something and then remembered whose question she was answering.

'I believe in our justice system to—'

'Fuck me, Stone. I don't even have my notepad out. That was just me asking you a question. One time, just one time, I'd like to have a normal conversation with you.'

'Well, when you retire, give me a call and—'

She stopped speaking as she caught Bryant's subtle sideways glance.

She understood the message, and maybe he was right.

'Okay, my gut isn't as confident as I'd like it to be that we're going to secure a conviction,' Kim admitted. 'And that stays in this car.'

'Hardly profound, was it? Trust me, that's not a headline that's gonna sell newspapers. So why the doubts?'

Kim stared forward. No way was she answering that one.

After a few seconds, Frost groaned. 'Bloody hell, Stone, you have some serious trust issues. Okay, I'm concerned too and I'm happy to tell you why.'

'Please do,' Kim said, wishing Bryant could travel to Keats as the crow flies to get them there quicker.

'Okay, the cynic in me wonders what will be different this time around. In fact, I think the CPS faces even more of a challenge on their second crack at it.'

'Go on,' Kim said. Frost hadn't yet said anything she disagreed with.

'Well, Nick Morley did nothing prior to his first trial. Arrogant bastard thought he was literally gonna get away with murder. And he almost did because of the jury's perception of him. In the time since, he's made the most of his image, exploiting the very thing that caused the hung jury in the first place. He's been hard at work, but there's no new evidence, so I feel the scales have tipped even further in Morley's favour.'

And there it was, the reason Kim wasn't wholly convinced of the outcome.

'Where the hell are we going anyway?' Frost asked as Bryant turned the car into the trading estate.

At the top of the estate was a single road that ran straight through, with side roads branching off. There was no activity at the top of the site, so Bryant drove slowly, both of them looking left and right around dilapidated signs listing the names of businesses, many of which were no longer there. There was a time that the small town of Lye had been a thriving hub of small businesses and local shops, but each recession had beaten it down bit by bit and sole traders had been forced to close.

'Didn't know this road went this far down,' Kim observed as the other units began to ebb away.

'There,' she said as Bryant followed a slight bend that took them out of sight of the rest of the trading units.

Keats's van was sandwiched between two squad cars at the entrance to what had once been a lawnmower wholesale warehouse. The property was approximately the size of two football pitches and lay a quarter of a mile away from its closest neighbour.

'Are we going to a crime scene?' Frost asked excitedly.

'We are. You're not,' Kim said. 'Park here, Bryant,' she instructed, wanting to keep as much physical distance between the reporter and something that didn't concern her as possible.

Kim turned in her seat. 'Frost, you stay in this car. I mean it. You dare not move or so help me I'll—'

'Okay, okay, keep your bloody hair on. Jesus, you are one uptight—'

Kim got out of the vehicle before she heard the rest, and Bryant followed.

'Can't you lock her in?' Kim asked as they moved away.

'Thing is, guv, even dogs have to have a window left open.'

She didn't have time to argue with him as she passed two constables, looking a bit green, standing either side of a middle-aged man who stank of vomit.

'Here, guv,' Bryant said, handing her a pair of protective slippers. She put them on and headed through the roller shutter door, the view of which had been obscured by the vehicles.

Her feet stopped moving as her eyes took in the scene before her.

'What the fucking hell is this?' were the only words that came out of her mouth.

CHAPTER FIVE

Kim tried to make sense of the image that greeted her.

A man of indeterminate age had been cuffed by his hands and feet to a roller cage, similar to ones used by stores to transport supplies around the business. The man was naked. His arms and legs had been spread so that he formed a grotesque star shape.

Every inch of his skin that she could see was burned and blistered with raised white sores, varying from the size of a fingernail to a golf ball. There were areas where the blisters had burst, revealing angry red skin beneath.

She forced herself to look away from the horrific scene to where Keats was standing.

Three metal burning bins stood in a triangle, their exterior coloured brown from the intense heat they'd contained. The lids had been placed on the bins so that the smoke would have come out in funnels, slowing its exit from the bin.

Kim looked around the vast space and wondered how long it would have taken to fill with smoke.

She opened her mouth and closed it again.

'Yes, speechless,' Keats observed. 'Which is a first for me and even rarer for you, I should imagine, Inspector.'

Kim ignored the jab, pleased to see that his voice had returned to normal.

She took another good look around the space, which was empty, except for the incongruous sight right before her eyes and a single metal chair twenty feet away.

'What the hell went on here?'

'This man was slowly and horrifically tortured,' Keats stated.

'No shit, Keats?'

Yes, she'd worked that out for herself.

'Guv, shall I?' Bryant asked, nodding towards the entrance.

He didn't wait for a reply before heading out to the guy sitting on the ground. She didn't blame him. If she could have left she would have.

Most crime scenes stayed in the memory of police officers. Some were closer to the forefront of the conscious mind and were harder to file away. She knew many officers who had turned to alcohol or drugs to numb the horror and offer some respite to the images they'd seen. But there were some crime scenes you knew would remain with you until the day you died, no matter what you used to try and erase it. And this was most definitely one of those.

She took a slow walk around the body that was tied to the steel cage with four sets of handcuffs. One on each wrist and one on each ankle, spreading his body as wide and open as it could be spread.

The stench of the charred flesh had hit her the second she'd entered the property. As she'd stepped into the warehouse, the acrid smell had mixed with the lingering aroma of smoke and the dirty, ashy waft from the bins.

Every inch of the visible flesh was flame red or blistering. His hair remained remarkably intact. Kim remembered reading somewhere that hair didn't undergo physical change until it was subjected to radiated heat in excess of 240 degrees Celsius.

'May I?' Kim asked, pointing to the cage.

Keats handed her a pair of latex gloves.

She pushed gently on the roller cage.

'Jesus,' she said, realising how easy it was to push around, even with the dead weight of an average-sized male on board.

It was obvious that the man had been cuffed to the cage for ease of movement and to continually turn his flesh towards the heat. The three bins had remained in place, and the victim had been turned and wheeled around it.

Even more offensive to her was the chair. The bastard responsible had taken the trouble to bring a chair and watch the spectacle, as though sitting beside a barbecue waiting for the steak to cook.

'Sick, absolutely sick,' she breathed, walking around the immediate area again.

'Want some?' Keats said, offering her the Vicks menthol VapoRub to dab beneath her nose.

'You not been showering again?' she asked, waving him away. She didn't want any respite from the stench. It was a characteristic of the crime scene that she would take away with her. It helped form the complete picture and reminded her of what had taken place here. It also kept fresh in her mind the type of person she was now looking for.

'Some kind of psychopath?' Keats asked, reading her thoughts.

'Has to be,' she agreed. 'No person with an ounce of feeling could do this.'

'You'd come close,' he chimed, paying her back for the shower comment.

'Especially if it was you up there,' she responded as Bryant returned and came to stand beside her.

'Yeah, it really is as bad as I thought it was,' he said, casting a quick glance at the victim, as though his moments away had altered the scene. 'Seamus O'Halloran,' he continued, speaking of the guy sitting on the floor outside. 'Scottish guy. Okay, just kidding, Irish guy, been here for seventeen years. Thought our shop doorways would be better than the ones in Belfast, happened upon the body as he was taking a shortcut through the trading estate to get to Cradley Heath.'

'But what made him…? Oh, no, don't say it,' she said, holding back a groan.

Bryant nodded. 'Sorry, guv, he came in here because he thought something smelled good.'

The groan escaped, and Kim wondered if this poor fellow in the roller cage could have any more indignities heaped upon him.

'Thanks, Bryant. So, Keats, how long are we talking?'

'I'm going to say around twelve hours, but I'll know more once I get him home.'

She turned to walk away and realised her mistake. She turned to the pathologist. 'Is there anything else I should know?'

'Well, his name and address, I should think.'

Kim sighed loudly. She had assumed, as there were no clothes, that all his personal possessions were gone.

She held out her hand.

He took an evidence bag from his pocket and held it towards her.

She took out her phone and snapped a photo of the driving licence.

His name was Keith Phipps, and he was thirty-eight years old. The photo on the driving licence bore little resemblance to the scorched face hanging down in front of her.

She handed it back. 'Keats, I swear—'

Kim stopped speaking as a loud female scream filled the building, followed by a loud thud.

Oh no, she thought, running for the entrance. She had forgotten one little thing.

Tracy fucking Frost.

CHAPTER SIX

'You sure you're gonna be okay?' Kim asked the reporter as they pulled into the car park at Halesowen station. The journey from the warehouse had been made in silence.

Her initial rage at the woman for defying her instructions back at the crime scene had dissolved when she'd looked down at the heap on the ground. All colour had left her face in the seconds before she'd passed out.

The two PCs she'd slipped past had helped her to a seating position against the wall of the warehouse, and she'd opened her eyes to Kim towering over her with her arms folded. Confusion had creased her features until her brain had re-presented her with what she'd seen. It was at that point she'd turned to the side and vomited.

Bryant, ever the gentleman, had produced a handkerchief and told her to keep it.

'You couldn't possibly imagine that I asked you to stay in the car for your own good?' Kim had asked, once Frost had wiped her mouth.

'No,' Frost had answered with certainty.

'So you know we've gotta cut you loose now?' Kim asked, turning in her seat.

'Oh yeah. Got it,' Frost answered, and Kim would swear she heard a hint of relief in her voice.

'And you know that what you saw is off—'

'Stone, to write about it would mean remembering it, and I'm going to be trying to get that picture out of my head as soon as I can.'

The hint of colour she'd regained appeared to be ebbing away at the very thought.

'You gonna be okay?' Kim asked again, feeling a bit guilty for the wan expression still on the reporter's face.

'Yeah, I'm fine. Thanks, guys. It's been a blast,' she said, getting out of the car.

Kim watched her hobble to the Audi, with her oversize bag slung over her shoulder. The woman had offered no argument when Kim had explained they had no choice but to cut her loose.

She'd expected more resistance, had anticipated Frost trying to force herself into an active murder investigation, but she'd had the feeling that Frost's mind had already been elsewhere.

Kim got out the car and headed towards the station.

Tracy Frost was no longer important.

Kim had a psychopath to find.

CHAPTER SEVEN

Frost took a few deep breaths once she was in the safety of her own space. It wasn't the first time her body had betrayed her, and she cursed it for doing so.

She had been following her natural instinct of needing to know everything when she'd got out of the car. How many reporters got to steal a front-row seat to a fresh, juicy crime scene? The opportunity had been too good to miss. What she'd expected to see was a figure lying on the ground, mainly obscured by people. She'd been anticipating a glimpse of an item of clothing or a hair colour, maybe a fatal injury like a single stab wound. She hadn't been expecting to see a naked man pinned to a roller cage with most of the flesh burned from his body.

As the stars had appeared before her eyes, Frost had seen DI Stone standing close to the body, studying it, analysing it, viewing it as some kind of clue. How the hell did she do that?

Yes, the sight had been horrific, but her own reaction to it had surprised her. She'd always visualised police officers attending crime scenes and viewing bodies objectively from the outset, much the way she'd view a plate of scones before deciding which one to choose. She had assumed there was no emotional reaction from them at all, just part of the job. But how did one even prepare for a sight like that? How could you be mentally ready to absorb and process such a scene?

She took out her notebook and began to jot down thoughts. She knew Stone had been surprised that she hadn't asked more questions about the murder or the victim, but quite frankly she didn't want to ask anything that was going to keep that picture in her mind. As juicy as it was, Fitz was going to have to pass this one along to someone else.

She couldn't write a story about what she'd seen, but other thoughts about the morning were whizzing around her head. Police officers rarely knew exactly what they were turning up to at a crime scene. They had no clue of the horror that awaited them. How did one train for that? But what if they got too emotional? What if they were overwhelmed by the sight and couldn't function? Though what did it say about them as individuals if they could?

When Stone had finally returned to the car, she had been distant and closed. For years Frost had thought the woman owned only one expression, but she had come to realise that the scowl had different emotional shades and variations, depending on the situation.

It was no secret that the two of them didn't get on, despite their shared brush with death a couple of years earlier, but she did like to think there was a modicum of respect between them. Frost knew there were times when she'd done little to earn that respect in her current position at the *Dudley Star*.

She had nothing but admiration for the real journalists who hot-footed it to war-torn countries: reporting on life and death situations; putting themselves in harm's way against rebel groups, corrupt or secretive governments, to get the story to the people. Those same people reported on famine and genocide and the plight of refugees, starving and dying children, and she knew they were made of much sterner stuff than she was.

A couple of years ago, she'd been snapped up by an east London daily paper after a high-profile case she'd covered in the Midlands. And she had lasted little more than two months.

At first, she had loved the excitement of being in and around the big city, but it hadn't taken long for her to see the dark side: the drugs; homelessness; poverty behind the bright lights.

The crunch had come when her boss had insisted she do a story about a mother's neglect, which had led to a fifteen-year-old girl overdosing on heroin in Hackney. She'd used every trick in the book to get herself an interview with the woman. Instead of a neglectful mother, she'd found a woman who had taken her eye off the ball for a moment while holding down two jobs, due to a seventy per cent rent increase from her slum landlord. She had wanted to run with that story instead, but her editor had refused and insisted on the neglect angle for the piece.

At that point, they'd agreed that though she was ruthless, she wasn't ruthless enough.

Luckily for her, the editor at the *Dudley Star* had not filled her position and had welcomed her back. She now knew that not only was the grass not always greener on the other side, sometimes it wasn't real grass at all.

She took another deep breath as she started the car.

It had been a very eventful morning and she'd seen something that would stay in her memory for ever, and yet that wasn't the uppermost thought in her head as she reversed out of the space and drove away.

CHAPTER EIGHT

Kim was surprised at the amount of time it had taken Frost to drive away, noted only as she poured coffee from the fresh pot. Perhaps the experience had affected her more than she'd thought. Or she was making notes of what she'd seen in case she forgot. It made no difference. Woody would never let it through, whatever kind of article she chose to write.

'Thanks to whoever,' she said, turning back to her team and raising her mug in the air.

Penn raised a hand in acknowledgment.

Thank goodness. As Stacey drank neither tea nor coffee, her efforts did not yield the best results.

Bryant had quickly briefed the team while she had updated Woody. And during that conversation, despite the news of what she'd been called to, he had still asked if she'd actioned 'the other thing'. He knew full well that she would use a major murder investigation to put it off for just a little bit longer, and he wasn't going to let her get away with it. And she had resolved that she was going to address it in just a few minutes.

'Okay, post-mortem is at three.'

Penn's head shot up expectantly.

Kim nodded. 'It's yours but get ready: it's a grim one.'

'No probs.'

'Penn, yowm a weirdo,' Stacey said, shaking her head.

'What was your first clue?' he asked with a bright smile.

'That you listen to headphones with no sound,' she answered.

'Who says there's no sound?' he asked, crossing his eyes.

'Okay, enough you two,' Kim said. Left to it, the two of them could banter for hours and right now they didn't have those hours to spare.

Their first task was finding out if this was a victim- or killer-led murder. Where was the thread that they would need to grasp by the fingernails and unravel? Would Mitch, the lead techie, find forensic evidence that would lead them to the killer, or would the history of the victim lead to the killer's identity?

'Bryant and I will be heading off to the victim's address shortly, and while we're gone I want you to find me anything you can on our victim, as well as checking any CCTV in the area. This was well set up. The murderer had to have known the spot. It's not a building you'd just happen upon if you were passing by the trading estate. He must have been driving a decent-sized vehicle to transport the bins, roller cage, chair and fuel for the fire.'

Both were making notes as she spoke. She didn't need to be more specific. They would divide the jobs up between themselves.

But before any of that, there was something she could delay no longer.

'Stace, a word,' she said, nodding towards the Bowl.

Carrying her coffee, she stepped in and closed the door behind the detective constable.

'Sit down, Stace.'

'I'm okay, boss, but you're starting to freak me out.'

'You've done nothing wrong. In fact, quite the opposite; now please take a seat,' Kim said, sitting behind the desk. The position felt alien to her, and she felt more at home with her behind parked on the edge of the spare desk in the squad room.

Stacey sat.

'Woody and I have been talking about your performance and h… we feel that you're ready for the next stage in your career.'

'Okay,' she said, clasping her hands together.

'It's time for you to go for the sergeants' exam.'

Stacey looked surprised. 'Okay,' she repeated. 'I mean, if you think I'm ready.'

'You're ready,' Kim said without hesitation. 'You've grown in both confidence and ability, and you've always been mature beyond your years. You'd be an asset to any team.'

'Th... Thanks, boss. I don't really know what to say. I appreciate your faith in me, and I'll give it some—'

'Great. Leave it with me and I'll get the ball rolling, okay?'

'O... Okay, boss, thanks,' Stacey said, rising from the seat.

Kim logged into her computer to start the process.

She had been lucky enough to witness the growth of the constable, but the time had come for change.

CHAPTER NINE

'I know what that was about, you know,' Bryant said, once they were in the car.

'Good work, Sherlock,' she retorted. 'If this chauffeuring thing doesn't work out, you could always try—'

'You do realise that if she makes sergeant, one of us will have to go.'

'And you'd better hope I don't get to choose which one,' she snapped, knowing full well that he was right; but the choice would not be up to her. A team of four wouldn't contain three detective sergeants. The likelihood was that Stacey would be moved on to another team. Not a thought that appealed to her, but the woman had too much potential to be ignored.

'It's the right thing, Bryant,' she said more to herself than anyone.

He paused for a moment and then continued. 'On a lighter note, it was kinda funny that Frost passed out, don't you think?' he asked with a devilish smile.

They had chosen not to share that detail of the crime scene with the rest of the team. Funny as it was, it only served to remind them that Frost wasn't quite as tough as she'd have them believe. It was about the only funny thing at the crime scene, she thought, looking out the window as Bryant continued to drive in silence.

There were many aspects to this murder to consider. The logistics of the crime told her their murderer was organised. He'd scouted a location where he could torture and kill at his leisure. He had planned exactly how he wanted to do it, got all the equipment there and sat and watched. And that was what she kept coming back to. It had to be one of the most horrific crime scenes she'd ever witnessed. What kind of monster were they dealing with and why this victim? There were few crimes that deserved such punishment.

'I think it's just up here,' Bryant said as he turned off the main Halesowen Road onto a side street in Old Hill.

A line of six small, terraced houses backed onto a chip shop and a small fastener supplier.

'Never even knew this was here,' she observed as Bryant pulled into a space at the end of the road.

'Yeah, it is kind of hidden.'

Kim got out of the car still weighing up just how much she was going to share with the family members.

The question of whether a victim suffered came up with most grieving relatives. There were times she could dodge the question and avoid the truth, but there was no way of sugar-coating this one. Eventually they would have to know. Pain upon pain.

'Ready?' Bryant asked before knocking on the front door.

'No, but best do it anyway.'

The door opened before Bryant's arm rested back at his side.

The woman who answered was tall and slim, similar to Kim's own five foot nine height. She wore faded jeans, ankle boots and a sweatshirt. Her hair was a short, sleek, chestnut helmet.

'Mrs Phipps?' Kim asked, and wasn't surprised at the shake of the head.

'I'm her sister, Leanne. Who are you?' she asked without stepping aside.

Both she and Bryant offered their identification. Panic shot into her eyes but still she didn't move.

'Is Mrs Phipps here?' Kim asked.

'She is but what's this about?'

Kim had patience for a grieving family, but it wasn't an endless supply. Especially for people who were delaying her efforts to do her job.

'It concerns her husband, but I'd rather speak to Mrs Phipps.'

The woman seemed to consider this as though it was her decision to make.

Kim moved forward. 'If we could just—'

'Okay, you'd best come in,' she said, stepping aside.

It was only when she stepped into the small reception room that Kim realised the heavy velour curtains were partially closed, leaving only a gap for a head to look out.

'Migraine,' Leanne explained, opening them.

Kim wasn't sure if she meant herself or her sister.

'Hey, Leanne, do you…?'

'Police officers, Diane,' Leanne said, cutting her off.

The woman entering the room was petite and fair, unlike her sister. Her light skin was without make-up and appeared blotchy in places.

'Mrs Phipps, would you mind sitting down? I'm afraid we have some bad news about your husband.'

Diane looked to her sister and sat.

Before she spoke, Kim's gaze passed over a photograph on the mantelpiece. Two pre-teen boys, probably a couple of years difference in age, dressed proudly in school uniform. Her heart sank even further into her stomach.

'Mrs Phipps, I'm afraid there's been an incident involving your husband.'

Leanne moved to sit beside her sister. She didn't clutch the woman's hand, as Kim would have expected, but instead lay a hand on Diane's forearm.

Fear shone from Diane's eyes, and Kim would have loved to reassure her that she had not come to bear the worst possible news.

'I'm afraid to say that your husband is dead.'

Diane opened her mouth, but it was Leanne who spoke.

'Are you sure it's him?'

Diane waited hopefully for the answer.

'We're certain,' Kim said. Despite the burns to his face, he had still been recognisable as the man on the driving licence.

'Was it some kind of accident?' Diane asked as her brain tried to compute the news. Kim hid her surprise that the question on the manner of death had come so quickly.

Kim shook her head. 'Your husband was murdered.'

Diane's eyes went immediately to the photo on the fireplace. 'Oh God. Oh no, what about—?'

'Will the body need to be identified?' Leanne asked, cutting her off and showing no emotion at all.

'Yes, but it can wait for—'

'I think the sooner the better, don't you?' Leanne said, standing.

Kim noticed a red mark on Diane's forearm where Leanne's hand had been.

Kim frowned and made no move to leave.

'Given the circumstances, we'd prefer to ask your sister some questions before we get to that,' Kim said, looking pointedly at the woman who had just had her life destroyed. 'Mrs Phipps, when did you last see your husband?'

Kim needed to establish a timeline.

'Two days ago,' she answered.

Although everyone expressed their grief differently, Kim was surprised that Diane Phipps hadn't yet cried. It was as though her own emotional reaction had been shelved in favour of something else. How she was going to tell those boys might be at the forefront of her mind, Kim reasoned.

'It was Saturday morning. He left to get a paper like he did every Saturday. After an hour, I called him but his phone went to voicemail. I tried again later, but the same thing happened.'

'So what did you do?' Kim asked as her gut began to react.

'I called my sister, and she came to stay with me.'

'Did you call his friends, colleagues, places he liked to go?'

Diane shook her head. 'He's a loner. He doesn't really have friends. He works in construction, for J. Norris and Sons, but he doesn't really mix with any of the others.'

'Did you report him missing?' Kim asked, trying to accept the story at face value.

'It's not the first time,' Leanne interjected as Diane shook her head. 'Now and again he goes on a bender, disappears for a few days, comes back like nothing ever happened.'

'He had a drinking problem?'

'He wasn't an alcoholic,' Diane defended quickly.

'Just needed to blow off steam a bit probably, which is why Diane didn't call the police. She didn't want to waste anyone's time. She expected him to walk back through the door at any minute.'

Kim appreciated Leanne's response, but she would have preferred his wife to be answering the questions. She again turned her attention to the woman most affected by the news. 'Mrs Phipps, can you think of anyone who would want to hurt your husband?'

'Definitely not. No. He was a kind man. He didn't mix with many people,' she said, shifting in her seat.

'Could he have upset anyone on one of his benders?'

A drunken brawl would hardly have been a motive for what he'd suffered, but Kim desperately needed some kind of foothold on the type of person Keith Phipps had been.

'No, I don't think so. He wasn't that kind of drunk. He wasn't aggressive or confrontational. He was gentle and… Oh my God, how am I going to tell our boys?'

Again, Leanne stood. 'I think that's enough for now. She needs to get her head around all this before you ask her any more questions. I'd like to assist with identifying the body, and I think it needs to be done immediately so that Diane can accept that he's gone.'

Kim really felt like telling the woman to stay in her lane but wondered if she might find out more if Leanne was away from her sister, maybe details of the couple's marriage.

'Okay, I'll make a call on the way to the hospital. Do you want to come—?'

'I'll take my own car,' she said, taking her keys from the windowsill. She turned to Diane. 'I'll pick the boys up from school on the way back.'

'Mrs Phipps, we are so sorry for your loss,' Bryant offered quietly as Leanne held open the front door for them to pass.

At the last second, Leanne turned back into the room and said something that Kim didn't catch, followed by something that sounded like 'and make sure you lock the door'.

CHAPTER TEN

'What the hell was that in there?' Bryant asked as soon as they were in the car.

'You felt it too?'

'Is that a serious question? I'm steady not dead. Weirdest dynamic I've ever seen between two sisters. Not one tear shed by either of them, and one of them can't wait to bloody see him. Very weird.'

'I'm wondering if she'll be any less strange alone.' Clearly she wasn't close to her brother-in-law, but Kim was now just as interested in the dynamics of the Phipps' marriage.

'Is that why you agreed to the early identification?' he asked. 'I thought you were going to tell her to jog on with her demands.'

Kim would have done had she not wanted to separate the two women.

'Talking of which, best give Keats the heads-up.'

She pressed his number and tapped her fingernail on the back of the phone until he answered.

'Inspector, I said the post-mortem was—'

'Yeah, Keats, you may need to postpone slightly. We have a family member en route to identify.'

He laughed.

'I'm not joking.'

He stopped laughing. 'Stone, you'd better be.'

'Only time they can make it,' she lied. She could have told Leanne it was impossible to view the body so quickly, but she needed to speak to one of these women alone. There was something here she didn't like the smell of.

'Stone, we've only just removed his body from the roller cage. It's taken a while, as I'm sure you can imagine. We'll be leaving the site shortly, so any time after lunch would—'

'No can do, Keats. We're on our way with the relative, so I suggest you get back to the morgue and I suggest you do it fast.'

CHAPTER ELEVEN

'You all right, Stace?' Penn asked, watching his colleague closely.

They had divided the jobs between them. He had taken CCTV, and Stacey was checking background on Keith Phipps. The boss had told her to research the victim first and then spread out to the wider family; only Stacey didn't seem to be checking a whole lot of anything.

She had slid back into her seat after her meeting with the boss, absolutely beaming from ear to ear. But she hadn't spoken a word since.

'Yeah, I'm fine.'

'Okay, Stace, now I know you're not fine cos every time you've opened your mouth for the last two weeks, it's been to tell me you're now a married woman. I say: "Do you want a drink?" You say: "Of course I do, I'm a married woman." I say: "Can you pass that folder?" You say: "I can't do that cos I'm a married woman."' He frowned. 'You get divorced in the last half an hour?'

'No, I'm still a married woman, but the boss just took the wind out of my sails. She wants me to go for sergeant.'

'And?' he asked. The only person surprised by this news was Stacey herself.

'I dunno, it's…'

'Stace, you're so ready for it, and the boss knows it. You should be a DS.'

'You think?' she asked.

'Stace, in all honesty, I forget you're not. To be fair, it's great that the boss has recognised the fact.'

'Yeah, I'm just a bit stunned I think. But I'm chuffed to bits.'

There was something in her voice that said otherwise.

She turned back to her screen, and he followed suit, receiving her message loud and clear.

She didn't want to talk about it.

CHAPTER TWELVE

Frost pulled up outside the property and switched off the engine.

As a reporter, she shouldn't care all that much about trudging around someone's despair and unhappiness, but she hesitated before approaching the home of Penny Colgan, and she wasn't sure if it was more for herself or the woman inside.

All she knew was that she hadn't wanted to leave earlier. She had wanted to spend more time with Penny, listen to what she had to say. Let her talk about her dead sister.

She put her own feelings aside, got out the car and knocked the door.

Penny opened it and didn't even try to contain her look of surprise.

'I'm not here in any official capacity, Penny. Trisha's story struck a chord with me, and I'd like to hear more about her.'

'Mum's still at the park,' she said, stepping aside.

'I'm sorry we had to rush off,' Frost said, taking a seat.

'It's okay. I know there's nothing any of you can do. We think he's going to get away with it and, despite her assurances, I know that police officer thinks so too.'

'To be fair, they've done as much as they can do against Nick Morley's propaganda machine,' Frost said, feeling a strange need to defend the police on this occasion.

'I know and we're powerless to do anything about it. Somehow this thing has become all about him. I read every single article and Trisha's name barely gets a mention. She's the victim. He systematically broke her down physically and mentally and then murdered her, and right now no one is hearing about how special she was before she met him, or the shit she went through while she was with him.'

'Tell me about her,' Tracy invited.

'Oh God, where to start? She was the reason for the cliché, and she truly did light up a room. I was five when she was born, and from the second her pudgy little hand grabbed my thumb, I was sold. I enjoyed every part of her childhood. She just loved everything. She saw the positive in everything.'

A smile turned up her lips as she remembered something. 'When Trisha was about five or six, our mum was pulling up weeds in the garden. Trisha was horrified, cried, saying they were living things and that Mum was killing them. She gently took out the last weed from between the slabs and put it in a plant pot. She watered that bloody weed until it grew way too big for the pot. She insisted that we take it to the park and plant it so it could grow freely. And that's what we did,' she said, as though she could hardly believe herself what they'd done. 'I'm not sure if that's one of the memories that drives Mum to the park every day. We used to go there a lot.'

'Did she rebel at all?' Tracy asked.

'Nope. She stayed out late one time, saw how it worried Mum and she didn't do it again,' Penny said, glancing at the photo. 'She was beautiful both inside and out.'

'How did she meet Nick Morley?'

'Human League said it best. She really was working as a waitress in a cocktail bar, or more accurately, the casino next to the zoo. She worked there three nights a week to pay for university. She was nineteen; he was ten years older. He asked her for her number, and three weeks later they were inseparable. He tried to get her to leave university, but she wasn't having it. She got her degree, and they were married six months later. None of us were comfortable with the marriage, but though we wanted to support her and stay in her life, it became increasingly hard to do.'

'How so?'

'They moved to the rural part of Romsley, which doesn't sound like miles away, but Trisha hadn't learned to drive. She was out in the middle of nowhere, not a neighbour for miles and one bus daily, which was three miles from her door.'

'Was he controlling before they married?' Frost asked.

'In subtle ways, yes. He offered her advice but didn't push it. If he suggested a different outfit and she refused, he let it pass. He showed his disapproval but didn't force it. She used to laugh about it, only with me. I questioned her, but she said he'd met his match with her and she loved him.'

'And that changed?'

'On the wedding night. He pushed her to the floor because she refused to pick up his suit and fold it. Obviously, she thought he'd had too much to drink, that it was a one-off and she forgave him. Not because he bought her a huge bouquet of flowers the next day, but because she truly believed he was sorry and that it wouldn't happen again.'

Frost felt a shiver run through her. She knew this story as well as if she'd written it herself and, in some ways, she had.

She'd had her own brush with domestic violence nine years earlier. A guy she'd been seeing for a couple of months had pushed her to the ground during a heated argument. He had been apologetic and remorseful afterwards. She had forgiven him but had been ever aware afterwards that he had introduced something new into the relationship. He had introduced fear. Any cross word after that she'd found herself backing down, agreeing with him to prevent an escalation. She'd toned herself down to please him, to avoid a repeat of the violence, until one night she'd exploded and fought back in an argument. Maybe she had wanted to know how far she could push him. Perhaps she'd been trying to force him to go against his promise. And he had. His right fist had met with her jaw. She had ended it that night and threatened him with the police if he ever contacted her again.

Maybe that's why she'd felt compelled to return to Penny to hear more about Trisha. The reason for the shudder was that she could have been the woman they were talking about.

She tuned back in to what Penny was saying.

'… obviously it didn't stop there. The violence got worse and worse. She lied, of course, explained away the injuries by accidents and clumsiness.

'We begged her to go to the police, but the more we got on her, the more she retreated. Seeing the bruises was bad enough, but for the last couple of months it was like she'd changed into a whole other person. Especially after my accident, she stopped—'

'Accident?'

'Yeah, I was rear-ended. Had whiplash, nothing too serious. The guy coughed to it and I was compensated, but it was like she stopped talking to me, stopped sharing because I had problems of my own. But I still saw the weight loss, the nervousness, the light disappearing from her eyes, the anxiety if her phone rang.' Penny blinked back the tears. 'She was missing for seven days before the police investigated, and three more days before they found her remains.'

Frost knew that bones and teeth had been found in an ash pile at the edge of the countryside property.

'I read those articles about him and realise that my sister and her ordeal are becoming less and less of the story, and what makes it worse is that Trisha was warned and still couldn't find the courage to leave him.'

'Warned?'

'Yeah, she was contacted by a woman on Facebook about two years after she and Nick married. She was a previous girlfriend of Nick Morley apparently, told Trisha she was in danger and to get out.'

Something in Tracy switched, as though a button had been pressed. She'd come back here to let Penny talk, following their chat earlier being cut short, but the more she listened, the more she felt the urge to do something.

A feeling that was alien to her was growing stronger with every minute.

She wanted to make a difference. She wanted to help.

She took out her notepad and pen.

'Do you remember the woman's name?'

CHAPTER THIRTEEN

'How much longer?' Leanne asked as they waited to enter the morgue viewing room.

So far, it had been around ten minutes, and the woman had checked her watch a dozen times.

Kim had seen Keats's van pull into the hospital grounds as Bryant had parked the Astra Estate, and knew the pathologist would be working as quickly as possible to prepare the victim for as sensitive an identification as possible. He would work hastily but he wouldn't rush.

Kim had to wonder if his efforts in sensitivity would be in vain anyway. She was starting to think the woman could have viewed her brother-in-law in situ at the crime scene in all his horrific glory and she still wouldn't have allowed any emotion to leak from her pores.

'I'm assuming you weren't close to your brother-in-law?' Kim asked as Leanne paced in front of her for the fifteenth time.

'Not really.'

'Any particular reason?' Kim pushed.

'Not really,' she repeated.

'He wasn't violent to your sister?'

'No, he wasn't that kind of guy.'

'Did he mistreat her in any other way? Did he leave her alone a lot? Did they argue?' *Bloody hell, give me something*, Kim thought.

'No more than anyone else, and no, he didn't mistreat her.'

'The boys?' Kim asked.

'No, he loved his boys,' she answered, pacing back.

She glanced at Bryant, asking a silent question.

He shrugged but got the message.

'So it was a happy marriage?' he asked. The woman wasn't responding to Kim at all.

'Same as most. Had their ups and downs. They weren't rolling in money, so had to stretch what they had.'

'Any issues with extended family?' he asked.

'It was only them… and me,' she added. 'There's no other family.'

Kim found it strange there were no other family members on either side, but Leanne had no reason to lie.

'How old—?'

'You can come in now,' Keats said, opening the door to the viewing room.

Leanne stepped inside, and she and Bryant followed.

Keats left by the door on the opposite wall of the room.

Kim would have liked to ask more questions, but it didn't seem right as they stood in silence awaiting the arrival of the body.

In all honesty, Kim hated this room more than the morgue. Relatives never made it down to the business end of the department, but this clinical, uninviting room was the place they finally had to accept that a loved one was dead.

Maybe that would inject some emotion into the woman standing between her and Bryant, she thought, as Keats's assistant opened the door to allow the trolley through.

The stark white sheet normally evoked some kind of reaction in relatives, but Kim was surprised to see there was none. She sensed only a growing impatience to get this done.

Keats brought the trolley to rest and then looked across all three of them.

Normally Kim would have asked the family member if they were ready, just to allow them another few seconds to compose themselves. Leanne looked as though she needed no such consideration.

Kim nodded for him to continue.

Keats plucked the top corners of the sheets and gently folded it back to reveal a face that, although not as badly burned as the rest of his body, still showed signs of trauma.

Kim watched Leanne's facial features closely. There was initial shock at the reddened skin and blisters on the cheeks, but there was no horror or distaste.

'You lied, didn't you?' Leanne asked, turning towards her. There was no accusation, just an observation. 'You said he didn't suffer.'

'Actually, I didn't answer the question,' Kim corrected.

'It's him,' Leanne said, turning back to Keats. 'This is definitely Keith Phipps.'

Keats re-covered the man's face and moved to open the door to wheel the trolley back.

'Is that it? Can I go now?' Leanne asked as the body disappeared.

'I was hoping we could talk more before—'

'I have to get back to Diane and collect the boys.'

'Okay, but we'll need to speak to Diane in more detail later, once the news has sunk in a bit.'

'Right, give us until seven to tell the boys and then I think we'll be able to answer you more fully.'

Seemed reasonable, Kim thought. At least the woman was trying to meet her halfway.

'Okay, just one thing before you go. Can you think of anyone at all who would want to hurt Keith Phipps?'

'No, Officer, I absolutely cannot,' she replied quickly before she turned and walked away, leaving Kim with a niggle in her stomach.

There was no doubt in her mind that the woman had just lied.

CHAPTER FOURTEEN

'I ay finding a lot,' Stacey said, sitting back in her chair.

'And I'm finding way too much,' Penn said, also sitting back.

'Keith Phipps is present on absolutely no social media platform whatsoever.'

Penn rolled his eyes. 'However did we manage before Facebook?'

'Says the man who has over five thousand friends.'

'Folks ask and I don't like to say no.'

'Why not?' she asked, momentarily distracted. She rejected requests all the time.

'I have this theory that there are some real fruit loops on Facebook.'

'Given that there are more than 2.7 billion users I'd say that's a fair assumption,' Stacey replied.

'So what if one of them sends me a friend request, I refuse and it pushes him or her over the edge? They might track me down and kill me in my sleep.'

Stacey laughed out loud. 'You are kidding?'

'Only about the last bit. I honestly don't like saying no. It's not like I interact with them or anything.'

Stacey was tempted to ask what the point was, but she had long ago realised that she would never understand the enigma that was Penn.

'So my show and tell was unexciting. What have you got?' she asked her colleague.

He consulted a piece of paper. 'Of the fifty-five units originally built and let at the Hayes Trading Estate, there are thirty-six still operating. There is one fixed CCTV camera at the entrance to the site. It captures vehicles coming in but doesn't have the scope to see where they go.'

'But that's good news, isn't it?' Stacey asked. They knew there was no other way onto the site, so their killer had to be on there somewhere.

'In the twenty-four hours prior to the rough estimated time given by Keats and the last time Keith was seen alive, there are 183 vehicles big enough to be carrying what our guy needed to execute his plan.'

'Aww shit,' Stacey said. Trying to match those up to the premises they were attending was near impossible. And even if Penn managed to do that, there was no guarantee that the killer wasn't also a genuine visitor to one of the units. He had to have known about the abandoned building somehow.

'That's bad, Penn, but I'd rather have your problem than mine. How is it that out of a family of four, not one of them is on any social media platform?'

'I'm sure it's not that unusual, Stace,' he said, checking his watch. 'And on that note, I've gotta go.'

'Could you not be quite so excited about attending the post-mortem of a man burned to death?'

'Not excited, eager to learn,' he corrected, grabbing his jacket from the chair.

She rolled her eyes as his back disappeared out the door. Once she was sure he was gone, Stacey took out her phone and keyed in a message to her now wife, Devon.

Hey, D. Boss is putting me forward for DS!!!

Instead of putting the phone down, she held it and waited for a response.

She saw Devon's icon move down to signal that she'd read it.

Stacey already knew that the process involved four steps. The first step was demonstrating competency in her current rank. If the boss was telling her to go for it, she knew that was in order. The minute she requested the Candidate Registration Form, the FEO would send her line manager an Endorsement Form. She had no live written improvement notices and had achieved a satisfactory rating in the appraisal process.

The second step probably unnerved her the most. The legal knowledge exam was multi-choice but she had a habit of freezing in exam conditions. Third came the assessment against rank-specific competencies followed by a twelve-month temporary promotion. It wasn't a fast process, Stacey knew that. It took a couple of years, and she'd been through a similar process to make CID.

Stacey didn't realise she was holding her breath until it burst out of her once Devon's response appeared on the screen.

Stacey smiled as she instantly saw the overload of emojis in the message. There were fireworks, smileys, champagne glasses and hearts.

Amongst the pictures were the words:

Great news. Congratulations, hun. Will pick up a Chinese on the way home to celebrate. Whoop Whoop.

Stacey keyed in a response of hearts and kisses before putting her phone aside.

It really was great news. She was flattered and proud, and it was definitely the way she wanted her career to go.

What she wasn't sure of was why she seemed to be seeking everyone's opinion on the matter to define how she felt about it herself.

CHAPTER FIFTEEN

Housing estate was a bit of an overstatement for the houses that were going up on the edge of Blackheath town.

As Bryant parked the car, Kim counted a row of six properties shoehorned into the space of a decent-sized garden. Behind the scaffolding, new brick formed the narrow homes with gaping holes that would eventually house doors and windows.

A short, squat male approached the metal gate before they could enter.

'You all right there, gor... sorry, not these days,' he said, removing his hard hat. A circle had indented around the top of his forehead.

He stepped outside the gate. 'Sorry, even if yowm from planning I cor let yer past without a—'

'We're not from planning,' Kim said, taking out her warrant card.

A loud wolf whistle sounded from the upper level of the scaffolding.

'Smurf, button it,' he called over his shoulder.

'Sorry about that,' he said.

'It's okay,' said Bryant. 'I get it all the time.'

'Bill Murray not the actor,' the man said, holding out his hand. Bryant shook it.

'And what can I do you for?'

'We're here to talk to you about Keith Phipps,' Kim said, putting her ID away.

'He's fired and yow can tell him that from me.'

'I'm sure that's the least of his problems,' Kim said. 'I'm sorry to tell you the man is dead.'

Bill looked at her for a long minute before speaking.

He scratched his head. 'How?'

'I'm not going into detail, but I'd like to know more about the man he was.'

'You've come to the wrong place, love, I mean, marm… I mean… shit, what the fuck is the right thing to say anymore?'

'Officer or Inspector will do,' she offered, hiding a smile.

Political correctness and all the ISMs, as she liked to call them, had been filtering through different industries at different speeds, and she was guessing that construction was one of the last trades to get the memo.

Bill glanced behind him and took a few steps away from the gate.

A quick glance told her that his workers were beginning to congregate and listen to what was going on.

'I'm sorry the man is dead,' he said when he felt they were far enough away. 'But there ay much I can tell yer about him.'

She nodded back towards the site. 'Can you get us someone who—?'

'There ay no one,' he said, glancing back to where the sawing and hammering had resumed. 'Smurf, who whistled your colleague here, he's worked with me for nine months. I know his wife's name is Gloria, and they've got a teenage daughter who stays out too late but gets straight As at school. Spike, my carpenter, has been with me for just under six months. His girlfriend is named Sandy, and he's saving his money to buy a ring to propose at Christmas. Noodle, who eats nothing but pasta, still lives at home, and I reckon he likes the boys, but he dow say nothing and neither do I. He's been with me almost a year. I employed Keith Phipps almost three years ago, and I dow even know his wife's name.' He frowned and scratched his head. 'Come to think of it, he never even told me he was married. I assumed he was cos of his lunchbox.'

'His what?' Kim asked.

'His grub, his lunch. Most guys who bring a sarnie box have a missus, whereas the single guys will nip to the café or grab a Greggs. I mean, I don't mean to generalise but—'

'Seems a decent indicator to me,' Bryant said.

'So he didn't talk about himself much?' Kim asked.

'Not at all. Not one thing. Never came on a night out to the dogs or the Christmas meal. When invited he'd just shake his head and say thanks for asking. Always on time, never missed a shift and I was joking when I said he was fired. It was the first shift he'd missed.'

'When?' Kim asked.

'Saturday morning. Had to give 'em all Friday off cos of the storm that was forecast, but they were all supposed to be here for a few hours catch-up at eight o'clock sharp. He was the only one didn't come.'

Kim did the calculations between the last time Diane had seen him on Saturday morning and Keats's rough estimation of time of death some time on Sunday, and guessed that Keith Phipps would have far preferred to have been on the job site, instead of enduring his fate.

'Any enemies?'

'Not one that I know of. Kept himself to himself, sat on his own on breaks – guys stopped asking him after a while and let him get on with it. He was a solid worker and couldn't do enough to help out. Other guys got used to him in the end. To be honest, I can't imagine Keith having a cross word with anybody. He just wasn't the type.'

Kim was having trouble establishing just what 'type' Keith Phipps was.

'Okay, well if you think of anything else, give me a call,' she said, handing him a card. 'And I want you to know that your efforts to join the equality of the twenty-first century are appreciated.'

She expected a smile in return or an acknowledgment, but Bill was frowning.

'You know, I remember something from the early days. It's probably nothing but…'

'Please, anything,' she said.

'Well, like I say, it was early on and the other guys were a bit weirded out by him, and I gotta say that a group of men gossip just as much as a group of women. Rumours start and before you know it the blokes had him down as a paedo.'

'Why that assumption?' Kim asked.

He shrugged. 'I suppose it's cos he never asked one single question of anyone else. Like he was scared they'd return the favour and ask him a question back. He didn't want to engage with anyone.'

'So there was nothing to suggest that was the case; no inappropriate comments or sharing of images?'

'Nah, nothing like that. It was just clear to the lads he was hiding something, and that was the worse something they could imagine, so I did my job and pulled him aside. Asked him if he'd lied on his application form. His face reddened up brighter than a bricklayer's arm. Looked right terrified. My heart was going like the clappers. For a minute, I thought he was a paedo, so I asked him outright. He shook his head and swore he wasn't. To be fair, I checked the sex register anyway, but it was really strange now that I remember it clearly.'

'What was strange?' Kim asked.

'Well, here's me asking him outright if he's a paedophile, and the guy seemed relieved that that was the question I was asking.'

CHAPTER SIXTEEN

It was three o'clock before Frost got to knock on the door of her boss, Glenn Fitzroy – or Fitz, as he was known to them all.

The man's career path had followed a similar route to her own, except he had spent twenty-seven years in the nation's capital.

Unfortunately for him, he'd been a casualty of a national newspaper that had closed down amidst the phone-hacking scandal. Editor of a local daily paper was a far cry from the career he'd once had, but she'd found him to be a half-decent boss.

'Hey, Fitz, got a minute?' she asked, putting her head around the door.

'I'd best say yes, seeing as you've been watching my door for the last half hour.'

She stepped in and closed the door, blocking out the sound of phones ringing and people talking. It wasn't the environment of a chaotic newsroom that people imagine; it was just a very small office with eight hot desks being used by around fifteen staff from reporters to photographers and a couple of admin staff. Luckily, they weren't all there at the same time, but now and again it was two to a desk.

His observation didn't surprise her. Fitz was the kind of man who gave the impression he was offering only thirty per cent of his attention and yet he never missed a thing.

'Is this about your tag along this morning?'

'It was cut short,' she said, taking a seat. 'Active investigation.'

Although there'd been no official announcement from West Midlands Police, the news of an incident at the Hayes Lane Trading Estate was all over the Internet.

'You make it to the crime scene?' he asked, giving her his full attention.

'Ha, I wish,' she lied. 'The outer perimeter was the closest I got before Stone dumped me back at the station.'

If she told her boss what she'd seen, it would be the screaming headline. He was a decent man, but he was an editor and it was his job to sell papers. It was an exclusive view that she hadn't been expecting. There were no sources to check and verify. It was what she'd seen with her own eyes. If she told her story, it would outsell every edition to date this year. It would also destroy any relationship she had with West Mids Police or any other force.

'You're telling me you got nothing?' he asked. 'I thought you were in there writing up the article right now.'

'Sorry, Fitz, I saw the outside of a warehouse,' she said, shrugging.

'Bloody hell, Frost. You were right there.'

She said nothing. Despite her reputation, she did believe in the public's right to know but not before family members, and she wasn't prepared to jeopardise that.

'You want me to put someone else on it?' he asked, offering her a mild threat if she didn't step up and get the story.

'Actually yes,' she said, taking the wind out of his sails. That was exactly what she wanted.

'Fucking hell, Frost, what's th—?'

'Tagged along to a quick meeting with the family of Trisha Morley.'

He rolled his eyes before turning towards his computer. 'Sick of hearing the Morley name. His team is doing a great job of campaigning. Forget a conviction. I can see this guy running for prime minister.'

As a newspaper, they had run no features on the case and had only reported the facts.

'The family is suffering, Fitz. They can't compete with his PR machine and, to be fair, they shouldn't have to. The crime is being forgotten. No one is talking about the fact this man allegedly killed his wife. The family knows that Trisha's name is being forgotten while he is becoming larger than life.'

Fitz shrugged and continued staring at his screen.

She took a breath. 'I want to run some articles focusing on Trisha and the crime.'

'You're joking?'

She shook her head.

'You want to be a dinghy in a tsunami?'

'I want to do what's right, Fitz. If this guy goes free and we did nothing, we'll—'

'It's a waste of your time and column inches. This isn't even a story of David and Goliath. You'd be the sand beetle beneath David's shoe.'

'Sand beetle?' she asked, raising an eyebrow.

'Impact wise, yes. Do you know how much money he's throwing at this?'

'Absolutely – he's trying to buy his freedom.'

Fitz began to turn away, and she knew she was losing him.

'Imagine if it was your daughter, Fitz,' she said, using her last card. 'Imagine you've watched her being controlled and beaten for years, and then you lose her altogether and there's nothing you can do to stop her killer getting away with—'

'Okay, enough of the emotional manipulation, Frost. You sure go low when you need to.' He did a quick calculation in his head. 'You've got three thousand words in print each night until it's over and unlimited online.'

She smiled. It was more than she'd hoped for. Using his daughter had served her well.

'But everything comes through me, even the online, got it?'

'Absolutely, Fitz,' she said, heading towards the door with a spring in her step.

It was time to start a bun fight.

CHAPTER SEVENTEEN

'I've never seen anything like it,' Penn said, walking around the naked body of Keith Phipps.

He didn't know a lot about burns. Jasper had suffered a couple due to his passion for baking. The first had been a superficial burn affecting just the outermost layer of skin. When he'd touched a hot pan.

A bit of redness on his fingertips had been eased by running the hand under cold water.

His brother hadn't been quite so lucky when he'd spilled burning caramel onto his bare toes, causing the skin to blister. A trip to A&E had resulted in painful cleaning and bandaging to prevent infection. These were just two of the reasons Jasper was not allowed to cook without supervision.

But anything he'd seen before paled beside this victim.

'Death would have been a welcome relief to this poor fellow,' Keats observed. 'He was dead long before he took his last breath, I'm afraid.'

'How so?' Penn asked, always eager to learn.

'You know about the rule of nines?' Keats asked.

'Kind of,' he answered honestly.

'It's an assessment system used by paramedics and hospitals worldwide to establish the surface area of the body affected and the likelihood of the injuries causing death to the individual.'

'Likely to cause death?' Penn questioned. 'Surely if a burns victim is alive when found there's a chance of recovery?'

Keats shook his head. 'Not the case, I'm afraid. Let me explain. The body is split into sections that are either divisions or multiples of nine. The front of each leg accounts for nine per cent each, the back and front torso count for eighteen per cent each, and the front and back of each arm counts for four and a half per cent each. Got it?'

Penn nodded while looking over the body of Keith Phipps and trying to do the maths.

'By using the approximation of the body surface damaged and adding the victim's age, you can establish the likelihood of the person dying from their injuries. The closer the total is to one hundred, the more probable it is a person will ultimately die days or even weeks later even if found alive.'

'Of what?' Penn asked.

'Shock, septicaemia, heart attack. If we look at our man here it would appear that approximately eighty-nine per cent of his body is covered in second-degree burns, which are worse, in my opinion, for this fellow than third-degree burns.'

'How so?' Penn asked. It was his understanding that third-degree burns were the most severe, causing damage through every layer of the skin.

'There's a misconception that third-degree burns are the most painful, but the damage is so extensive there may not be pain because of nerve damage. Do you see these reddened areas?' Keats asked, pointing to one of a hundred marks over the body that varied in size from a centimetre to approximately five centimetres.

'These are blisters that have popped open to reveal painful scorched skin, which has then been subjected to more heat from the fire.'

'Bloody hell,' Penn said, trying to imagine the agony of having the burns reheated.

'Eventually fibrinous exudate may have developed over the—'

'Fibrinous what?'

'Scab,' Keats clarified. 'Every single one of these blisters would have been prone to infection. The worse the blister is, the longer they take to heal. The pain from even a tenth of these would have been excruciating to live with. Even the most basic movement would have been agonising, and any skin graft would have been out of the question.'

Penn knew there was nowhere on his body from where the healthy skin could have been taken.

'It is highly unlikely he could have survived any form of treatment, and there is little your killer could have done to make this poor man suffer more.'

'Why is the face less burned than the rest of him?' Penn asked, walking around the metal table.

Keats dropped his head forward onto his chest, to demonstrate. 'I would imagine from falling in and out of consciousness due to the pain.'

Penn was beginning to agree with Keats about the man surviving. He stared hard at the pus-filled blisters that rose up from the skin like bubble wrap. Perhaps it was merciful that the man had died.

'Okay, lesson of the day is over. So, to recap our findings in terms your boss will understand, we have a 38-year-old male in reasonable health who was once a heavy smoker. No evidence of him being a heavy drinker. Teeth would indicate he didn't have access to the best health care as a child. Various broken bones around the body, especially the hands but nothing more recent than five years ago. I would confirm my estimate that he died early evening on Sunday, and that his first burn was approximately twenty-four hours before that.'

'Twenty-four hours,' Penn repeated, shaking his head.

'The cause of death would be shock. Quite simply his body could take no more.'

'Thanks, Keats,' Penn said as he began to remove his protective clothing.

For once he was happy to leave the morgue as quickly as he could. It was fair to say that he enjoyed the process of learning all that he could about the body's mechanics, but in today's case every minute of this guy's suffering was staring at him from every angle. The only thing he'd seen was the horrific torture this man had suffered.

'And if your boss wants to know, his last meal was eggs and toast.'

'Yep, deal-breaker,' he said, heading for the door as Keats took the white sheet and began to cover the body.

'Good night for now, my... oooh, wait one minute,' he said as the sheet hung in mid-air. 'What on earth is this?'

Penn stepped right back into the room.

CHAPTER EIGHTEEN

'You do know that five o'clock isn't seven o'clock, guv?' Bryant asked as they parked easily in front of Diane Phipps's house. Kim was relieved to see Leanne's Ford Kuga was no longer there. Maybe this time they could get more than a couple of words out of the victim's wife without her sister butting in every other word.

'Yeah well, when I agreed to leave them alone for a few hours, I didn't realise we were going to get nothing more than a name confirmation from a man he's known for years. We know as much about Keith Phipps now as we did when we walked away from the body.'

'To be fair, we know way more about his physical appearance than—'

'You happy to take the boys?' she asked, knocking the door. On occasion, Bryant turned squeamish about interviewing kids too soon, but these were not babies. Judging by the photo she'd seen, Tommy and Darren Phipps were early and pre teen and may well know something about their father that their mother did not.

'I'll take 'em,' he replied as they waited. 'At least I won't be waterboarding them for information.'

'Funny,' she said, knocking again.

This time she listened carefully.

'Hear that?'

'What?' he asked, listening at the door.

'Exactly,' she said, stepping to the side. The heavy curtains she'd noticed earlier that day were pulled tightly shut.

'Okay, you get top and I'll get the bottom.'

'You want to break in before we've even—?'

'Bryant, her husband was kidnapped, tortured and murdered. How do we know he didn't want the whole family?'

He stepped back and looked at the house. 'We have a duty to check all points of access…'

'Duly checked, rule boy, on my head it is. Now get back here and help me break this door down.'

'Since you asked so nicely,' he said, getting into position.

'One, two, three,' she called as Bryant threw his shoulder against the top of the door and she kicked hard at the bottom.

The door burst open and bounced against the back of the two-seater sofa.

Kim pushed it aside and entered.

'What th—?'

It was clear to her immediately that the house was empty. Not only of people but of possessions.

A gaping space was now where the TV and game system had been just a few hours ago. The photo above the fireplace of the boys had gone, leaving a rectangular piece of clean wallpaper.

She moved further into the house as a feeling of dread began to form in the pit of her stomach.

The kitchen diner showed plates and cups left on the side. All appliances were present except for a kettle, which she assumed had been next to the beverage canisters. There was no handbag or car keys, and a small cupboard with coat hooks had been left ajar. She opened the door wide to find a couple of pairs of men's shoes and a man's lightweight jacket. Keith's jacket.

'Check outside,' Kim said as she headed upstairs, though she doubted there was anything there.

The upstairs rooms followed the same pattern. The larger furniture items had been left in the boys' room. Their school uniforms had been discarded on the bed. Drawers had been opened and emptied. Bedside cabinets were bare. Some books and toys remained.

She ventured left into the master bedroom and saw the exact same picture. Shoes and clothing had been removed from one side of the wardrobe. All of Keith's possessions appeared to have been left. No longer needed.

Kim moved on to the bathroom. The cabinet door was open. There was a single toothbrush but nothing for the boys. Towels and sheets had been left folded tidily in the airing cupboard.

'Nothing to see outside, guv. Back gate is locked and secure.'

He took a quick look around the rooms as she tried to get her thoughts in order.

'Took what they needed and didn't hang around,' he observed.

Hence Leanne's instruction for them to return at 7 p.m. She had already known what they were going to do. She remembered Leanne's hushed words to her sister as they'd left for the morgue, obviously issuing instructions to pack while she was gone.

'They certainly didn't hang around, Bryant, but the question is why? What exactly does this family have to hide?'

CHAPTER NINETEEN

'I count thirty-seven,' Keats said after his second check of the body.

Penn had waited patiently after Keats had discovered a single needle mark just one inch up from the man's belly button.

'And I have absolutely no idea why,' he said, scratching his head.

'There was a pricking torture once used under the guise of a test for the Devil's mark during the witch-hunting trials,' Penn offered.

Keats raised one eyebrow as he headed to his computer in the corner of the room. 'Penn, how do you know this stuff?'

Penn continued: 'It was felt that a witch would carry the mark of Satan and that the mark could be visible or invisible. Could be birthmarks, moles, warts and stuff, but if they found nothing obvious, the witch finders decided that if any part of the skin was insensitive to pain or did not bleed when punctured by the sharpest of implements, it must be an invisible badge of the Devil. King James the first said the absence of blood while pricking was an infallible sign of sorcery.'

'Hmm…' Keats said, staring at his computer screen.

Penn walked around the body. 'The women would be stripped naked, have their hair shaved off then the witch finder would systematically pierce all of the poor woman's body, until he could discover a spot that failed to yield blood or the accused no longer cried out in pain.

'The test was always successful, because as a result of the continuous torture, the woman's body would have become insensitive to pain through shock or because the woman would cease to give any indication of pain to make the torture stop.'

'Very interesting,' Keats offered.

'I think—'

'Not you, this,' Keats said, tapping his screen. 'Any fire involved with the witchcraft torture?'

Penn shook his head. 'Not at the same time but fire was—'

'Back in ancient times, the tyrant Antiochus ordered a torture on naysayer Areth, whereby he was tied to a pillar by a fire that was lit at such a distance so as not to fatally burn him. He was pricked all over his head, face and body to allow the heat to penetrate deeper into his skin.'

'For what purpose?' Penn asked.

'The purpose, my boy, was to roast him alive.'

CHAPTER TWENTY

It was almost six o'clock when Frost pressed the 'Publish' button and the first article went live.

Without realising it, the office had emptied around her. Only Fitz and the sports photographer remained. The phones were quiet, the chatter had gone and the desks had been left in an array of chaos, ready for the next day because news happened on its own schedule.

She sat back and rolled her head from side to side to release the tension in her shoulders. She had worked non-stop on the article after being given the green light on the idea.

'I'll make you coffee you won't drink again, Frost,' the photographer said, walking past her desk.

'Sorry, Brad, got caught up,' she said, touching the side of the mug. It was stone cold.

'Wanna go get a fresh one at—?'

'I'm good, thanks. Gonna just see this online.'

'No probs,' he said brightly. 'See you on the morrow.'

She held up her hand in response as she clicked onto the article. Admittedly, it had been a rush job. She'd used the piece as an introduction, a refresher on the whole case: Trisha's background, her family and basic information. Fitz had made a couple of small changes, but overall he'd been happy with her approach.

She grabbed her notebook and began scribbling ideas for how she saw the features playing out in her mind. She wanted to report it in a linear fashion. The article today had focused on

Trisha as a person. Frost had made sure to include photos of the fun-loving, carefree girl she'd been before meeting Nick Morley and to mention her name as many times as she could. She looked at her own list and nodded with satisfaction, a clear direction now formed in her mind.

Tomorrow her article would focus on the abuse, the injuries sustained over the course of the relationship.

On Wednesday, she'd focus on the murder, and the evidence against Morley.

Thursday she'd write about the mistrial, and then end with a sum up on Friday of the whole case, just in time for the new trial next week.

A small part of her felt as though she was speaking to an empty room, but she cast the thought aside. At least she was opening her mouth.

She turned to a fresh page in her notebook and began sketching out aspects of the abuse. She wanted to cover the first incident of intimidation, isolation and shame. Her pen flew over the page with ideas. When she next looked up, she'd written seven pages of notes and Fitz's office had darkened behind her. She'd never even heard him leave.

It had been a long day and she knew she should go home, but there was a niggle in her mind that she was missing something in the abuse angle.

'Past behaviour,' she said to the empty office. She needed to demonstrate that he'd done it before. That it was a pattern.

She flicked backwards in her notepad to the first thing she'd written. The first thing she'd noted when talking to Penny Colgan earlier in the day.

She stabbed the pad with her pen. 'Okay, where are you, Ariane Debegorski?'

CHAPTER TWENTY-ONE

As she stood outside the empty house, Kim did her calculations.

'This took more than two people,' she said. 'Given the time they had, the space in two cars and the volume of stuff that's gone, there had to be more people involved.'

'Agreed, but why?' Bryant asked. 'Her husband has just been murdered, and she's done some kind of disappearing act with her two kids.'

'Clearly they know something we don't,' she said, knocking on the door of the neighbour.

'Well you took your— Oh,' said the woman opening the door, clearly expecting to see someone else.

Kim guessed the woman to be early forties. Her short, dark hair had a purple hue that matched her nail varnish.

Loud voices suddenly sounded from the rear of the house.

'Kill each other quietly,' she called over her shoulder, stepping out of the house and pulling the door behind her.

'Twin boys, thirteen, and every day I don't kill 'em is a bonus.'

'Similar in age to the boys next door?' Kim asked.

'Sorry, who are you?' she asked pointedly, folding her arms. Clearly not prepared to say another word until they'd identified themselves.

They both offered their warrant cards.

'Bloody hell, I only phoned the landlord out of courtesy. I didn't expect—'

Her words were cut short as the door swung open behind her.

'Mum, Kieran's hogging the Xbox and won't—'

'If you boys don't let me have an adult conversation for ten minutes, you'll lose the game system for a week. Go do the maths on that one,' she said as the boy retreated and closed the door.

'Can you tell I'm a stay-at-home mum?'

Kim couldn't help the smile that played on her lips. It was a parenting style she appreciated.

The woman held out her hand. 'Rachel Carson, feral kid wrangler and resident snoop.'

Kim returned the handshake briefly, hoping they'd fallen lucky here.

'You said you'd called the landlord?' Kim asked.

'Not long after you left with that other woman, a grey Transit van turned up. Two guys got out and started loading stuff in. Diane was bringing out bags, then the other woman came back with the boys, and twenty minutes later they were gone. I called the landlord in case they were doing some kind of flit to avoid paying the rent, but he said they were all up-to-date, that he was on his way back from Lanzarote and would swing by tomorrow to check for damage. Didn't seem too fussed, so I cracked on with the ironing.'

'And the landlord is…?'

'Stephen Jenner from Wilson Fairbanks Limited, and his number is…'

Bryant took out his notepad and took it down as a thought occurred to her.

The women were of similar age and they both had two boys. She was surprised they weren't sharing a glass of wine over the back fence every night.

'You weren't friends then?'

You didn't call the landlord on your mates.

Rachel shook her head. 'Not for the want of trying.'

'Go on,' Kim said.

'Family moved in five years ago, only about a year after we did. I'll be honest and say I was excited when I saw they had two boys.' She looked left and right. 'No other kids here, so I had visions of barbecues over the fence, kids playing together. My own two were missing their old mates in Leicester, but I was soon disabused of that notion.'

Kim listened, allowing the woman to just speak.

'I knocked on the door the day after they moved in, just to introduce myself. She gave me her name and that was pretty much it. I asked her round for coffee, but she said she had too much to do so I left it. A few days later I saw the three of them, mum and boys, in the street. I tried again to engage her, tried to speak to the boys, but she answered for them. I never heard them speak once. It was as though she was scared they were going to say something wrong. Of course, that could purely be the outlandish musings of a woman spending too much time at home with her kids.'

Or maybe not, Kim thought.

'I saw her in the back garden once. We were both hanging out our washing. I made some kind of lame joke. She smiled tightly and went back inside. Two days later, they had six-foot fence panels delivered, and her husband spent the weekend putting them in.'

Friendly family, Kim thought.

'And how about the husband. Was he any warmer?' Kim asked, wondering if they'd had any better luck than his workmates.

Rachel shook her head. 'Nah, my guy, Mick, asked if he wanted any help with the fence panels. He politely declined, so Mick left him to it. Blokes don't try as hard as us women. We like to bond with like-minded ladies, but guys just want a drinking buddy.'

Bryant nodded. 'Yeah, it's true.'

'What about the pub? Did Mick ever see him down the local?' Kim asked, recalling the reasons Diane hadn't reported him missing.

'Never. I don't think the guy ever went out alone. I don't think he was a drinker. Once he got a job he'd come back at five every night and that was that. I sometimes heard them all out in the garden, the boys playing together, but when it was just the two of them they spoke in low, quiet voices that I couldn't hear. And to be honest I did try.'

Kim liked the woman's honesty.

'Keith Phipps had no job when they moved in?'

'Don't think so. Didn't see him leaving the house at a regular time until they'd been here a few months. Maybe six or seven.'

'And what about Leanne, was she here often?'

'Who's Leanne?'

'Her sister: the woman who was with Diane earlier. The one who picked up the boys.'

'Oh, didn't know that was her sister. I saw her a couple of times when they first moved in, and maybe once or twice over the years, but we never spoke.'

Kim had got the impression the sisters were closer than that. They had to have a decent relationship or Leanne wouldn't be a named person at the school, able to collect the boys. Schools didn't allow just anyone to take kids out on behalf of the parents.

Kim had to accept that however observant the woman appeared to be, she must have missed some comings and goings. She did have teenage boys to contend with.

'And did you ever hear or see anything strange – visitors, shouting, arguing?'

'They had the occasional loud argument where she would scream that it was all his fault. But don't we all do that – blame our partners?'

'Yep, sounds right,' Bryant chimed in.

'Any suspicion of violence between the couple or the boys?'

Rachel looked genuinely shocked at the question.

'No way. There was barely anyone who knew they were alive, so I don't imagine anyone having any grief with them.' She narrowed her eyes. 'Is he dead?'

'Thank you for your time. You've been an incredible help,' Kim said not unpleasantly.

'You're welcome. I suppose I'd best go shower my two with E numbers as a reward.'

Kim smiled as she walked away.

'Well, don't you want it then?' Rachel called after them.

'Want what?' Kim asked.

'The registration number of the Transit van.'

CHAPTER TWENTY-TWO

Kim felt the exhaustion of the day seep into her bones as she perched her behind on the edge of the spare desk. There was no way that it had only been that morning that Woody had hit her with the Frost drive along. Looking around her team, it appeared they all felt the same way.

'Okay, guys, quick catch-up and then time to call it a night,' she said, glancing at the board, which had been updated with very little detail.

'It ay registered, boss,' Stacey said, waving Bryant's piece of paper in the air.

She took a look. 'That's definitely what she said: try it again.'

The Transit had to be registered to someone, and yet a part of her felt it had just been too easy.

'No such number,' Stacey said again. 'Maybe the neighbour got it wrong.'

The woman's front window was probably ten feet away from where the van had been parked, so Kim doubted that. Just another mystery in the case that appeared to be going nowhere fast.

'And the family themselves?' Kim asked, sticking with Stacey and her task of finding out more about the Phipps.

'Absolutely nothing on social media for any family member. Nothing for the parents or the kids.'

Kim recalled that she hadn't noticed any computers or devices when she'd been at the house.

'Sorry, boss,' Stacey offered. Kim knew the constable hated days where she had nothing to show for her time.

'I'm gonna move on to medical records tomorrow. See what I can track down.'

'Good idea,' Kim said, feeling the knot in her stomach tighten. A whole family with no social media presence seemed a bit off to her. She wasn't a huge user, but to have nothing at all with boys of that age struck her as odd.

'Okay, we have some big questions to try and answer. We know the family kept to themselves and took their privacy very seriously. Even after five years, the neighbours knew nothing more than their first name, that Keith Phipps would never hurt a fly and—'

'That makes no sense, boss,' Penn chimed in. 'Our killer wanted Keith to suffer unimaginable pain. He tried to roast his organs. You don't do that for no reason.'

'But it might not be about him,' Bryant added. 'He might have been in the wrong place at the wrong time. The victim may be unrelated, and we've just got some sick and twisted psychopath who likes to inflict horrific suffering.'

Kim thought Bryant made a valid point. Not every murder was about the victim, and she might have agreed with him if the family had not acted so strangely and then actually disappeared.

'There's a link somewhere,' Kim said. 'The family is running from something. It's too coincidental and, much as I'd love to go with the mindless psychopath theory, I'm just not feeling it.'

Bryant was not offended at her disagreement. One of his key strengths was in offering an alternative point of view to be considered. He was the team's resident devil's advocate.

'Anything of interest at the post-mortem?' Kim asked.

'Other than the pricking thing I messaged you about, it appeared that our killer tortured him for more than twenty-four hours. He had eggs for breakfast, a few broken bones and appeared to live a reasonably healthy lifestyle now, despite apparent lack of dental care as a child.'

'Evidence of heavy drinking?' Kim asked, remembering Diane's reasons for not reporting her husband missing.

'None,' Penn answered.

'Hmm… so why didn't she report it?' Kim said more to herself. Diane had known full well that her husband wasn't on a bender, but she still hadn't called the police. So far, they appeared to be exhibiting a real issue with the authorities. They had lied, avoided, distracted and now run away from the police. From what the neighbour had said, the family had definitely gone willingly, but that didn't rule them out of being in danger.

What the hell was this family hiding?

'Okay, folks, time to call it a night. Be here fresh and early in the morning. We have to try and find this family.'

Everyone grabbed their belongings and headed for the door. They all knew that finishing before 10 p.m. was a luxury they might not be afforded later in the week.

Only Bryant paused at the door. 'You okay to…?'

'I've got the bike,' she said. A ride home on the Kawasaki Ninja was just what she needed to clear her mind.

He said his good nights and left.

Damn it. She'd forgotten to ask Stacey if she'd started the process for promotion yet. Now that Woody had the bit between his teeth, she knew it was going to come up every time they were face to face. She knew that a part of Woody felt that she didn't put enough time into developing her team or pushing them towards the next rung of the career ladder, and that she kept them stagnant for her own personal reasons.

It wasn't true. Admittedly, the team dynamics between the four of them worked well. Yes, there had been an adjustment period when Penn had replaced Kevin Dawson, but he had found his niche and the team had rearranged itself. But that wasn't the reason she didn't push. She knew that not everyone had the same career goals, regardless of skill and capability. Just because they could, didn't mean they should. For instance, Bryant had made it clear he had no aspirations for the detective inspector position, and she wouldn't force him. Penn had recently lost his mother after a prolonged terminal illness, so she wouldn't be pushing him either. Despite her conviction that people should make their own decisions on their career path, Woody was leaving her no choice.

She sighed heavily as she reached for her jacket. As it was halfway on, her phone signalled a Google Alert. She still got them for articles posted by Frost since their last major case, where reports posted by Frost had been the primary form of communication between herself and a killer.

'Oh, Frost, what have you… what the hell?' she said, reading past the headline.

Kim felt her anger rising. 'You ruthless, manipulative bitch.'

The godforsaken woman had taken advantage of the situation of meeting the family of Trisha Morley and was now jumping on the bandwagon.

She chose to ignore that this had been Woody's plan all along. There was just something about the fact they had allowed Frost access to the family and that she was now writing about them that made her want a steaming hot shower and a bottle of bleach.

The more she read, the more incensed she became. All of this information had not come out during their visit, which could only mean one thing: Frost had gone back and intruded again, bothering the family at a difficult time, and that wasn't what Woody had had in mind.

'Frost, I swear,' she said as her thumb hovered over the 'Contact' icon.

Bryant's voice sounded in her head, urging caution. Telling her to breathe before she acted.

She returned to the article and read it properly – twice.

She noted all the references to Trisha's childhood: her upbringing; her relationship with her sister; memories they shared. The piece wasn't about Trisha the victim, it was about Trisha the person.

It was exactly what they'd wanted her to do. The article hinted at more to come.

A slow smile spread over Kim's face as she put away her phone.

'Fair play, Frost,' she said, walking out of the door. 'Bloody fair play.'

CHAPTER TWENTY-THREE

Stacey took a breath and placed a smile on her face as she put her key in the lock. She wasn't sure why, as she'd never felt the need to do it before. This was her home, her safe haven. It had been Devon's flat, but she'd felt at home here since the first time she'd visited. She'd had no complaints on making this their home, as it was bigger than her old place, had a second bedroom and a Juliet balcony that looked out onto a row of back gardens. The day after the wedding her name had been added to the lease.

'Hey…' she called, hanging up her coat in the hallway, another facility her own flat had lacked.

'Hey, babe. I'm in the kitchen,' Devon called back.

Stacey could smell the delicious aromas of her favourite Chinese meal being kept warm in the oven.

As she stepped into the kitchen, Stacey caught her breath as she always did.

Devon was dressed in low-slung deep red joggers that hugged her slim hips but showed off her toned stomach. A V-neck T-shirt with cut-off sleeves hinted at the body beneath.

The body was killer, but that wasn't what took Stacey's breath away. It was the soft skin, lighter than her own, that disappeared beneath the shortest, tightest curls that were cut close to the head and dyed blonde. Devon had never had a weave in her life and didn't intend to.

It was that face and the love that emanated from it that sent Stacey's heart hammering in her chest. For a long time, she had felt unworthy of such a creature, with her own dark Nigerian skin and the extra few pounds she carried, but not anymore. She now knew that Devon loved her for the person she was and she trusted in that.

'How was your day, wife?' Devon asked, moving towards her.

Stacey forgot everything as Devon took her in her arms and kissed her passionately.

Stacey groaned out loud as the desire hit her immediately.

'Later, babe,' Devon said, moving away. 'First, we celebrate with your favourite wine,' she said, handing Stacey a glass. Although not much of a drinker, she did enjoy the odd glass of rosé.

'So, come on, tell me all about it,' Devon said, hitching herself up onto the work surface. 'I'm so proud of you.'

'Nothing to tell, hun. The boss just called me in and said she thought I was ready for promotion.'

Devon looked disappointed, and Stacey knew she hadn't presented it exactly the way it had happened.

'Oh well, as long as they're recognising how fantastic you are, which I always knew, of course.'

Stacey suddenly felt bad for playing it down when Devon just wanted to be excited for her and to show her support.

Stacey put down her drink and leaned into the woman she loved.

'Well, if you must know she told me how much I'd improved in both confidence…'

'Well, that's true,' Devon said, snaking her arms around Stacey's neck and pulling her close.

'She also told me how much my abilities have grown.'

'Also true,' Devon said breathlessly as Stacey caressed the skin of Devon's bare back.

'And that I always make the effort…'

'Oh yes,' Devon said, moving closer towards her.

'And that I always get results,' Stacey said, allowing her hands to wander.

'Absolutely,' Devon breathed into her ear.

'And that my skills…'

'Jesus Christ, Stace,' Devon cried, jumping down from the tabletop. 'You are bloody lethal, woman.'

Stacey laughed out loud before taking a sip of wine.

Devon took her hand. 'Come with me – I've got a surprise for you.'

Stacey couldn't help but hope she was being led to the bedroom. She tried not to let her disappointment show as she found herself being pulled into the lounge.

'Oh, what's this?' she said as she took in the rearrangement of the room.

The sofas had been moved into an L shape around the wall-mounted TV, to make way for a dressing table, brought out from the spare bedroom. A new lamp had been placed on top along with her laptop and a collection of notepads and pencils.

'It's your working space,' Devon explained. 'You're going to need to concentrate to study for your sergeants' exam. You can't do it lounging on the sofa, laptop on your legs while half-watching the TV. And look, I bought these so we can be together but you won't be disturbed by the sound of the telly.'

Devon held up a new pair of Wi-Fi headphones.

Her excitement demanded a response.

'Oh, D, I dow know what to say.'

It really was a sweet and thoughtful thing to do. They had supported each other's careers from the very beginning.

'I thought about setting you up in the spare room, but I knew you wouldn't have used the space.'

Devon was right. Many days at work she spent long periods in the office on her own, and whereas she didn't mind it there, she didn't want to replicate it at home.

It was the perfect solution. Devon really had thought of everything.

'I'm really blown away by—'

'Well, sit down and try it out. We've got to make sure you're comfortable.'

Stacey did as she was told and made her way towards the desk.

CHAPTER TWENTY-FOUR

'Morning, folks, hope you all slept well,' Kim said once her team was fully assembled.

The response was a collection of affirmative noises.

She had worked on her new project for a couple of hours, taken Barney for his late-night walk and then worked on the bike some more, hoping exhaustion would rid her mind of the images she'd seen. Every time she closed her eyes, the picture of Keith Phipps's scorched and tortured body had thundered into her mind. She had attended countless crime scenes during her career. She had seen bodies in the most horrific states, but for many she had been able to console herself that the victim's end had come quickly, that their suffering had been minimal. Never had she been faced with such a slow and horrific torture where there was no such consolation. Added to that knowledge was the basic understanding of the pain. All of them had been scalded by hot water at some point or sustained a minor burn from a hob or cooker and knew how uncomfortable it could be. Magnify that by a thousand and she suspected it wouldn't come close to what Keith Phipps had suffered.

She'd finally given up on sleep when a dream of a pig roast had woken her at 5 a.m. quicker than an adrenaline shot.

'Good, let's get to it. By the end of the day, I want to know everything there is to know about this family, and I don't care who you need to sleep with to get it.'

'Boss, I'm a married woman,' Stacey said with dramatic mock offence.

'Yeah, Stace, you might have mentioned that a few hundred times,' Kim said, rolling her eyes. 'It's all on you then, Penn.'

'Cool,' he said, taking the tie-dyed bandana from his drawer. It was his way of resigning himself to a day spent primarily in the office. If he ventured out, he would lose the bandana and apply some of the magic potion that kept his blond curls at bay.

'Okay, between the two of you I want those vehicles in and out of the trading estate whittled down to something sensible. I want you to track down the vehicle that assisted the Phippses in moving so quickly, and I want to know where the family is now. We need to confirm they're safe and find out what they're trying to hide.'

'What about after lunch?' Stacey asked with a smile.

'Get the medical records for the whole family, and once you've done that you can do some searches on similar incidents elsewhere. Enough?'

Stacey laughed out loud. 'Gor it, boss.'

'Sounds like they need me to stay and help,' Bryant offered.

'Oh yeah, Bryant, with your technical skills I'm sure you'd be a huge asset to them.'

'We're good, Bryant,' Penn offered with a smile.

Bryant clutched his heart, as though mortally wounded.

'Sorry, Bryant, but you're coming with me back to the crime scene,' she said, pushing herself off the desk.

And she had just one important call to make before they got there.

CHAPTER TWENTY-FIVE

Of course, the perception of journalism was nothing like the reality, Frost mused, as she typed the place name of Preston into the electoral register.

She'd once dreamed of the glamour of hopping on planes and trains with a moment's notice to cover a breaking story. The excitement and adrenaline of picking up a thread that led to an original piece that won prestigious awards. Writing something different to the facts every other tabloid or station was covering. Yes, that might be the experience of some of her peers, but it wasn't true for her.

In her case, there were many hours desk-bound, chasing down basic facts and figures. Not quite so glamorous. Added to that she'd never figured on being a detective or fathomed just how monotonous that could be.

Sometimes information didn't fall into your lap as easily as you wanted it to. Sometimes it was like digging a grave with a spoon.

Like now. There was nowhere she could go to find out where Ariane Debegorski currently lived. An old Instagram account had shown the woman at various beauty spots and places of interest around the Midlands. All searches of the electoral register locally had turned up nothing.

Further interrogation of her old social media showed her with friends who had visited from Lancashire. Logic told her that if a woman was scared enough to move out of the area, she might move somewhere with some familiarity, some people that she knew.

So she'd focused her search in the north-west of the country and was working her way through as many place names as she could find. It was one of those jobs that you felt might not get done before retirement; but then what if the next place you tried yielded a result? Using the advanced search, she could enter an age range to narrow the selection, but still she could search only by town and not county.

And so she continued to consult her map and type in the names.

Pendleton

No results found

'What?' she said out loud as her phone began to ring. 'Oh,' she mumbled, seeing Stone's number flashing on her screen.

She pressed the answer button and began to speak immediately. 'Look, whatever I've done to piss you off this time will have to wait. I'm busy.'

'Yeah, busy poking your nose into other people's business as usual,' Stone retorted.

Frost frowned. The words she expected but not the tone. It was maybe one or two degrees above the freezing temperature Stone normally employed with her.

'Why are you…?'

'I read your article last night. It wasn't bad.'

Frost felt a smile tug at her lips. High praise indeed.

'You got more to say on the subject?' Stone continued.

'Oh yeah, but it wasn't even your case so why the interest?'

There was a slight hesitation before the inspector answered. 'Trisha Morley is what we call a choke case.'

'Choke?'

'So-called because it sticks in the throat of every officer on the force whether it was their case or not. No one believes Nick Morley is innocent, but proving it is a different matter. At the centre of this PR circus is a woman who suffered for years, and your article last night helped remind the public of that fact. So, like I said, well done. You didn't fuck it up.'

Frost opened her mouth to reply, but the line went dead in her hand.

For a moment she considered the situation from the side of the police. They had done all they could to secure a conviction. They were fully convinced of his guilt, but once the evidence had been submitted to the Crown Prosecution Service they could do no more. That knowledge must torture them all but none more than Stone, who lived and breathed justice.

And that was the point of the call, she realised. The inspector was telling her that, regardless of their personal feelings, the police could do no more. But that she could.

With Stone's words ringing in her ears, she resumed her search for Ariane Debegorski.

Pilkington
No results found
Prestwich
1 Result found

Frost froze, not quite believing her eyes. There she was. For the last seven years, Ariane Debegorski had been living in Prestwich, just three miles out of Manchester city centre.

A slow smile spread across her face. That was the thing about long shots. It sure felt good if you managed to hit the target.

Frost wasted no time in grabbing her jacket and handbag.

Ariane Debegorski, I am coming to get you.

CHAPTER TWENTY-SIX

Kim ended her call to Frost as they entered the Hayes Trading Estate. She hoped the reporter had received her message loud and clear.

'You know you were almost civil to her then,' Bryant noted.

'Almost?' she asked. On her thermometer the conversation had bordered on almost warm.

'Well, the bit where you end a conversation without warning needs a little work.'

'I said what I wanted to say and I was done,' she replied, shrugging as she looked out of the window.

'It's a shame,' she noted, shaking her head.

There were other places she wanted to go, but it wasn't even eight o'clock. One person she knew who would already be hard at it was their top forensic tech.

'What's a shame?' Bryant asked, driving down the central road.

'The decline.'

She remembered tagging along with Keith, her foster father from the age of ten to thirteen, as he drove around such places, searching for parts for his motorcycle restoration projects. He'd drive over two hundred miles for an authentic air filter instead of using the many copies he could have sourced locally.

'But you can't even see it?' she'd queried as they'd headed north.

'But I'll know,' he said. 'If it's not an original part, I'll know that the bike hasn't been properly restored to its former glory. I'll have settled for less because it's easier. Does that make sense?'

It had made sense and it had stayed with her. As had many of their conversations. It had only been three years that she'd been in the care of Keith and Erica, but they had been the best three years of her life and had changed her for ever. There were still days when she wondered how different her life would have been had they not been killed in a motorway crash just after her thirteenth birthday.

She had always accompanied her foster father on his journeys, watched his eyes light up as he foraged through piles of metal at scrapyards, and she'd inherited that same excitement as though she was his natural child. She'd loved being with him in busy, industrious places, with the sound of machinery and vehicles in her ears. The places had been alive with activity of people working, producing and manufacturing. Every unit had been a different kind of business. Different sandwich vans had littered the roads, offering a quick meal to the workers. Those areas had been alive.

But now, as they passed one empty unit after another, it felt like an animal just waiting to die.

She pushed the thoughts away as Bryant pulled up between Mitch's van and a vehicle she didn't recognise.

'Hey, Inspector,' Mitch said, hearing her approach.

The area had been filled with three oversize tarpaulin sheets. The contents of each bin were in the process of being emptied onto its own sheet by techies using hand shovels and scoops. Kim noted that each shovelful of debris was being placed next to the one that had been scooped out before it.

Mitch and the owner of the car she didn't recognise stood at the mound of ash nearest the door.

'Please meet Nigel Adams, Fire Investigation Officer.'

He didn't extend his hand but simply nodded in her direction.

'Did you see our victim?' Kim asked.

'I did,' he said. 'And it's safe to say that your man knew exactly what he was doing to prolong the suffering and pain,' he said, leaning down to the pile of ash. He used his pen to poke into the pile. 'See here.'

Kim looked closer at a piece of cardboard around four inches square.

'The ash is being removed in layers, like a timeline if you will. The presence of intact material demonstrates that your killer never let the fire go out. He was constantly topping it back up to maintain a permanent wall of heat.'

'And that's the fuel he used?' Kim asked. She'd expected more than just cardboard.

'Looks that way. He didn't need anything more elaborate to achieve a temperature of 120 degrees, which is easy enough with cardboard and paper and would have inflicted the damage it did.'

'Ignition?' Kim asked hopefully as Nigel stood up.

'Matches,' he answered. 'A dog team is on the way to check for accelerants, but there's nothing obviously detectable.'

Kim moved away from the area as Nigel continued to poke at the ashes with the tip of the pen.

'You know, I can't imagine the kind of person you're dealing with here,' Mitch said, coming to stand beside her. 'To cause this amount of suffering to someone can only mean our victim did something heinous like murder a room full of kids or old ladies.'

Kim shook her head. 'Not even close that we can find.'

'Then he is one sick puppy, but bloody clever.'

Yes, Kim was beginning to suspect as much, but Mitch continued to put her thoughts into words.

'To have transported everything here undetected and to take so much time over the torture smacks of skill, patience and solid confidence. As yet, we've found nothing to help you identify him. So not only did he take his time with the act itself, but he took the time to clear up after himself. To have left nothing at all behind means his exit was measured, leisurely and controlled. He was in no hurry.'

'Yes, you're right,' Kim said as a thought occurred to her.

'Bryant, it's time to go,' she said, heading towards the roller shutter at speed.

People who were leaving in a hurry tended to leave things behind.

CHAPTER TWENTY-SEVEN

'So did you and Devon celebrate your good news last night?' Penn asked.

'Oh yeah,' Stacey said with a smile that was quick and genuine. From the glint in her eye, he wasn't sure she was talking about a shared bottle of wine.

'And she's even made me a cosy little working space in the corner of the lounge.'

'Now that is sweet,' he observed. 'That's showing you some love. I'm glad you had a nice evening. In my case, Jasper went into my room, farted and closed the door right before I went to bed.'

Stacey laughed out loud, and even Penn smiled at the memory.

'You gonna let him get away with that?' Stacey asked, smirking.

'Already taken care of,' he replied, winking.

Stacey waited for him to confess the nature of the retribution.

'Okay, I may have accidentally dropped cornflakes into his bed before I left for work this morning.'

'Accidentally? You missed his bowl by a room?'

He shrugged. 'Don't challenge the master.'

'You're both as bad as each other,' Stacey observed, and he didn't argue.

God only knew what their mother would be thinking, watching them from above; but they were now finding their rhythm. The first few weeks had been hard while they'd been working out what each needed from the other in the wake of their mother's death.

He'd spent many an hour fretting and worrying about the role he now played in the life of his brother. Older brother, parent figure, a bit of both. He'd eventually come to the conclusion that he would be what the situation dictated. If Jasper needed a firm hand, he could provide one, and if his brother needed a mate, he could be that too. As long as he was there for him in some form, he was confident they'd manage to get through.

'And anyway, I'll probably be out when he finds them,' Penn stated, thinking of his plans for the evening.

Stacey's head snapped up. 'You doing something nice?'

Penn laughed. 'Don't act so surprised. I do socialise sometimes you know.'

Stacey leaned forward. 'Tell, tell, tell.'

'Nothing exciting. Just meeting Lynne for a bite after work.'

Stacey raised an eyebrow. 'I'm gonna need more detail than that. Is it a date?'

Penn shook his head. 'Nah, nothing like that.'

'Where are you going?'

'The Bell, at Himley,' he answered.

'You're going to a nice pub for a meal and a drink and it ay a date?' Stacey queried.

'It's not like that, Stace.'

'Sounds like a date,' she said, returning her attention to her screen.

Penn opened his mouth to explain and closed it again. It wasn't like that between him and Lynne. They were mates, good mates. They liked the same films, the same music and shared a slightly warped sense of humour. They always had a laugh, and he liked spending time with her. He hadn't seen her since she'd helped build the bridge for him to cross back to his brother, and he was looking forward to her company.

'You know, it doesn't matter how many times I search the database for this vehicle, it's simply not there. The neighbour must have got it wrong,' Stacey said, interrupting his thoughts. 'If I've got any chance of trying to track down where the family has gone, I'm gonna need to at least start with the correct registration number.'

'Boss was pretty sure the woman was switched on,' Penn answered, taking the headphones from his drawer.

'So how do you explain it?' Stacey asked.

Penn paused with his own task. Ferreting through every vehicle that had entered the trading estate was a daunting task that was unlikely to yield any results this side of Christmas.

'Okay, Stace. Either she was right or she was wrong.'

'Jesus, Penn, I'd worked that much out myself.'

'You're convinced she's wrong, so go with that.'

'How does that help?'

'Okay, what's the registration number?'

'HL87 0RB.'

He wrote the registration number down on a plain piece of paper and held it up. 'So what did she get wrong? What letters are easily mistaken or confused? What letters could have been written in the wrong order? Don't be defeated by it. Treat it like a puzzle.'

Stacey regarded him silently for a moment.

'Penn, I may have a little crush on you right now.'

It was his turn to laugh out loud as he reached for his headphones again.

He would return to the vehicle-sorting task until the official post-mortem report came through.

Because he was convinced there was something there that didn't make sense.

CHAPTER TWENTY-EIGHT

Bryant pulled into the small street just as a smartly dressed man got out of a silver Lexus.

He appeared perturbed by the officer guarding the door.

As Kim exited the car into the bottle-necked street, she wondered what Rachel was making of the continued activity outside her front door.

'Mr Jenner of Wilson Fairbanks?' Kim called, holding up her ID.

He nodded and changed direction, heading her way.

After being given the name by Rachel, Kim had taken the time to research the landlord the night before.

In his late fifties now, he had started his own property management company at the age of twenty-four. With a small amount of inheritance money, he'd bought a run-down terraced house in the middle of Lye, taught himself different trades, renovated the house and rented it out. By the time he was forty, he had amassed a personal fortune in excess of ten million by doing what he was good at.

The last article she'd read had listed him as one of Britain's top ten wealthiest men, with over three hundred properties nationwide.

More interesting to her was the fact that he and his team actually took care of every one of those properties. This man was no slumlord, providing run-down properties for extortionate prices to vulnerable people. He charged the market rate for a decent place to live.

'Pleased to meet you,' she said, offering her hand briefly. 'But you can't have your house back yet,' she added to answer what she thought would be his first question.

'I can wear it, Inspector,' he said with the hint of a smile. The expression turned to concern. 'Is everyone okay?'

'Unfortunately not,' she answered. 'Which is why we need to ask you some questions. Did you know the family well?'

He shook his head. 'I have many tenants. Some are more time-consuming than others, but the Phippses never gave me any trouble. They were polite, not particularly demanding, were pleasant enough to the maintenance guys and were just a normal family. I would use the term unremarkable but not in a negative sense. Just seemed to keep themselves to themselves. I've never received one complaint from the other neighbours, which is not bad going,' he said, raising an eyebrow to indicate that wasn't the case in other properties.

'You own all six houses?'

Jenner nodded. 'Bought them all ten years ago, after a compulsory purchase order was placed for a new road that never got built.'

'So you got them cheap?'

'They were reasonably priced. All six tenants are on long-term leases.'

Kim knew from his portfolio that he didn't buy and sell, giving his tenants long-term security of having a roof over their heads.

'So you met the family how many times during the last five years?'

'Maybe three times.'

'And there was nothing that struck you as odd?'

'Only that they were a bit quiet and didn't invite conversation. They seemed like a decent family. To my knowledge they weren't doing or selling drugs, fencing stolen goods or conducting any other kind of criminal activity. They had no wild parties, caused no complaints, looked after the place and paid their rent on time for four and a half years.'

'Okay, Mr Jenner, thank you for… hang on,' she said, feeling the frown rest on her face. 'The neighbour said they'd been here for five years.'

Maybe nothing but the timeline could become important.

'Yes, they were. Almost five years to the day.'

'But you just said—'

'Sorry, I should clarify. The rent was never late for the duration of the time the Phippses were paying me.'

'Mr Jenner, could you explain?'

'Of course. For the first six months of their lease, the rent was being paid by someone else.'

CHAPTER TWENTY-NINE

It was after ten when Frost pulled into the narrow street in Prestwich. The traffic had been kind to her, and the Audi had greedily eaten up the miles of motorway.

She hadn't tried to call the woman, guessing she would refuse to speak to her. It was harder to do that when she was standing on the doorstep.

Frost locked the car and headed for number twenty-seven. She saw the irony in the fact the property was unassuming and brought no attention to itself.

She knocked twice on the solid wooden door before spotting a small camera and speaker to her left.

It buzzed into life.

'May I help you?'

Even through the electronic device Frost could hear the hesitancy in her voice.

'My name is Tracy Frost. I'm here to talk to you about Trisha Morley.'

'I don't know anyone by that—'

'Ariane, I know who you are. Please let me speak to you for a moment.'

'Please leave. I have nothing to say to you.'

'Just five minutes of your time,' Frost pleaded. 'If you've been watching the news, you know what's going on.'

'I can't help you.'

'I think you can. All I want is to talk for five minutes and then you can throw—'

The sound of the chain sliding across the door cut off her words.

The door opened to reveal a woman about the same height as herself. Her hair was short and severe but the style did nothing to detract from the attractive face.

She wore jeans and a V-neck sweatshirt. Her only jewellery was a pair of stud earrings.

'How did you find me?' she asked, stepping aside.

Frost noticed she took a look up and down the street before closing and locking the door.

'Many hours on the electoral roll,' Frost said, following her through a light and airy lounge to a kitchen at the back of the house.

'And your last name…' Frost added, in case that was something she wanted to address.

'Yeah, I've got my dad to thank for that,' she said, turning off a running tap. It appeared that she'd caught the woman immersed in a deep clean of her kitchen cupboards.

Was there any satisfaction to be gained from such a task? Frost wondered. There were things wedged in the back of her cupboards that had been there since the day she'd moved in. And for her they could stay there until she really could find nothing better to do with her time.

'You tried to warn Trisha about Nick Morley, didn't you?' Frost asked, taking a seat at the small wooden table.

Ariane sat opposite and regarded her cautiously. 'Why would I tell you anything? There's no way I want my name in the papers. Especially given what's going on at the minute. There's a lot of money and man hours going into trying to get Nick off the hook.'

'I understand and your name won't be mentioned. I'm writing a series of articles to try and address the balance.'

Ariane laughed out loud. 'You are joking me?'

Frost shook her head. 'Someone's gotta do it. Trisha deserves that much.'

Ariane stopped laughing. 'Nick has the best PR firm in the country working for him, and you think you can impact the image they're building with your local daily newspaper?'

'I can try,' Frost answered, trying to keep the edge out of her voice. She didn't need to be constantly reminded that she was throwing snowballs into a log fire. 'I mean, did you think trying to warn Trisha was going to do any good?'

Ariane shook her head.

'But you did it anyway.'

'And I now wish I'd done more,' Ariane said quietly. 'Because Trisha saved my life.'

'How so?' Frost asked, taking a notebook from her bag.

Ariane eyed it suspiciously.

'You have my word.'

'Because he left me for her.'

'Do you mind starting at the beginning?' Frost asked.

Ariane turned and took a pack of cigarettes and an ashtray from the drawer. Frost wondered who she was hiding them from. She hadn't seen evidence of a man or children in the small property.

'I met Nick when I was working in a Pret close to Snow Hill station in Birmingham.'

Frost guessed she was talking about the café chain Pret a Manger.

'He was working at a law firm around the corner and would pop in most days for lunch. He was incredibly good-looking and charming. He'd smile over at me even if I wasn't serving him. I started to look forward to his visits and tried to position myself so that I'd be the one taking his order. One day I was having my own lunch break outside, reading, when he asked if he could join me. We chatted and the time flew by. After that I started scheduling my lunch to coincide with his visits. Eventually, he asked me out on a real date, and he took me for a romantic meal in town.

'I don't even remember how it happened, but within three months I'd moved into his canal-side apartment.'

'There were no signs of violence?' Frost asked.

'I wish I had a pound for every time I've asked myself that same question. But there really weren't any clues. He was kind and gentle, funny and interesting. I really felt like the luckiest girl alive. Until I moved in with him. At first, I just noticed his sour moods. He'd get a bit snappy over nothing, and I realised it was best to just leave him alone.'

Adapting her behaviour, Frost thought.

'I tried not to annoy him. I knew he had a stressful job.'

Excuses, Frost realised. How quickly someone can fall into the trap, she realised.

'The controlling started probably a week after I moved in. I was getting dressed to go to a mate's hen party. He passed comment on the dress. He didn't like it. I did and wore it anyway. I thought nothing more of it, until two days later, when I was putting out the rubbish and found the dress cut to smithereens in the bin.'

'What did you do?'

'I confronted him. I was incensed. He laughed and said he'd buy me another dress. I wouldn't let it go, so he punched me in the mouth.'

Ariane took a deep breath before she continued, as though acknowledging that this was the point of no return. That it had been in this one moment she had sealed her own fate.

'He couldn't apologise quickly enough. He begged for my forgiveness, collapsed on the sofa and started crying, saying he'd never forgive himself for what he'd done. So quickly, I felt sorry for his anguish. I told him it would be okay, that everyone snaps sometimes. That we'd get through it.'

Frost shuddered, remembering her own reaction after that first shove.

'I'm sure you know already that it wasn't the last time. A month later, I was waiting in A&E with a broken arm. Two months after that I had two cracked ribs.'

'Didn't the doctors ask?'

'Of course, but I had my excuses ready. Nick would always tell me what to say, and I'd say it. They didn't believe me, but what could they do? I was too frightened to press charges. One time, I made the mistake of telling him I was going to leave, and he taught me a lesson I would never forget. We'd been together for eight months when I began to consider suicide. The shame of what I'd let him do to me was paralysing. That and the fear numbed me into silence. I couldn't tell anyone, and I just wanted to escape the fear that lived inside me every day. Then one night, he came back after an evening with his friends and told me to pack my stuff and get out.

'In my haste, I left half my stuff behind; but I filled a case, all the time thinking he was playing some kind of game with me. That he was going to stand in front of the door and laugh and tell me it was all a joke. He'd told me many times that he would never let me go.'

'And?' Frost asked, feeling the tension emanating from the woman as she lit another cigarette.

'I packed like the wind was behind me, all the while questioning his motives; but I wasn't going to look a gift horse in the mouth, when only moments before I'd been considering ending my own life.'

'Go on,' Frost urged.

'When I got to the front door, he was there, waiting. He told me that if I ever spoke of our time together I'd live to regret it, and I believed him. Of course, what I didn't realise at the time was that was the night he first met Trisha at the casino. I saw all the news headlines of the two of them together. It took me a long time to build up the courage to warn her.'

'You believed his threats?' Frost asked.

'Absolutely. He'd already shown me what he could do.'

Frost said nothing.

'I told you he gave me a warning when I threatened to leave him.'

Frost nodded. 'What did he do to you?'

'It wasn't me. He was way too clever for that. My father was involved in a car accident. He was rear-ended.'

Frost tried to keep the surprise from her face. Exactly what had happened to Trisha's sister, Penny.

'You really think that was him?'

Ariane took another deep breath.

'If you have to even ask me that question, you really have no idea who you're dealing with.'

CHAPTER THIRTY

'Okay, this is a complete and utter waste of time,' Stacey said, throwing her pen across the table.

Penn removed his headphones as the pen hit his coffee cup.

'Assault with a deadly weapon there, Stace,' he offered with a smile, while retrieving his cup and heading for the coffee machine. He knew not to offer her one and instead passed her a fresh can of Diet Coke.

'No luck yet then?' he asked, dropping in a sweetener.

'Nope, took a break and started fishing around social media for family background again, and it's like I said – not one person in this family seems to have any presence online. Found one account that might belong to Leanne, but it's locked up tighter than a duck's arse, so I cor confirm it.'

The account was Facebook's equivalent of sealing something in a lock box, placing it in a small safe and then locking the door in a dark corner of Fort Knox.

'I'm gonna go back to it once I've made some headway on this damn registration number.'

'Where you at with it?'

'I've tried every variation of the letters with no joy. It's what I said. The neighbour got it wrong.'

She pulled back the can ring and heard the satisfying hiss of the gas escaping.

Penn retook his seat.

'Hold the paper up,' he instructed. 'My mum always used to say that my dad couldn't see the wood for the trees, and right now, Stacey, I think you're lost in the damn forest.'

She'd heard that saying too, and she didn't disagree.

She held it up.

He looked at it for a full minute without speaking, then said the details aloud.

'HL87 0RB.'

He turned to his computer and spoke without looking her way.

'And you've tried all the letters?'

'Yes, I've tried variations of H and L and R and B. I've exhausted it.'

There were times when she really did question the workings of his mind, but this time she'd covered every base.

'Give me one sec,' he said, tapping furiously. Something was sparking in his eyes. A slow smile formed on his lips.

'Got it.'

'Are you kidding me?' she exploded.

'Grey Transit van belongs to a company called Matrix Enterprises. The zero has been changed with one single piece of tape across the middle to resemble an eight, and the zero in the second part is the letter O not the number zero.'

Damn it, she hadn't allowed for there being two potential errors in the number plate.

'You know, Penn, some days I love you to bits and other days you just piss me right off,' she said, tapping the details into her computer.

'You're welcome, Stace,' he said, giving her a wink.

She ignored him as her attention turned to trying to track down the whereabouts of this family.

CHAPTER THIRTY-ONE

'So the number plate had been doctored?' Kim asked as Stacey gave her the news.

'Yeah, boss – it was Penn who caught it.'

The woman would never take credit for anyone else's work.

Kim switched the phone to loudspeaker so Bryant could hear. They were about to start a detailed search of the upstairs of the Phippses' home. The lower level had yielded nothing.

'So the van belongs to a business called Matrix Enterprises.'

Kim stopped walking halfway up the stairs.

'The same company that was paying the family's rent for the first six months,' Kim added, revealing what they'd learned from the landlord.

Bryant turned her way to frown at the coincidence.

'Okay, get on it, Stace, I want to know everything about this company.'

'Got it, boss,' she said, ending the call.

'Okay, Bryant, you take the master and I'll take the boys' room,' she said as they reached the top of the stairs.

Following Mitch's words at the crime scene, her theory that something important must have been left behind in the family's hurry to leave had so far proven fruitless. Every cupboard and drawer had been opened and, although there was stuff, there was nothing that would offer any clues to their whereabouts or their secrets.

Mitch had been briefed to attend once he'd finished at the warehouse; however, if he found nothing to indicate a crime, they would have no choice but to hand the property back to the owner, who had assured Kim he would store the Phippses' remaining possessions for a period of three months.

There has to be something, she told herself as she closed the boys' bedroom door behind her.

In the corner, next to the wardrobe, was a pile of dirty clothes, most of it school uniform. Shirts, trousers and two blazers. The family had no intention of coming back.

She began the search in a methodical order, as she had with the other rooms, but there was a sense of sadness in this particular space. Like the other spaces, it bore all the signs of a hasty exit. Books and board games had been abandoned. She imagined the two young boys grabbing only their treasured possessions, making decisions on what to leave behind. Whatever the family's story, this had been their home for the last five years. They had made memories here. Had the boys known why they were being ripped from their home? Had they been frightened? Had they been fearing for their lives while throwing their most treasured possessions together?

She shook the thoughts away as she opened one drawer after another. The only way she could help them now was to find out who had killed their father.

Her heart sank as she searched the last drawer in the dresser. There was nothing.

As she had with all other rooms, she followed the process of walls, ceiling, floor.

There was no hatch on the ceiling, which left only the floor.

She dropped down between the two beds and lay flat on her stomach.

The door opened as she began to scan the space underneath the beds.

'Bad timing for a nap, guv,' Bryant quipped.

'You got anything?' she asked, ignoring his joke.

'Absolutely nothing,' he said, removing his latex gloves. 'It's almost like they were always ready for this. Like it had happened before or that they knew exactly what to grab.'

'Yeah, agreed,' Kim said, changing her position on the floor and laying her head down to get a better look.

'And they left absolutely nothing that will help— Ooh, hang on, what's this?' she said, stretching her right arm under the bed.

Her fingers closed around a single piece of folded paper, about to disappear between the floorboards.

She stood and opened it, feeling the disappointment settle like lead in her stomach.

'It's nothing,' she said, passing the paper to her colleague. 'Just a kid's doodlings.'

Bryant looked at the piece of paper that held the name 'Tommy Phipps' written over and over again, filling the page.

'Clearly likes his own name,' she said, dusting herself down.

'Not necessarily the case, guv,' Bryant said. 'Some people write things down repeatedly to remember them.'

'You think he needed help to remember his own name?'

Bryant shrugged. 'Maybe. Especially if it wasn't his real name to start with.'

CHAPTER THIRTY-TWO

'So, according to Companies House, Matrix Enterprises has been going for seventeen years and hasn't made a profit once,' Penn said.

'How the hell are they still in business?' Stacey asked. Every business could have a bad year or two, but seventeen years of making no money. Why were they still trading?

'Trust me it gets weirder. The company's profession is listed as people development, and every year their outgoings match their incomings to the exact penny.'

'Hiding profit?' she asked. Any auditor would see that this was impossible to achieve. Someone was cooking the books somewhere.

'Not sure, but the thing is, looking through their accounts for outgoings, the balance sheet looks like any normal business. You've got costs for rent and utilities, which isn't high, followed by vehicles, depreciation, expenses, accommodation. But the incoming amount equals exactly the total, and the revenue comes in one bulk payment listed only as sales.'

'Sales of what?' Stacey asked, wheeling her chair around to his screen.

'Great question. I have no idea.'

Stacey looked at the details he'd written down.

'This ain't no small-fry company,' she said. 'They're turning over hundreds of thousands each year.'

'Which is increasing by approximately twenty per cent annually.'

'But for doing what?' Stacey insisted.

Penn shrugged and pushed himself away from the desk.

'Can't answer you, Stace, no matter how many times you ask me the same question.'

'If this company paid the rent for the Phipps family for six months, what the hell did they expect in return?'

'Now that,' he said, grabbing his jacket, 'is a bloody good question.'

Stacey felt the anxiety building in her stomach as Penn left the room. What had this family got itself into? What were they so frightened of that they'd thought even the police couldn't protect them?

Stacey knew she had to try and find them, and so far she'd tracked the vehicle heading in the direction of Junction 3 of the M5 motorway in Halesowen. She was waiting on the images from one traffic camera, to ascertain if they'd passed the motorway island or continued their journey on the A456. She was praying for the latter.

Stacey knew there were approximately 1100 ANPR cameras across the motorway network. Each one read a number plate and instantly converted the information into non-unique reference numbers known as hashing. The cameras recorded fourteen million tags a day, making it near impossible to trace a particular vehicle using these cameras.

Speed cameras were a better source of tracking, but with more than 1800 of those, a direction of travel was necessary for a starting point. Once on the M5, the vehicle could be lost in the network of the motorway, making her job impossible.

Her email signalled the receipt of the requested footage of the camera on the A456, located on the other side of the motorway island. If it appeared, she had a chance of continuing to follow its journey.

She watched the ten-minute window she'd requested.
She returned to the beginning and watched it again.
The van wasn't there.
Damn it. The vehicle had entered the motorway.

CHAPTER THIRTY-THREE

Frost pulled into a service station once she figured she was about halfway home.

The chat with Ariane Debegorski had been both heartbreaking and rage inducing.

Once started, Ariane had talked openly about the abuse and her feelings. She had said that she couldn't see how she would ever trust a man again. That she would always swallow her own opinions for fear she might be physically attacked for answering back. Between the tears, she had explained how she had spent years trying to understand what it was within her that had given him the right to treat her in such a way. She talked of the guilt of escaping with her life when someone else had now lost theirs.

'Did you honestly feel he was capable of killing you?' Frost had asked.

There had been no hesitation in her response.

'Absolutely. In his rages, Nick became another person. There was no reaching him. The escalation of the violence convinced me my life was in danger.'

As she'd been speaking openly, Frost couldn't help but picture what a compelling witness she would be for the prosecution. A first-hand account of both the violence and the escalation.

She'd begged Ariane to consider it, but the woman had flatly refused and then asked her to leave.

She had respected the woman's request, though she had tried to drop a few earworms as she'd made her way to the door.

She took out her phone and dialled Penny's number, once she'd emailed her request for the court transcripts of the original trial, which would form the basis of her article this evening.

'Hi, Penny, it's Tracy Frost from—'

'Hi, Tracy,' Penny responded.

She was struck by two things. The warmth in her voice and the use of her first name. Everyone except her mother called her Frost.

'I read your article twice, and then me and Mum read it together and cried.'

'Penny, I'm sorry if—'

'No, please don't apologise. It was refreshing to read about her in that way. You captured her personality accurately. It got me and Mum talking about all the good times, all the years we had with her before she met Nick. It was good for us and it helped.'

Frost didn't know what to say. She couldn't remember a time she'd been thanked for something she'd written. But she had to give Penny a warning.

'Listen, you might want to give tonight's article a miss. It's all about the injuries Trisha sustained. I want people to know everything this bastard did to your sister. It may be hard to read.'

'We sat through it all at the trial. We know how she suffered.'

'And one more thing, Penny, just so you know, Trisha didn't stop trusting you. She didn't stop opening up because she wasn't close to you. It's the exact opposite. She was trying to protect you.'

'I'm sorry but how…?'

'Your car accident. You told me she stopped sharing with you when you were rear-ended. There's no way to prove it, but I'm absolutely sure Nick was behind it.'

Frost heard the sharp intake of breath but continued: 'The same thing happened to Ariane when she threatened to leave him. Her father was injured in exactly the same way. It was a warning and it worked. He knew that threatening the safety of the people

Trisha loved most was a solid way of controlling her. She stopped talking to you because she didn't want you to get hurt.'

Frost stopped speaking when she heard the gentle sobbing on the other end of the phone.

'Thank you, Tracy, I always wondered if I somehow let her down in those last few weeks.'

'You didn't.'

'That means more to me than you'll ever know, but Tracy, I have to ask: Why are you doing this?'

Frost opened her mouth to speak before realising she didn't even know the answer to that herself.

CHAPTER THIRTY-FOUR

Ormiston Forge Academy was the new name for what had once been Heathfield High School. Situated on Wrights Lane, in Old Hill, the school was less than a mile away from where the boys lived.

A woman in a navy pinstripe trouser suit appeared to be awaiting their arrival at reception.

'Anna Lennox,' she said, offering her hand.

Both of them held up their identification.

'Please, follow me,' she said, as though trying to get them out of sight as quickly as possible.

They followed into a small room, just off the reception area, which the woman opened with a single key. The office was a small, windowless room with a desk and a couple of chairs. The sparseness indicated it was a spare office no longer in use. Did the woman not want her own working space infected with their presence?

'Unnerving and distracting,' she explained. 'If the students see you wandering around, it'll disrupt their studies. Now, how may I help you? Are the boys okay? They've not come to school today, and I've had no call from their mother.'

The woman wrung her hands and Kim detected more than just concern for the boys, and she instantly guessed why.

'We have no reason to believe the boys are not in the custody of their mother and that they are safe and well.'

The pile of school uniforms told her that they'd returned home from school. This woman and her staff had done nothing wrong.

'You just never know. Even though the woman is an authorised party and the necessary checks were made—'

'What checks?' Kim asked.

'Well, most children have two nominated adults, often parents, but we allow more for the purpose of grandparents and other family members. Even so, we don't just allow the children to be collected at any time of the day by people we've never met before, even if they are listed on record.'

'So Leanne had never collected the boys from school before?'

Anna shook her head. 'No, it was always the mother and just occasionally the father. We called Mrs Phipps to verify that everything was in order, and she confirmed it was.'

'Did she offer any explanation for removing the boys in the middle of class?'

'No, she said only that it was a family emergency and that Ms King, her sister, was to bring the boys home.'

Bryant took out his notebook and made a note of the name. 'Address?'

'Yes, I can get that from the office before you leave.'

'And were there ever any issues with the boys?' Kim asked.

'Not that I'm aware of. I don't know every child individually; I rely on their form teachers to address any immediate problems but to keep me informed.'

'And neither of their teachers have alerted you to any concerns?'

'Not at all.'

'May we speak to Tommy's teacher first?' Kim asked.

'Yes, let me get him for you. He's a supply teacher, but he's been with us for some time.'

'Thanks,' Kim said. Clearly Anna was not going to let them leave the office.

The woman paused at the door.

'Of course, we don't know what kind of trauma the boys suffered before they came here.'

'Trauma?' Kim asked.

'Well, something had clearly happened some time in their past. Why else would they both need counselling?'

'Both of them needed therapy?' Kim queried.

'Yes, they both visited the same therapist once a week.'

CHAPTER THIRTY-FIVE

It was an athletic-looking man in his mid-thirties who knocked and entered the small office. His smile was warm and open.

'Liam Docherty, Tommy's teacher.'

Bryant stood to offer his hand and introduce them both, while Kim couldn't help but wonder how many of the girls he taught had secret crushes on him. Not that he appeared to do anything to emphasise his natural good looks. He wore a pale blue shirt and black trousers, but he wore them well. He sat in the seat previously occupied by Anna Lennox.

'Mr Docherty, we—'

'Please call me Liam. By the end of the day, I am sick to death of my last name.'

'Okay, Liam, can you tell us about the Phipps boys?'

'Well, I don't know either of them well. I probably spent just a little more time with Tommy, the older boy; even so, I didn't really know him.'

'But you're his teacher?' Kim queried. Teachers were trained to look out for all kinds of signs.

'I'm actually his temporary teacher. I'm supply, not permanent. I get called in to cover sickness, holiday, maternity leave. I'm here right now and could be in Staffordshire or Leicester next week. I teach many children, so rarely get the chance to form real bonds with them.' He smiled. 'I have all the same responsibilities: lesson plans, marking and all that.'

'But you prefer to be casual?'

'It suits me for now. I don't have to get bogged down in the politics of a place, the gossip. Let's be honest, every place has that, but as it doesn't affect me, I get to come in, teach and leave.'

He offered a smile that while not smug indicated he'd found a system that offered him the best of both worlds.

'So you didn't notice anything—'

'Aah, I didn't say that,' he said pleasantly. 'I said I didn't know him well. I immediately saw that he was what I would call a middle child.'

'A what?' Kim asked. Tommy had only had one brother.

'In my experience, a class is filled with three types of kids on the social spectrum: the introverts, who don't want to interact at all; the extroverts, who want all the attention; and the ones in the middle that would like to interact more but hold themselves back. Those are the ones you aim for, the ones you try and nurture towards confidence. I'd see Tommy in class, watching the extroverts shoving their hands in the air to answer every question. I could tell he wanted to contribute more, so I started to call on him for answers, but he'd always close right back down again.' He thought for a moment. 'It was like he was scared of letting go, of joining in. He was a clever lad, always writing things down.'

Like his own name, Kim thought.

'Did he ever reveal anything about himself or his family?'

Liam shook his head. 'They seemed like any normal family. A bit reserved but—'

'You met Keith and Diane?'

'Yes, parents' evening about four months ago. Though it wasn't a long meeting, they were very attentive.'

'It wasn't a long meeting because?'

'There were few issues to discuss with them. He needed a little more attention to Maths, but overall Tommy worked hard, got good grades and wasn't a disruptive child in class, which is why I chose to keep the one minor incident to myself.'

'Minor incident?'

'Just a scuffle with another boy. It was over in seconds. Just a disagreement. The boys shook hands and moved on.'

'Any idea what it was about?'

'Neither boy would say but both assured me it wouldn't happen again, and it didn't.'

Kim's interest was piqued. Given what she'd learned about the boy's tight control on his emotions, any sudden outburst had to be considered. Was this linked somehow to the therapy sessions the boys attended?

'May we speak with the boy concerned?'

'I don't see why not, seeing as you're not questioning him about a criminal offence,' he said, standing. 'Obviously, I'll remain…'

'Of course,' Kim agreed.

'Okay, if you'd like to follow me.'

'I get the impression Mrs Lennox preferred us to stay hidden for fear of disrupting—'

'I'm sure it'll be fine,' he said, opening the door. 'I'm confident that any kids that see you know you're the good guys.'

They both followed him out the door.

'Actually, probably better if just one of you comes along.'

'I'll be in the car,' Bryant said.

Kim fell into step beside the teacher.

'Am I allowed to ask if everything is okay, with the boys, I mean?' he asked.

'I'm sorry. I can't discuss it with you,' she said shortly.

'Okay, nice weather we're having this time of year.'

Kim smiled at his effort of making small talk. It was not something she did well.

'Just here,' he said, opening the door on his left.

Kim stepped into the classroom, and every eye was upon her, including those of a lightly bearded man sitting behind the desk.

He stood but didn't move towards them.

'That's Jacob Powell, my teaching assistant,' Liam said as Jacob looked away and took out his mobile phone.

Kim couldn't help but notice the pensive expression that rested on his face.

Liam clapped his hands, bringing the attention of the class back to himself.

'Okay, guys, nothing to worry about. As you were. Except for you, Robbie Weston,' he said, beckoning the boy with a finger and a smile.

The fair-haired kid with his tie messily done up came towards them.

Liam glanced at Jacob. 'You okay for…?'

'Yeah, I just gotta make a quick call,' he said, holding up his phone.

Liam appeared irritated but nodded.

Jacob left the classroom, mumbling about just needing a minute.

'Right, guys, I'm gonna be just here, so get on with your lesson,' Liam said, moving Kim and Robbie into the hallway.

He remained standing in the doorway so the kids were not alone and neither was Robbie.

'Hey, Robbie, I'm DI Stone and you've done nothing wrong. Can I talk to you about Tommy Phipps?'

'Okay,' he said, shifting from one foot to the other despite her assurances. His right hand started fiddling with the knot in his tie.

'You two had a bit of trouble?'

'He hit me,' Robbie said, putting his hands in his pockets.

'Why'd he hit you, Robbie?' Kim asked, feeling that unprovoked violence was out of character for the quiet, secretive boy.

'Dunno,' he said, staring at the ground.

'Robbie, look at—'

'It's okay,' Kim said, cutting off the teacher's words. She didn't care where he looked as long as he told her the truth.

'Do you hit people for no reason?'

He shook his head.

'But Tommy does?'

He shrugged.

'Does Tommy have many friends?'

'Nah, he's too quiet.'

'Does he bully other kids?' Kim asked, thinking it unlikely, but Robbie didn't seem to want to share the cause of their skirmish.

'Robbie, for what it's worth, I don't think Tommy is coming back to this school, so you can tell me the truth.'

'He hit me cos I made fun of him.'

'Why?'

'We were working on a joint science project, and we had to sign our work. I laughed at him cos he signed the name Ryan. I laughed cos he didn't know his own name. He belted me and said he'd beat me up if I told anyone.'

Kim's mind started turning as she thanked both Robbie and Liam and walked away.

The boy hadn't been writing his own name repeatedly for fun or because he was bored. He'd been practising to get it right.

CHAPTER THIRTY-SIX

I watch her take a seat on the bench. Every day she comes, and every day I watch.

What is she thinking? How is she feeling? What is she trying to recapture when she sits in that same spot every single day?

I can see the entrance to the park clearly from the studio flat, which is nothing more than a decent-sized room with everything fitted in. There has been an attempt at demarcation of the individual areas. A two-metre square of cool linoleum is fitted beneath the sink, two-ring cooker and storage cupboard. The dishwasher is a bowl in the sink.

A metal strip denotes the transition from lino to carpet, which covers the rest of the room. It is functional, biscuit-coloured and rough on my feet, but it is clean and intact. A single bed and chest of drawers occupy the far corner, and two chairs sit in front of the window. One faces outside and the other looks towards the small television mounted on the wall to the right of the bathroom door.

I understand that some might find it stark, but to me it's liberating. It holds nothing of my past and the person I was before I had to disappear. There are no memories of what I lost or was forced to leave behind.

My old life is lost to me. My family and friends are gone. I had no choice but to give them up, and yet I still wake each morning with the hope that can only come with a fresh, new day.

The thing I miss most is speaking. I say hello to the elderly lady who lives in the room below. She looks me up and down and greets me with kindness in her eyes. We comment on the weather, in passing, and I ache to say more: to chat, to pass the time of day, but I dare not. I am terrified of what I might give away.

The man who lives above sometimes helps me with my rubbish on a Friday morning. I think he waits to hear my door open and magically appears, whisking the bin liner from my hand.

'Give it 'ere – I'll take it,' he says.

'Thank you,' I say, retreating back into my room, grateful for such a small kindness.

Again, I would like to say more but I can't.

No one knows who I was before and they must not, will not ever find out.

I am safe.

We are safe.

And that's all that matters for now.

CHAPTER THIRTY-SEVEN

With only a first name to go on, Kim knew it wasn't going to help, but what she did know was that Tommy was not the child's real name.

'Did you miss me?' Bryant asked as she got back into the car.

'You were right about the name,' she said, ignoring his question. 'Tommy's real name is Ryan.'

'You reckon the whole family are using false names?' he asked.

'I think we need to assume so, but the burning question is why.'

'Well, I didn't come straight back to the car. I lost my way and ended up at the office of Mrs Lennox. Asked her if I could take a look at their previous education records. There are none. The school was told they were unavailable, and both boys had to sit tests to establish where they were in their education.' He lowered his voice, imitating the principal. '"They may have been travellers, you know."'

'Bloody hell, was this entire family born five years ago?' she asked in frustration.

'Maybe the psychologist can help,' Bryant said. 'While I was with Mrs Lennox, I thought I'd get us an address. He might be able to offer us something.'

'Let's go and find out, Robin,' she said, reaching for her seat belt.

'Anything else of interest?' he asked, pulling out onto the road.

'Teaching assistant didn't seem all that pleased to see me. Rushed off to make an urgent call.'

Bryant frowned. 'Bearded guy, mid-to late-twenties.'

'Yeah, sounds like him, why?'

'Sounds like a guy that passed me once I got back to the car.'

Kim was confused. He'd only left the classroom to make an urgent call.

'All I can say is he looked eager to get away, and he wasn't talking on his phone.'

CHAPTER THIRTY-EIGHT

Penn stood outside the registered address for Matrix Enterprises at the Five Ways Island on the edge of Birmingham City Centre.

The building was a vast expanse of metal and dark glass and appeared to reach up about fifteen storeys.

'Impressive,' he said to himself as he entered Staunton House. There had to be someone here who could tell him what the company actually did.

The reception was warm and tastefully decorated, with individual seating areas scattered around the space. Tables were littered with magazines, but not like the dog-eared, worn pages of *Woman's Own* you found at the dentist's office. These were thick, chunky copies of *Forbes* and the *New Statesman*.

Penn smoothed back his hair and approached the high reception desk, behind which sat a male and female, both wearing headsets.

The badged male named Brad finished first and offered a pleasant smile.

'Is this Matrix Enterprises?' Penn asked.

'Yes, how may I help?'

'Is there someone I can speak to about the company?'

'Do you have an appointment?'

Penn shook his head.

Brad's smile dimmed just a little.

'Let me just check.'

Penn waited as Brad made a call.

'No, I'm sorry but there isn't anyone there.'

Brad's tone told him that all his efforts were now exhausted.

Penn took out his ID.

Brad looked unimpressed.

'I'm sorry, sir, it doesn't matter what you show me, it won't make someone there.'

Penn was not warming to Brad's attitude.

'Are you telling me there isn't one person in the whole of this building that can come and speak to me about its purpose?'

Brad appeared surprised. 'I'm sorry, Officer, but Matrix Enterprises don't use the whole building. Far from it,' he said, pointing to a double directory board behind the door Penn had opened to enter the building. There were at least forty names on the list.

'The first thirteen floors are for resident businesses. The top two floors are serviced offices. Matrix Enterprises is on floor fifteen.'

Penn knew how serviced offices worked. You literally rented a single room and got a phone line and a postal address.

This company was turning over thousands and thousands of pounds each year. How did they do that from a serviced office?

'May I go and—?'

'There's no point,' badged-up Andrea said, ending her call. 'There's no one there. There's never anyone there.'

'Are you sure? What about paying the rent, post?'

'We don't receive any post. They pay their rent monthly by direct debit. They keep the office, but I've been here almost eight years and I've yet to meet one soul who works for Matrix Enterprises.'

CHAPTER THIRTY-NINE

The office of Doctor Michael Crewson was not what Kim had been expecting. In fact, it wasn't really an office at all. It was a detached home with a gravel driveway that sat on the Halesowen and Bromsgrove border, with a nameplate that was only visible once you were at the door.

If the man had earned the property through his work as a psychologist, Kim could only wonder how the Phipps family had afforded his prices. As far as she knew, only Keith Phipps had been working.

'Best guess?' Kim asked, knocking the brass door handle. It was a game they often played: guessing the house prices.

'Seven twenty,' he answered.

'Not bad. I'd say more like—'

Kim stopped speaking as the door opened on her words.

The man before her was a similar height to herself, with a short, dark haircut that didn't eradicate all the grey at his temples. He wore dark jeans and a white polo shirt. A pair of glasses hung around his neck.

Kim was quick to offer her identification to his questioning gaze.

'May we come in, Doctor Crewson?'

'Regarding what?' he asked, making no effort to stand aside.

'Regarding one of your patients.'

'Which one?' he asked, still withholding any invitation to enter.

'A fourteen-year-old boy named Tommy Phipps.'

'You have to know that any clients of mine are protected by confidentiality laws?'

'I understand that, Doctor Crewson, but we're investigating a murder.'

He raised an eyebrow. 'Tommy Phipps murdered someone?'

'No, but he is closely related to our victim, so will you please allow us into your house?'

He shook his head. 'I don't see the point for what will be a very brief conversation. If Tommy Phipps poses no danger to himself or—'

'Are you being deliberately unhelpful, Doctor Crewson?' Kim challenged.

'Absolutely not, Inspector, but I will not be breaking any confidences.'

'You did hear the word murder?' Kim snapped.

'Your problem not mine. I am tasked with providing a safe, secure environment for my clients so—'

'Mr Crewson,' Bryant said, stepping forward. Kim was guessing her colleague had seen her fists clenching at her sides. 'We would never ask you to compromise your professional integrity, but we are trying to catch a killer who may strike again, which, as you say, is definitely our problem not yours, but any help you can offer to help us save innocent lives would be greatly appreciated.'

Exactly what she'd been about to say. Almost.

'I shouldn't reveal anything at all without a court order.'

'Feel free to speak hypothetically, Doctor Crewson,' Bryant advised.

The doctor thought for a moment, and Kim realised there was no way he was letting them into his home, which made her want to get in there all the more.

'I treat people for many different reasons: depression; anxiety; stress; behavioural problems; phobias. You name it, I've treated it. Some cases are deeper than others. Some require years of therapy, and for others it's a problem of adjusting to a new situation. Big change can be harder for children than it is for adults and can last for years. It's like a grieving process.'

'We understand that the family moved into the area around five years ago. Was Tommy still receiving treatment this far on?'

'I won't discuss specifics, Officer, as I've already said. I can only tell you that a sudden move for children is a traumatic experience. The effects can last for years.'

'But why was the move so sudden?' Kim asked.

The doctor said nothing.

'You know, don't you?' she pushed, feeling this man held the key to unlocking all of the Phippses' secrets.

'I'm sorry, Inspector, but for that you are definitely going to need a court order,' he said, closing the door in her face.

CHAPTER FORTY

Michael Crewson only let out the breath he was holding once he heard the car pull off the drive.

Damn, that woman knew he was privy to the Phippses' past, and she would be back with a piece of paper that would force him to hand over the records.

He had known the minute the car pulled on to the drive that it was police officers, and they only ever visited him for one reason. He had been determined not to allow them access to the house, fearing they would find some clever way to get into his paper records: some kind of diversion or sleight of hand.

He had played the only card he had. A polite refusal when first asked was acceptable, even to law enforcement. Not complying with a court order was another matter entirely.

'Damn, damn, damn,' he cursed aloud as he headed back into his office, unsure of his next move.

The last thing he wanted to do was piss off Matrix Enterprises. It wasn't that they gave him a lot of business, but they were happy to foot the bill for as long as he deemed necessary.

Yeah, of course Tommy Phipps had experienced problems when the family first moved to the Black Country. Who wouldn't? He was a kid. And on his monthly report to Matrix, he'd listed issues like 'displacement anxiety' and 'past life grief', but the kid kept coming back, still talking about missing his friends, his school and relatives. All perfectly normal, but he was being paid a handsome amount per hour to listen.

He wanted to maintain the trust of Matrix, and he had no idea what would happen if his records got into the hands of the detective inspector.

He took out his phone and scrolled down to the contact listed as 'Babysitter'.

The call was answered on the second ring. The voice was breathless. 'What?'

'It's Doctor Crewson,' he said, unlocking the filing cabinet.

'What is it?'

The voice was short and sharp.

'The police were here, asking about Tommy.'

'Shit. What do they know?'

'Not a lot,' he said, placing the file on the desk. 'They're fishing, but I'm pretty sure they're going to be back.'

'Okay, let me think.'

The phone went silent, and he listened for the response. He wasn't surprised when the three words came.

'Destroy the file.'

He leaned over and switched on the shredding machine.

'Okay,' he said as the tension started to ease out of his body. 'And thanks for your help, Leanne.'

CHAPTER FORTY-ONE

Frost dropped her reading glasses onto the court transcripts and rubbed at her eyes. It made for depressing reading – but more than that.

She was well aware that there was nothing she could do to change the direction of the forthcoming trial. Her motivation in writing the series of articles had been to bring Trisha Morley's name back into the spotlight, to refocus the public on what the man had actually done, instead of the saintly image that was filling column inches.

Reading the transcripts in full, she could see why the jury had struggled to convict him.

The Crown Prosecution's case had focused not on the forensics so much as the pattern of behaviour of Nick Morley. Cleverly, the defence had not disputed that Trisha Morley was dead, just that Nick Morley was the one who had done it.

But the strategy of the CPS had been flawed. Yes, Trisha's medical records showed a litany of horrific injuries – but there was one major issue, Frost realised, as she read once again through the list she'd made.

Injury – Broken finger… Reason – Hammering a nail.
Injury – Facial swelling and bruising and cut lip…
Reason – Walked into a door.
Injury – Broken foot… Reason – Slab dropped on toes.

Injury – Dislocated shoulder… Reason – Fell over in bathroom.
Injury – Broken arm… Reason – Tripped over quilt cover.
Injury – Fractured rib and severe bruising to abdomen… Reason – Fell down the stairs.

And the list went on. Every injury had an explanation. Every bite, scratch, cut, punch and kick had been hidden behind a claim of clumsiness, and every explanation had been offered by Trisha herself.

Without a full understanding of the fear and conditioning of domestic abuse, the jury had questioned Trisha's refusal to seek help, especially when it was made clear that she had been alone in the consulting rooms. The defence had insisted that Trisha had had every opportunity to tell the truth, seek refuge and escape by telling just one doctor who would have alerted the police.

In her opinion, the CPS had done a terrible job in not calling enough experts to explain the thread of fear that bound Trisha to Morley, even when he wasn't around. And Trisha had seen evidence of his power. He hadn't been threatening her, he had been threatening her family. For herself she would have taken his wrath, but the car accident involving her sister would have both magnified and cemented the power he held over her.

And that was why his team was focusing on PR for his image. If the jury had struggled to find him guilty before, they had no chance now.

There was a part of Frost that was tempted to approach DI Stone and seek help, but the inspector had made it clear that there was little more they could do, no matter how strongly they felt about the impending injustice. She also knew the woman's hands were full with her current investigation.

She also knew beyond a shadow of a doubt that without any fresh evidence from the CPS, Nick Morley would soon be a free man.

CHAPTER FORTY-TWO

'What do you mean empty?' Kim asked, pouring a coffee from the machine.

'A bit like Bryant's wallet when it's his round at the pub,' Penn offered.

'Jesus, that empty?' Kim asked as Bryant pulled a face.

'The staff never see anyone go in or out,' Penn continued, updating them on his visit to the Matrix offices. 'Parking space is never used. Apparently, there's a desk and a phone, which is just enough to keep the space. Rent is paid weekly without fail, but receptionists have never met anyone associated with the company.'

'Post?'

He shook his head. 'Probably a redirection in place at the Post Office.'

'Damn,' Kim seethed. The Post Office was notoriously one of the hardest places to get information from.

Looked like the rest of her day was going to be spent applying for warrants and court orders.

'Medical records, Stace?'

'Requested and waiting. Checked on previous cases, but nothing like this is unsolved. I've logged a few Google keyword alerts for anything new.'

'Okay, so it's almost two and, so far today, we've learned a grand total of fuck all?'

Her team nodded miserably.

'In fact, we know even less than we did yesterday, because now we don't even think this family are using their real names.'

No one disagreed, and Kim tried to remember any other case that had taken them backwards.

She looked at the whiteboard that was glaringly sparse with information.

'We know that for whatever reason, someone hated Keith Phipps enough to torture him to death. We know that the rest of his family have fled their entire life, and they were helped by someone with a van that is registered to a company that spends hundreds of thousands of pounds, makes no profit, and has no physical employees.

'We know that one of the boys was in therapy for something, but that his doctor was never taught how to share.' She paused. 'Have I missed anything?'

'Only the dodgy teaching assistant that took a dislike to you and fled the school.'

'Hardly ground-breaking that someone didn't warm to me, but note his name down, Stace, and just do a bit of—' Kim stopped speaking as wedding bells chimed from Stacey's phone.

'What th—?'

'Google Alert, boss,' Stacey said, looking sheepish.

'What? You could choose the actual sound that—'

'Hang on, give me a minute while I… ooh… it's pinged on the word torture— Oh my God, come take a look at this.'

CHAPTER FORTY-THREE

'So who'd you speak to in Somerset?' Bryant asked as they pulled out of the station car park.

'Detective Inspector Lynes. Helpful kind of chap. Said he'd hold the body in place until three thirty, so I might need you to find that fifth gear, Captain Slow.'

Stacey's Google Alert had turned up a fresh, new crime scene being handled approximately ninety miles away, in Clevedon. The initial holding statement from the press liaison had actually used the word 'torture', causing it to show up on their radar. A quick call to the local force, a brief explanation and she'd been transferred to the DI at the scene.

Avon and Somerset Police was responsible for the county of Somerset and also the districts of Bristol, Bath and South Gloucestershire. The force employed almost six thousand people and covered a population of just under two million. The team consisted of around three thousand police officers and was responsible for the eleventh largest geographic area in England and Wales.

They were heading to Clevedon in north Somerset. Using the M5, Kim's satnav told her they were now 88 miles away and would be there in an hour and a half. Ten minutes too late. Bryant was going to have to haul ass to get them there in time; she wanted to see this body that had apparently been slowly tortured to death.

'Did he say anything else about the body they've found?' Bryant asked.

'Only that he'd never seen anything like it in his life.'

CHAPTER FORTY-FOUR

'Finally,' Stacey said as an email landed from the Cedar Vale medical practice. She'd fired off emails to the school secretary at Ormiston, requesting details on Jacob Powell, but had received no response, but it was the medical records of the Phippses that she was really interested in.

The message had four attachments. One for each member of the family.

'Hmm… that's strange,' she said, noting the size of the files.

'Strange is good,' Penn said, raising his head.

Stacey clicked into the first file, which was that of Darren Phipps, the youngest of the two boys.

'The file only goes back five years.'

'Wasn't that when they moved into the area?'

'Yeah, but medical files follow you around. There must be some kind of mistake.'

Stacey wondered if the surgery had started new electronic files when the family had joined the practice but not bothered to attach the old ones.

She reached towards the phone to call them and stopped. It had taken long enough to get this much.

'Youngest boy has asthma,' she said, reading through the notes, but Penn's interest had already been lost. Other than an ear infection, there was nothing to note.

She clicked onto Tommy's records and found little more there. A couple of minor infections, but no ongoing health concerns like his brother.

'There's no referral,' she said out loud.

'Huh?' Penn said distractedly.

'To see a therapist. There's no mention here of any adjustment problems, anxiety, depression.'

'Must have just gone private,' Penn said, reaching for his headphones. 'Still waiting for something strange, Stace.'

To her that *was* strange. The NHS had vast resources available for mental health issues. She could see no record of anything being mentioned about Tommy's state of mind. It made no sense. The Phipps family had not been rolling in money, so why go private instead of using the NHS?

The question stayed in her mind as she clicked onto the third file. The record of Keith Phipps. The man had a repeat prescription for Naproxen for arthritic pain in his hands. A job in heavy construction must have played havoc with that condition. Rare in a reasonably young man but not unheard of. Beyond that he'd visited once for a flu injection the previous winter. This family certainly didn't drain the NHS of resources. It appeared they visited the doctor only when absolutely necessary.

Right now, the family's medical records were posing more questions than they were answering.

She clicked into the final record of Diane Phipps and noted it was another short summary.

Her gaze passed over the generic information at the top of the page.

'Now that really is strange,' she said loud enough for Penn to hear.

'Make it worth my while this time, Stace,' Penn said, uncovering one ear.

'Oh, I think this one is worth it,' she said, checking again the section at the top on family relationships.

'Diane Phipps ay even got a sister.'

CHAPTER FORTY-FIVE

'Bloody hell, Stace,' Kim said as Bryant entered the coastal town of Clevedon.

It took her a second to digest the news about Diane and Leanne, even though a part of her was not surprised. There had been something missing in their interaction; a bond born of familiarity, history and knowledge. She'd seen no affection demonstrated between the two women, not even when Kim had informed Diane of her husband's death. Yes, Leanne had sat beside her on the sofa, but Kim recalled the squeezing of Diane's arm. It wasn't for comfort but control. But what was she trying to control? And if she wasn't Diane's sister, who the bloody hell *was* Leanne King?

'Gotta go, Stace, but keep at it. I want to know everything about that woman. And good work.'

'On it, boss,' Stacey said, ending the call.

'Okay, Bryant, you've got two minutes, so make 'em count.'

The satnav told her they would reach their destination in two minutes: it was 3.28 p.m. She hoped DI Lynes was true to his word and wouldn't move the body a moment before.

Kim caught a quick glance of the pier as they headed towards Walton Common.

They approached the external cordon at 3.29 p.m. The officer took what seemed like an age to check his clipboard before moving the cone for them to pass.

She was liking DI Lynes more and more, given he'd had the foresight to put her name on the list.

Bryant parked to the side of the pathologist's van from which a stretcher was being removed.

Thank goodness he'd kept to his word.

She approached the inner cordon and cast her eyes over the people standing around.

On cue, a short man in a three-quarter-length rain mac turned and headed her way.

'DI Stone, talk about taking it to the wire,' he said, holding out his hand.

She shook it. The man had been more than obliging.

'Suit up and come on through,' he said as two forensic suits were held towards them.

Keats wasn't normally as stringent at their own crime scenes, but she wasn't at her own. She had asked permission to come and trample all over someone else's crime scene. Their rules.

Once they were zipped up, an officer held up the cordon tape for them to cross.

'You got something similar back in Yam Yam land?' Lynes asked as they approached the activity.

She didn't object to his reference to the Black Country, so-called due to many folks saying 'Yow am' instead of you are. It might have been a different story if he'd called her a Brummie.

'If you're talking long and horrific torture, then yes.'

'Well, our guy is some piece of work, let me tell you,' he said as the crowds began to part.

'What the bloody hell?' she asked as her eyes tried to process the scene before her.

A naked man in his late twenties lay on his back, tied to an oblong wooden frame. His hands were stretched above his head, and his feet tied at the ankles to the bottom edge of the frame.

Her first thought was that the grotesque sight had been framed. She walked around it, trying to take in every single detail.

The frame had been formed of four pieces of wood. At the bottom corners a hole had been drilled and metal rods hammered into the ground, keeping the lower portion of the contraption in place. The two top corners of the frame had wheels at each corner. As she looked more closely at the centre of the long pieces of wood, she could see that it was two pieces of wood, one overlaying the other.

'Does the top half of the frame move?' she asked Lynes, who was following her around the body.

'Yes, there's a rope mark here,' he said, pointing to a jagged cut into the area right between the man's bound wrists.

Lynes took a few steps and pointed to the ground, where the grass was flattened.

'You think he stood there and pulled?' she asked.

Lynes nodded.

Her gaze eventually rested on the portion she'd been avoiding: the stomach, where most of his intestines had spilled out and were hanging over the side of his torso.

She tried to capture everything in her vision.

'What does all this mean?'

'DS Baldwin,' he said, calling over a female detective from his team. 'Care to explain?'

The sergeant nodded and smiled in her direction.

'It appears to be a makeshift rack, similar to the type used in the 1500s. This one is called the intestinal crank, where an incision is made in the abdomen to separate the duodenum, the first and shortest part of the small intestine, from the pylorus, the part that connects to the stomach. The constant pulling would extract the intestines from the gastrointestinal cavity of the victim.'

'How do you know all—?'

'Wait, there's more,' Lynes said, crossing his arms.

'By using a rope to keep pulling a bit at a time, the murderer was stretching the victim's body in the process. There would have been loud popping noises as his cartilage, ligaments and bones snapped under the tension. Additionally, once muscle fibres have been stretched past a certain point, they lose their elasticity and are unable to contract.'

Kim was impressed. 'Wow, that's erm…'

'That's what three years of medical school gets you before you leave to become a police officer,' she said with a smile.

'Thanks, Denise,' Lynes said. 'She knows some proper weird shit as well,' he said as she walked away.

If Kim was into matchmaking, she would have tried to get her number for Penn.

'She's impressive.'

'She's my right-hand person,' he said, smiling.

'Yep, I've got one too,' she said, warming to the man that reminded her of Columbo.

Bryant stepped forward.

'Her name is Stacey,' Kim clarified.

Bryant offered her a look, which she ignored.

'So how long?' Kim asked.

'Pathologist reckons five to six days but will tell us more once she liaises with the forensic entomologist and analyses the critters.'

Kim had known immediately that this victim had come before their own. Exactly how long before she would be interested to know.

She fought the urge to ask him who had found the body. Had they started viewing CCTV? When was the post-mortem? All questions she would have been asking if it had been her crime scene. But it wasn't and she could only push the DI's tolerance and good nature so far.

'Anything here to help you?' Lynes asked, giving the pathologist the signal to carry on with removing the body.

'Not sure yet,' she said, removing her gloves.

She thanked him for his time and headed back to the car. She had an urgent phone call to make.

'If we can assist further, give us a call.'

She called out her thanks over her shoulder.

That was probably an offer he was going to live to regret.

CHAPTER FORTY-SIX

Despite having his headphones on, Penn somehow knew when Stacey was mumbling away in the background to herself or when she was addressing him directly.

'What's up, Stace?' he asked, removing one ear pad for the fifth time.

'What are you doing?'

'Scrolling through 670 photographs.'

'Of what?'

'Dodgy-looking men.'

'Hey, save that for your own time.'

'You still got nothing?'

She shook her head. 'Not found anything on anyone called Leanne King. Any suggestions?'

His own task was giving him enough of a headache, even though the feeling in his stomach told him he was onto something.

Ever since the post-mortem, Penn had been wondering about the numerous broken bones in both hands: injuries normally sustained from boxing. He'd tried searching for 'Keith Phipps boxer' which had brought up no results, so he'd gone to the only thing he had: a driving licence photo. He was unable to use the post-mortem photos of the man's face due to the disfigurement caused by the burns. The tiny photo on the driving licence hadn't been too much better. He'd enlarged it a few times, but the magnification had reduced the integrity of the image. It was the best he had though, so he'd scanned it into the facial recognition software, and the program had offered him hundreds of possibilities. His only choice was to scroll through them all, looking for a match.

'You got a photo?' he asked, wondering if she could use the same app he was using.

She shook her head.

'You think that's her real name?'

Stacey dropped her head onto the desk. 'Don't take away the only bit of information I've got.'

'But was it always her name?' he asked, pressing the mouse button to continue his search.

'I've gone through birth and marriages a few—'

'I've got him,' Penn cried out, cutting her off.

'You're kidding?' Stacey asked, coming around to take a look.

He put the two photos side by side. 'You reckon?'

Stacey studied it for a few seconds and nodded before returning to her desk.

'So who is he?'

'Jackson aka "Jacko" Birch. An amateur boxer from the East End.'

'What the hell is he doing with a different name in Old Hill?'

'Dunno, Stace, but according to this article Jacko Birch vanished into thin air five and a half years ago.'

CHAPTER FORTY-SEVEN

'Sir, I want access to a murder enquiry in Somerset,' she said as Bryant took the slip road onto the motorway. They were heading back to Halesowen, and she wanted her request logged immediately.

'Stone, what the hell are you playing at?'

She'd momentarily forgotten that she should really inform her boss if she was leaving the county, especially if she intended to interact with another police force, just to pre-empt any complaints that might land on this desk. But he'd given her about the same amount of notice regarding Frost. Karma was a bitch.

'Sir, I think it's the same guy. The planning, the execution, the torture. I need access to every bit of information they get.'

'Bloody hell, Stone, you can't just go invading the crime scenes of other forces with your size nine hobnail—'

'I'm size six, sir, and I tiptoed,' she explained. 'To my knowledge, I didn't piss anyone off. I asked permission to attend, and I'm glad I did. This sick bastard is travelling the country to torture people and I need—'

'Hang on, Stone, I have another call.'

The line went dead as he switched to the other call. She groaned inwardly, already aware of what the call would be. DI Lynes had been co-operative and obliging, but she was willing to bet his superior officer was not so accommodating, and once he heard of her presence would have got on the phone. So right now, one DCI was talking to another DCI about her lack of etiquette and professionalism. She knew that Woody would field the complaint, support her publicly and bollock her privately.

She braced herself as the line opened up again and Woody returned to their conversation.

'Okay, Stone, you've got it,' he said tightly.

'Got what, sir, the sack?' she asked, momentarily confused.

'Access to the case in Somerset.'

Her relief turned to gratitude and then went straight for suspicion.

'Why, sir?' she asked, frowning. That had been way too easy. She hadn't had to sell a relative or anything.

He said nothing, and the unease in her stomach cranked up a gear.

She'd got exactly what she'd wanted, even though it was not what she'd expected. There was something here she wasn't being told. Woody hadn't had the time to make the calls necessary to get her unrestricted access. Who the hell had he just spoken to?

'Sir, we're on our way back, and I think it's best if I come up and see you right away.'

'Yes, Stone,' he said gravely. 'I think that's a very good idea.'

CHAPTER FORTY-EIGHT

It was almost five thirty when Frost pressed the 'Publish' button on her second article of the week, and in truth, she was quite pleased to see it go.

She'd spent the whole afternoon reading through every one of Trisha's unfortunate incidents and injuries. As Nick Morley had been found guilty of no crime, she'd had to cloak the article in an 'unluckiest woman alive' tone without any accusation towards her husband. She'd rewritten the article four times when her own voice and opinion had crept into the piece. At times, she had felt as though she was reliving every injury she was recording: the broken bones; the cuts; the bruises; two dislocations. And Frost knew that this victim could very well have been her.

She sat forward and clicked on the article, surprised to see the piece already had seventy-three comments. It had been live for no more than a couple of minutes. She scrolled through them and was delighted to see that the majority of them were speculating about domestic abuse. There was the odd smart-arse comment from their regular trolls, but she was happy with the result. The more people that questioned Nick Morley's innocence the better.

'Hey, Frost, get in here,' her boss called from his door.

The seven people left in the office looked up from their work. Such a summons was never a good thing. Well, not in her experience anyway.

It couldn't be the article, she assured herself as she threaded her way through the desks and enquiring glances. He'd checked it.

She closed the door behind her, even though his booming voice carried straight through it when he was angry.

But he didn't look angry, more a mixture of puzzled and amused.

'Just had a call from Nick Morley's lawyers: Fumble, Prickface and Dipshit.'

She laughed out loud and then sobered. She'd done nothing wrong. There was nothing in that article that was libellous. Nick Morley's name had only been used once in the reference 'Wife of' and then she'd left well alone.

'Yeah, I think it was Dipshit who called. Really nice guy – polite, friendly, professional.'

Frost folded her arms and waited. From the glint in his eye, her boss was playing with her.

'Invited me out to lunch tomorrow at a fancy restaurant in Birmingham.'

Devious bastards, Frost thought, and arrogant too. There was nothing in her articles that was not fact. They knew they had no legal argument against her or the newspaper. But it was clear they were watching everything, and she must have been setting off their Google Alerts like a brass band over the last couple of days. She wasn't surprised at their arrogance in thinking they could control the entire news cycle around their client. If they couldn't shut her up legally, they were going to try and manipulate her boss.

'And what did you tell them, Fitz?' she asked, crossing her arms.

He patted his ample stomach with a smile.

'I told Dipshit I was on a diet.'

Frost was still smiling when she left her boss's office. She was glad he had turned down their offer for what she knew would have been a subtle, underhand attempt to persuade Fitz to block the articles. In refusing their meal offer, he had refused their request and she was free to continue her series.

But they had noticed what she was doing and the readers and comments that were being attracted. They could see that Trisha's name was being mentioned on a daily basis.

Stick that in your pipe and smoke it, Goliath, she thought as she returned to her desk. *Now what are you going to do?*

CHAPTER FORTY-NINE

'Okay, so far I know that Jacko Birch started boxing competitively when he was sixteen years old,' Penn said, interrupting Stacey from her furious keyboard tapping.

'Hang on, let me just send this chaser email to the school about Jacob Powell. There, done. Continue,' she said, giving him her full attention.

'He was almost picked for the Olympic Games back in 2004 but just missed the list. He turned professional and entered the circuit early in 2005. Had reasonable success and won more than he lost for the first six or seven years, and then the tide turned. Almost overnight the balance shifted as he lost seventy per cent of his fights.'

'Age and fatigue?' Stacey asked.

'Probably. He'd maybe passed his prime but couldn't see it.'

'Or just wanted to keep making the money,' Stacey said. 'Talking of which, where is that money? He and his family were hardly living a lavish lifestyle.'

'Now that, Stacey, is a very good question. There's no mention of him retiring. He lost a fight in the second round and just disappeared. No more mentions and no more fights.'

'And a move to the Black Country with a new name.'

What did you do, Jacko Birch? Penn wondered as Stacey returned to tapping her keyboard.

'You still trying to find a search engine for Deed Poll?' he asked, taking his mug to the coffee machine.

'How are we not able to just search their database?' Stacey asked. 'And by us I mean the police. We wouldn't want any old Tom, Dick and Harry getting in there but surely…'

'Deed poll records aren't held in one place,' Penn explained. 'The National Archives in Richmond, Surrey, hold records dating back to the 1760s. The Supreme Court of Judicature keep records of enrolled deed polls for five to ten years, after which they're logged in the National Archives, and any more recent deed poll enrolments from the year 2000 are held by the Royal Courts of Justice in London.'

She sat back and stared at him with her arms folded.

'Stace, it's not my fault you've hit… oooh, actually, I do have an idea. Search the archives of the *London Gazette*.'

'Errr… why?' Stacey asked. 'Leanne doesn't live in London.'

'No shit,' he said, retaking his seat. 'If I remember correctly, every deed poll application since 1914 has to be published in the *London Gazette* prior to the name change.'

'You're kidding?' she asked, sitting forward.

'Nope. There's actually no legal requirement to make a deed poll for a name change. Often a letter from a responsible person like a GP, stating that the person has been known to them under both names, is enough to satisfy most organisations, but not when it comes to the issue of a passport. No UK passport or driving licence will be issued without a public announcement, a statutory declaration or a deed poll. The deed poll is the quietest way to obtain an official record so—'

'Shush,' she said as her fingers flew over the keys. Penn couldn't help but stop and watch the abnormal speed at which she tapped.

'Got one,' she called out.

'I'm only here, Stace,' he said, waving across the desk.

'Oh, okay, so, I've got a record here of a female who changed her name to Leanne King seven years ago. And her name before that was Karen Jarvis, so let me just put that in a separate search.'

Penn took a swig of his coffee and waited.

'Hold the bloody phone,' Stacey cried out, startling him.

'Jesus, Stace, what…?'

'Look at this, Penn,' she instructed, turning her screen fully towards him.

'No way,' he said, taking in the image of Leanne King/Karen Jarvis smiling widely for the camera, dressed in full police uniform.

CHAPTER FIFTY

Despite her eagerness to get to the bottom of what was going on, Kim did think to knock briefly before storming into Woody's office. And once she saw the person sitting at Woody's meeting table, she was glad she had.

'Oh, should I…?'

'No, Stone. Superintendent Wexford is here for this meeting. Please take a seat,' Woody said, moving towards the meeting table himself.

What the hell was going on? This man was not Woody's boss. He was Woody's boss's boss.

'Pleased to meet you, Stone,' he said, offering a nod instead of a hand. His words aroused instant suspicion. No one was ever pleased to meet her.

Wexford was a similar age to her boss, but that was where the similarity ended. His skin colour was a dusty white, as though it had never seen the sun. His face was thin and pinched, as though permanently contorted by stress.

'Inspector Stone, it is imperative you understand that you divulge nothing of what you learn in this room to anyone.'

She looked to her boss who said nothing. She offered no response, as that was something she wasn't prepared to commit to. Her brain continued to work as Wexford went on to explain the severity of the situation. Her mind flew over the facts of the last two days. The secrecy; the family's isolation; the name repeated on the piece of paper; this sudden involvement of the top brass.

She got it.

'Witness protection,' she said as the truth dawned on her. 'The whole family is in hiding.'

Wexford nodded. 'And we can't allow that fact to go public.'

She sat back, allowing the enormity of the situation to filter into her brain.

Oh yes, she'd bet it couldn't go public. If the police couldn't provide adequate protection, no one would testify at a trial again.

'Clevedon?' she asked of the crime scene she'd just visited.

'Yes,' Wexford answered gravely.

'Jesus,' she said. Two witnesses murdered in two days.

'This is a programme that cannot be compromised, Inspector. Potential witnesses must have faith in us to keep them safe.'

Kim bit back her obvious retort and remained silent.

'The UK Protected Persons Service, UKPPS, is responsible for approximately three thousand people and is governed by the National Crime Agency. The service is delivered regionally by local police forces. When witnesses enter the scheme, they become a protected person, which has a legal status and places a duty on police for protection.'

She wondered how that was working out for Keith Phipps or whatever his real name was.

'So how does this work locally?' Kim asked, wondering how it could be going on under their very noses.

'Regional Protected Persons Units will work to keep the location discreet and help a family rebuild a life in the new area. The UKPPS is part of UK law enforcement. It works independently of police forces in providing protection arrangements and concentrates solely on keeping people safe. The Central Bureau, the national headquarters of the NCA, provides strategic and practical assistance to officers supporting protected persons.'

'Matrix Enterprises?'

He nodded with an element of surprise that she'd got that far.

'The budget for the scheme comes directly from the NCA. Referrals can only be made to UKPPS by police forces, NCA and other law enforcement bodies.'

'Well, the Phipps family didn't get rich out of the scheme,' she observed. She too had heard stories of crooks and criminals being set up in luxury for their co-operation.

'Doesn't happen. Big payments can't be made, as defence lawyers could argue that witnesses have been induced to provide false testimony. An average case can cost up to fifty thousand a year. Much of that is spent paying rent and bills and wages until a new home and job can be found, sometimes a car. If there's a shortfall in house sale, the difference will be paid, but actually giving someone a new name costs as much as buying a new passport. The witness chooses a new name and signs a memorandum of understanding that there will be no criminal activity. Once in the scheme, a witness is assigned a police officer who doesn't work on criminal investigations but is solely committed to protecting and hiding vulnerable witnesses.'

'Leanne King?' she asked.

'Yes, she is a trained protection officer. One of about two hundred around the country.'

That explained so much that Kim had picked up on: the absence of the bond between the sisters; Leanne's take-charge attitude; the obstruction to all her questions. The woman hadn't been trying to stop Kim doing her job – she had simply been trying to do her own. Though Kim hadn't liked her one little bit and that was not going to change, whatever the superintendent told her.

'But what about the family's history?' Kim asked, thinking of all the dead ends they'd found along the way.

'Destroyed. Witnesses are removed from the electoral roll and other publicly accessed databases. You see, the knowledge of someone being found and killed is catastrophic. No one outside the scheme knows where witnesses are located, and officers use different computer systems to prevent corrupt officers getting access to data.'

'Weren't a couple killed some years ago?' she asked.

'John and Joan Stirland were shot dead in 2004 by gangsters in retribution for a murder their son had committed. They'd moved house but weren't put into witness protection. Many murders remain unsolved due to great reluctance for people to enter the scheme. The witness is provided with new medical records, national insurance numbers, bank accounts so that it minimises the chance of someone stumbling by chance on the person's true identity. Some are given a panic button or a programmed phone to bring police assistance with one touch.

'Of the thousands granted since 1978 when records first began, only a few have been spotted. Almost always because they didn't follow advice. The scheme is an unprecedented success.'

Tell Keith Phipps that, Kim thought but instead said, 'Until now.'

He opened his hands expressively.

'Our killer found the Phipps family somehow. The information has to be recorded somewhere,' Kim said.

'A WS1 and WS2 threat assessment is completed for every family member that needs one. Completion, storage and movement of documents is done in accordance with strict protocols. The forms must be downloaded onto disc and then uploaded onto a secure stand-alone computer for completion. Referrals must be supported by at least DCI status. Signed copies are hand delivered, and all Protected Persons Unit operatives identify themselves by first name only, to minimise the risk of compromise. The degree of protection measures will differ in each case and are dependent on threat levels.'

Kim had heard enough about the process and now cared only about how all this affected her efforts to find the killer of Keith Phipps.

'Is someone having this same conversation with DI Lynes right now?'

Wexford shook his head.

She looked from one to the other.

'You're not going to tell him?'

'The less people that know the better. It is imperative that—'

'Yeah, I get it. I heard it the first three times, but how is he supposed to run a murder investigation when he doesn't have access to the full facts?'

'He'll continue to run it like normal. He'll gather witness statements, forensic evidence and personal details about the victim, all of which might lead to the killer; but only you will have full knowledge and access to everything.'

The sour taste in her mouth was growing stronger. She knew she couldn't divulge the truth to the man. There was no question in her mind that she would lose her job. Only a few hours ago she had wanted access to everything and now there was nothing she wanted less.

'Inspector, even your own team needs to be kept in the dark about—'

'No chance,' she said with finality. 'You're not going to tie my hands and cut my legs off. And to be honest, they're probably about five minutes away from working it out themselves.'

Wexford's face hardened. He was between a rock and a hard place with all that he'd divulged.

'I can assure you they can all be trusted.'

'If this gets out I will—'

'Sack all four of us, sir, because it won't be leaked by any member of my team.'

She could tell he wasn't reassured, but he nodded his understanding anyway.

'So Keith Phipps particularly?' she asked, wanting to know more about the man tied to the roller cage.

Woody held up his hands. 'It's after seven, Stone. You'll get more specifics tomorrow. There's an expert coming in first thing, so I suggest you go and brief your team.'

Kim stood and waited for her brain to digest all the information, as though she'd just been to an all-you-can-eat buffet.

She would brief her team on everything. Let them sleep on it and tomorrow await the arrival of their expert.

CHAPTER FIFTY-ONE

'Shall I close the door, boss?' Penn asked as she entered the squad room, confirming to her that the team had worked it out. They never closed the door.

She nodded and headed for the coffee machine. Despite the time of night, she was pleased to see that Bryant had had the foresight to make a fresh pot.

'Thanks for staying late, guys, and sorry if you had to cancel any plans.'

'No probs, boss,' Stacey said. Penn nodded his agreement before looking away.

'I'm assuming you've guessed what we're dealing with?' she asked.

'Had an idea, boss,' Penn answered. 'When I saw Keith… err… Jacko's background—'

'Stick with the names we know. It was what they'd chosen for themselves.'

'So with Keith's background as a boxer, his sudden disappearance after a run of bad luck in the ring, and then Stace finding out about Leanne, the pieces started to fall into place.'

'Matrix Enterprises is the financial hub that pays all the bills, which is why there's no profit and loss. The money is fielded that way to avoid detection,' she explained.

'So did Keith piss off someone in organised crime?' Bryant asked.

'We're getting more details on that tomorrow, as well as an expert on witness protection. But before we go on, I have to stress to you all that this…'

'Not a word, boss,' Penn said.

'Sealed lips,' Stacey added.

'Obviously,' Bryant said.

Kim didn't feel the need to spell out the repercussions and damage any leaks could do. They were all intelligent enough to understand, and it was that same intelligence that had led to them uncovering the truth.

Now for the hard bit.

'We're being granted full access to the murder in Clevedon, but they're going to be working the murder blind.'

'Bloody hell, guv, that's gonna be tough,' Bryant said.

'It is, but we have no choice. The less people that know the better. They'll follow the evidence, and we'll be looking at the bigger picture.'

Kim knew that wouldn't sit well with any of her team. They all had the ability to put themselves in the same position. If there was a way she could have let Lynes know, she would have done, but just one error could cost lives.

'They're definitely connected then?' Stacey asked.

'Manner of death was horrific, planned and executed with the same level of creativity and intelligence. We'll have an identity tomorrow and then we'll know for sure,' Kim said, draining the last of her coffee.

The clock above the wipe board told her it was almost nine.

'And that's enough for tonight, so take yourselves home and be back bright and early.'

They all knew that was code for a 7 a.m. start.

Her team grabbed their belongings and started to head towards the door.

'Wanna lift, Stace?' Penn asked as they left the office together.

Bryant hesitated at the door and turned. 'So who exactly is this expert?'

She shrugged, but it was something she wanted to know too.

CHAPTER FIFTY-TWO

Frost was still smiling at the response of her boss towards the sneaky invitation offered by Morley's solicitors when she got in the car. She wasn't even sure that he held her same conviction in running the stories, but he was a man who didn't appreciate being told what to do.

She considered taking a bit of a drive out, as she sometimes did, before going home. The journey from work to her home was barely four miles, and the distance did nothing to widen the gap between her working day and her free time. The mood she was in when she left was still upon her when she walked in her own front door.

But not tonight. Maybe a long soak in a red-hot bubble bath would ease the day out of her.

As she pulled up at the traffic lights at the bottom of Pedmore Road, she debated quickly nipping into Merry Hill Shopping Centre to grab a cheap bottle of wine to accompany the long soak she was already picturing. Nah, she was sure there was half a bottle of something in the fridge from a few nights ago.

The lights changed as she saw a black Transit van in her rear-view mirror, travelling towards her at speed.

'Slow down, buddy,' she said, reaching down to release the handbrake.

The force of the van hitting the back of her vehicle propelled her car forward into the intersection of the four roads. She felt her body try to lurch forward before the seat belt restrained her and threw her back. It took a few seconds of slow-motion surrealism before she realised what had happened. The nausea began to rise in her stomach as she vaguely noted a dark shadow pass on her right-hand side.

The trembling in her body began before the pain registered in her neck. For a moment, she couldn't remember her own name, or where she was, or where she'd been going.

A knock on the window startled her as the world started up again.

'Are you all right?' asked a middle-aged woman right up against the glass.

'I think so,' Frost answered, trying to open the door.

Her shaking hands couldn't grasp the handle.

The woman opened it for her.

'Stay where you are, love,' she said, pointing to her own car. 'We were right there, waiting to cross after you. Eric's ringing an ambulance. We saw the whole thing,' she said as Frost tried to turn in her seat. Pain shot through every part of her body.

'Stay still, love, help is coming. Now, does anything feel broken? I did a first aid course a few months back.'

'I d-don't th-think so,' Frost said through chattering teeth. She felt as though her entire body was trying to close down on her.

'It's okay, love, it's just the shock,' the woman said, removing her jacket.

Frost tried to protest, but the woman was already placing it gently around her shoulders.

'We couldn't get a licence plate number cos the van was side on to us, and he sped off like a scalded jack rabbit. Probably had a drink after work.'

It took Frost a few seconds to understand that the driver of the other vehicle had fled the scene.

Rear-ended in a hit-and-run. Where had she heard that before? Her throat dried up even more when she made the connection: Penny Colgan and Ariane Debegorski.

The trembling intensified as the phone in her handbag started to ring.

'Let me get that for you, love,' the woman said, coming around to the other side of the car. She opened the car door and fished out the phone, handing it to her.

It was a number she didn't recognise, she realised, as she heard sirens in the background.

On the third attempt, she hit the answer button.

'Hello…'

'Hello, Ms Frost, this is Daryl Winston of Winston Associates.' She immediately recognised the name of Nick Morley's PR firm. 'I do hope I haven't caught you at a bad time.'

The ebbing sickness rose like a tidal wave in her stomach.

His slimy, smarmy voice told her he knew exactly at what time he'd caught her. The timeliness of his call left her in no doubt that this had not been an accident.

'Y… You…'

'We'd like to meet with you, Ms Frost. At your convenience, of course, to discuss an exclusive interview with Nick Morley, who I'm sure would be happy to answer any of your questions.'

The sirens grew louder as Frost understood that meant in return for her not writing any more articles about Trisha Morley.

She wasn't stupid. She knew she'd got herself into something bigger than she'd anticipated. She should have known they would not take kindly to her heckling their well-constructed news cycle.

She couldn't deny that she was scared. But so were they.

'So how about it, Ms Frost – shall we try to schedule a meeting?'

The sirens were growing ever louder, and the trembling that gripped her body was leaving her exhausted.

She pulled the kind woman's jacket around her.

'K… K… Kiss my fucking arse,' she said, before ending the call.

CHAPTER FIFTY-THREE

It was almost eleven by the time Kim switched on the iPod in her garage. She knew that many people held all their music on their phones, but she preferred to keep hers separate, away from everything work-related.

Barney had brought his carrot to the doorway between the garage and kitchen and was munching happily after their late-night walk. It was the spot he always chose to lie on, and Kim understood that it was so he knew if she left the garage and went back to the kitchen. The place where all the food lived.

Eventually, when he accepted that he'd had his last treat of the day, he would saunter over to the king-size sheet which covered the floor and curl up about a foot away from her, tired and content.

'If only life was that simple for us all, eh, boy?' she asked, positioning herself beside the bike frame she'd acquired from Dobbie the scrap merchant a few weeks ago.

She still smiled when she remembered the look on his face when she had handed over the money they'd already agreed upon, despite his efforts to swindle her once he'd realised there was a demand for the frame.

And it didn't look much right now, she admitted to herself. But back when it was introduced at the 1948 Motorcycle Show at Earl's Court, it had been a machine ahead of its time. When tested by the respected *Motorcycle Journal* they'd concluded 'it is a connoisseur's machine: one with speed and acceleration far greater than any other standard motor cycle'.

Vincent HRD in Stevenage had been renowned for their design innovation, engineering excellence and high performance, but that wasn't the reason she'd been on the lookout for this particular frame. It was the bike her foster father had always dreamed of restoring.

Tracking down genuine parts to put it back to its former glory was not going to be easy, but if she wanted easy she'd have chosen a much more popular model, where the spare parts were plentiful.

'And where's the fun in that?' she asked Barney as he plonked himself beside her.

She stroked his head and reached for the wire wool. He looked at her dolefully. 'Oh, all right then,' she said, dropping the wire wool and stroking him some more. His tail swished over the sheet as she leaned down and rubbed both hands all over his head and around his collar. He stretched his neck to accommodate her.

When she was sure she'd scratched every inch of his neck, she gave him a final stroke of the head and reached for the frame.

She started rubbing gently at the larger rust spots that were stuck to the metal like barnacles. She was careful not to remove every spot, not wishing to completely destroy its history.

This was her therapy. This was her happy place. Beethoven's Symphony No. 5 playing softly behind her as she brushed a piece of metal lightly and chose between rust spots.

The phone ringing startled her. She reached for it and was even more surprised to see the person calling was Penn.

'Hey,' she answered.

'Sorry to disturb you, boss, but I just did a log check before bed and saw something you might want to know about.'

Checking the incident logs last thing was something they all did, to see if anything had happened that could be related to their current case. But if it was anything serious, she would have received a call.

'Go on.'

'It's Frost, boss. She was involved in a hit-and-run earlier tonight. Rear-ended at the bottom of Pedmore Road.'

'Is she okay?'

'Ambo was called and she was taken to Russells Hall Hospital. No major injuries.'

'Okay, Penn, thanks,' she said, ending the call.

Normally, she'd put any car accident involving Frost down to the reporter herself. Kim had seen the way she drove the Audi TT, but if it was rear-end damage, even Frost wouldn't deliberately reverse at speed into the front of someone's car. And people didn't flee the scene of an accident if they had nothing to hide.

She reached for her phone, her first instinct being to check that Frost was okay. No major injuries, Penn had said. She was probably already on her way home.

'Not our business, is it, boy?' she asked, putting down the phone and retrieving the wire wool.

Barney raised his head.

'She's as hard as nails, matey – she'll be fine.'

Barney stared at her.

'What? She's not my problem, so quit staring at me.'

She waited for him to lower his head back onto his furry paws. He didn't.

'Jesus, what are you, my conscience?' she asked, reaching for her phone again.

She scrolled through her contacts and hit the 'Call' button. The phone rang out continually, and Kim was about to give up when Frost's voice sounded on the line.

'As if my head ain't hurting enough. What do you want?'

Kim felt the corners of her mouth lift up. She wasn't seriously hurt.

'What you been up to and who've you pissed off now?'

'What do you care and how do you even know?' she asked groggily, and Kim was tempted to explain that Barney cared more than she did.

'Where are you?'

'Just got out of a taxi after four hours at Russells Hall.' Kim heard Frost's front door close behind her. 'And if you don't mind, all I want to—'

'Did anyone get the licence plate?'

There was a hesitation before she replied. As though weighing something up.

'No, the bastard just drove off.'

Why the pause before answering?

'Frost, do you know who it was?'

'Bloody hell, Stone. I think you need to arrest me and give me access to a lawyer before asking me this many questions.'

'I've asked one question.'

Silence.

'You do know, don't you?'

Kim heard a sigh as Frost sat down.

'Okay, let's just say I received a very timely call from Nick Morley's PR firm. But obviously, I can't prove anything.'

So the articles were causing quite a stir.

'You were warned off?'

'Not in so many words, but let's just say even I can put two and two together and make four.'

'Are you gonna listen and back off? For your own safety?' Kim asked. She was not a police officer, and these people were not playing games.

'Not now I've found…' Her words trailed away as she seemed to regret what she'd said.

'What have you found?'

'Nothing that will help the court case, but it does show a pattern of behaviour.'

'A previous victim?' Kim asked, feeling a tingle in her stomach.

'Not one that will ever testify in court, and don't ask me anything else. I gave her my word I would reveal her identity to no one.'

'But she could—'

'Not happening, Stone.'

Kim was fighting down the urge to physically extract the information from the reporter and talk to the woman herself. A first-hand testimony of Nick Morley's brutality had the power to tip the scales of justice at the second trial.

Frost continued: 'For what it's worth, I tried to persuade her to come forward, but she's too frightened of Nick Morley's powerful reach. And I can kind of see why.'

Kim heard the weariness that had crept into her tone. She reminded herself that the woman had just been involved in a car accident. She couldn't help the pang of guilt gnawing at her. The woman had been hurt.

'Look, Frost, I know I said—'

'Don't even flatter yourself that I'm doing this because of your little permission call this morning. I had the articles mapped out for the week before the first one was even written.'

'Yeah, that was before you got rammed up the behind by some random stranger. You gonna give it up now?'

'Would you, Stone?' Frost asked, and Kim found herself unable to give the right answer.

'That's different. I'm paid to—'

'We're both paid to find the truth.'

'I get that but—'

'Well, thanks for the call, Inspector, and I appreciate your concern,' Kim heard before the line went dead in her ear.

CHAPTER FIFTY-FOUR

The team was assembled at two minutes to seven, looking keen and ready to start.

'Thanks for the heads-up last night, Penn,' Kim said and then took a moment to explain the accident to the others.

'I've logged an urgent response request to calls from her address, but Frost will continue to do what she wants to do. As you all know, she's a difficult woman to deal with.'

Bryant offered a small cough, which earned him a warning glance from her.

'Stace, anything back from the school on Jacob Powell?' she asked, trying to tie up all the loose ends in her mind.

The constable shook her head. 'Two email chasers sent and a message left for Mrs Lennox to call me back.'

'Okay, Stace, keep at it, but I want you working with DI Lynes in Somerset, so set up protocols for information sharing and ensuring we get access to everything they have. We want the identity of the victim the second they have it. Also, I want Penn to be able to view the post-mortem remotely.'

Stacey made a note. 'Boss, are they gonna be amenable to all this intrusion?'

'It's a fine line, Stace,' Kim admitted, which was why she'd put the constable as the intermediary, as she was probably the most sensitive out of all of them. 'They know they have to share the information, but they don't know why. We can't tell them, and we don't want to stamp all over their investigation.'

'Subtle is my middle name, boss,' Stacey said with a smile.

'In the meantime, Penn, I want just about everything you can find about the former life of Keith Phipps and—'

Kim stopped speaking as a figure appeared in the doorway.

'I believe I'm here to help you with that.'

Kim made no effort to hide the repulsion that made its way onto her face.

'What the fuck are you doing here?'

CHAPTER FIFTY-FIVE

The expression on Leanne King's face matched her own, but she stepped into the room anyway.

Good of the desk sergeant to let her know he'd issued a temporary pass and directions to their visiting expert.

'Team, please meet Leanne King, the most unhelpful police officer you're ever likely to come across.'

To their credit, the half of the team who hadn't met her offered courteous greetings, while Bryant muttered something about getting popcorn.

Leanne's face didn't change as she took a seat at the spare desk. Kim hoped she wasn't going to be staying long enough to warm it up.

Kim had to admit she'd taken a dislike to the woman's superior and cold attitude when she'd thought Leanne was Diane's sister, but since finding out she was a police officer, that dislike was now drenched in resentment. You didn't do things to hamper people who were fighting on the same side. Leanne was the player who put a ball in the back of her own net.

She knew she had to find a way to let it go. All they needed was information, and the quicker they got it, the sooner this woman would be gone. There was no point in allowing her true feelings to escape from the other side of her lips.

'You must have really enjoyed watching us chase our own tails,' Kim said.

And sometimes she just couldn't keep them in.

The dark brown eyes that met hers were impossible to read.

'There was no entertainment for me, Inspector. I was simply doing my job, exactly as I have been trained.'

'But you're part of a team…'

'I have no team. I work alone, and I do what I've been trained to do, and nothing is more important than the safety of the people I'm being paid to protect.'

There was so much that Kim wanted to say, but doing so would only prolong the woman's presence, which Kim was already developing an aversion to. There was no apology in her expression, and Kim guessed they would have to agree to disagree on the conduct of a police officer.

'Okay, tell us everything you can about Keith Phipps,' Kim said, moving to the top of the office and crossing her arms. The words 'and then you can leave' hung between them.

'Jacko—'

'Keith,' Kim interrupted, informing the woman they would stick with the names they knew.

Leanne rolled her eyes but obliged. 'Keith was born into abject poverty in the East End of London. He was the youngest of five brothers and learned quickly how to take care of himself. By the time he was fifteen, he'd dropped out of school and was doing the only thing he did well. Fight.'

'He was boxing at fifteen?' Bryant asked aghast. 'He was a kid.'

Leanne nodded. 'But he was a tough kid. Many start before they're ten years old, but the sport for kids is governed heavily. Not so much in the circles Keith moved. It was a blood sport, where kids knocked the shit out of each other for the enjoyment of paying adults. Once he turned eighteen, he was recruited by someone called Eddie Flint, who worked for the Tyler family.'

Kim shook her head, although the name seemed familiar.

'The Tyler family is one of the most powerful crime families in London. Freddie Tyler and his brother, Paul, have their fingers in more pies than Aunt Bessie.'

No one laughed at her poor attempt at humour, but they were all listening intently.

'So Keith started boxing for the Tylers. It was legit at first and the money was rolling in. Keith got himself a wife and a couple of young kids before they started telling him which fights to throw. He wasn't keen, but he wasn't so light on his feet anymore and the family knew it. They could make more on the betting scams, and he needed to keep making money so he did what he was told.'

'Explains his sudden string of losses,' Penn observed.

'So what happened?' Stacey asked.

'Keith knew a fair bit of the Tylers' enterprises, and he turned a blind eye to most things, but he did have a hatred for drugs. His oldest brother had died of a heroin overdose and another was addicted to prescription drugs. He heard a couple of guys talking about a particularly big shipment of cocaine, and he snitched.'

'He turned informant?'

Leanne nodded. 'His intel got three shipments caught before they reached the docks. The Tylers aren't stupid and started taking steps to track the mole. At that point, he was pulled out and put into witness protection.'

'Did he testify?'

Leanne nodded. 'Got the brothers sent down for three years.'

'And they're out now?'

'Oh yeah, and back running their lucrative business in our nation's capital.'

'Well, isn't that the obvious place to start looking?' Kim asked. 'Surely the Tyler family has found him and suitably punished him. They must have police officers on their payroll. Someone has given them the information.'

'Possible but unlikely,' Leanne said, cutting her off. 'Our records are—'

'Kept remotely and as secure as the Crown Jewels. Yeah, I know that, but our killer got his information from somewhere.'

'Our files show no evidence of being hacked, and it's not their style.'

'It's not the style of a crime family to track down, torture and kill a man who snitched and put their main players away for a few years?'

'Not this particular family. Gratuitous violence isn't their style. I'm not saying they're averse to making people disappear, but that's how they do it: quietly, covertly and with no links back to themselves.'

'How many times these guys been put away?'

'This was their first stretch.'

'So it's safe to say they might be willing to make an exception on the manner of death for someone who cost them a shitload of money and put them in the slammer?' Kim pushed.

'It's too showy, too flamboyant for the Tylers. It's not how they do things.'

Kim nodded towards Penn, who made a note to investigate further.

'So you were their sole protection against a renowned gang of criminals with limitless resources, who wanted Keith Phipps dead, and you chose to leave the family alone to identify the body and collect the boys from school?'

Leanne raised one eyebrow. 'Inspector, the moment Keith Phipps was late coming home, a second protection officer was installed in the flat above the chippy at the end of the road. At no time was the family left alone.'

Kim was relieved to hear it.

'Well, one thing is for definite,' Kim said, 'we need access to Diane and the boys. Now we really do need to establish if they saw or heard anything suspicious in the days leading up to—'

'They didn't,' Leanne said. 'They've all been questioned extensively and none of them saw or heard anything.'

'Forgive me if I choose not to take your word for it. I'd prefer to question them myself.'

'I can't help you,' Leanne said, opening her hands.

'Did your special training cover how to obstruct a murder investigation at every opportunity?'

'No,' she said, showing no emotion at all. 'I can't help you because I no longer know where they are.'

CHAPTER FIFTY-SIX

'So they've been moved to a different borough?' Stacey asked.

'Probably,' Leanne said with a disinterested shrug.

'And their names will change again?' Penn asked.

'I don't know,' Leanne snapped. 'Are you lot bloody stupid?'

'Leanne, a word outside if you don't mind,' Kim said, striding the aisle that separated the four desks.

Kim came to a halt about ten feet away from the door. Leanne followed with her hands thrust deeply into her pockets.

'Right, let's get one thing straight here. I couldn't give two shits about your attitude towards me. I've made it as plain as the scowl on your face that I'm not your biggest fan, but do not treat my team with the contempt you think they deserve. They've been nothing but courteous to you and don't deserve the disdain oozing from your pores.'

Her face reddened. 'How dare you try to control how—'

'Shut up and listen. It's your whole demeanour. You've assessed their importance to you and discarded their input. I can see it in your face. You're not used to being part of a team, I know that, but you still get to use the good manners I'm pretty sure you still possess.'

Leanne's expression told her she was not particularly receptive to the advice being offered.

'Okay, I do not need your assistance enough to tolerate your rudeness to my team. If you can cast your mind back to your initial police training, you'll recall that we don't much like folks being tortured and killed. That team in there will work day and night until we catch the bastard responsible. If you can help us without the attitude, great. If not, piss off,' Kim said, striding back into the squad room.

She'd either follow or she wouldn't.

By the time Kim had poured a coffee, Leanne was back at the spare desk.

'So how does this all work out for you?' Bryant asked, breaking the silence.

Kim watched as Leanne consciously adjusted her expression and met Bryant's gaze. 'Diane and the boys have been moved to another safe house out of the area. They'll be the responsibility of another force now and I'll be reassigned.'

'It's that simple. You don't get attached?'

'It's my third placement, and it's my job. I go where I'm told.'

'And you feel no connection at all?'

'Absolutely none,' she said, looking away.

'So the other two families?' Kim asked.

'Inspector, are there any other questions you'd like to ask me about this case?'

She couldn't be clearer that she was not prepared to talk about her previous placements.

'Okay, how were you assigned to the family and how did it work?'

'The Phippses had asked to be relocated in the Midlands. I'd just been relieved of my last assignment.'

'Which was with?' Kim asked, playing with her just a little bit.

'None of your business.'

'And it ended because?'

'Again, none of your business.'

Kim felt a stirring of interest about how or why assignments ended.

'Any of them get killed?'

Kim saw a flash of anger.

'No,' Leanne spat.

Like it or not, Kim had no choice but to consider Leanne's involvement. Few people knew the Phipps family's true identities, so anyone they came into contact with was a suspect.

'Please continue.'

'I was instructed to attend a bed and breakfast in Dudley, where I was briefed on the family.'

'You knew nothing before you got there?'

She shook her head. 'They received instructions and were there with plain-clothed police. Over a few days, the officers gradually disappeared while arrangements were being made. By day three, they were moved into the house in Old Hill and I was their sole contact. We spent that time choosing new names and developing a brief back story they could all stick to.'

'Hard for the boys,' Kim observed.

'For all of them. Leaving your entire life behind, choosing new names and then behaving normally is impossible. Dealing with the external factors is bad enough: the physical changes of place, etc., but the emotional toll is far greater. Grief for the life you had, displacement, rage at the injustice.'

'Of what?' Kim asked. They were being given the opportunity of a new life, protection, a fresh start.

'The injustice that the people he helped put away were out in three years, while his sentence was for life. They got to go back home to their lives and families. The Phippses didn't. They had the luxury of living a lie for the rest of their days for doing the right thing.'

'But they're looked after, right?' Stacey asked.

'Define looked after?' Leanne said.

'Support, counselling, a fresh start and—'

'You don't get it, do you? Imagine having everything familiar ripped away from you: friends, family, places. There's lots of people telling you you've done the right thing at first, and when it's all over you're left with access to one psychologist and one police officer. Some are happy to have a fresh start and think they'll have a better standard of living, but they don't. Many people in protection are former criminals of some kind. It's the only life they know. If they commit any crime, they're thrown out of the scheme and left to fend for themselves. Many can't cope with a new way of life. The programme helps to find them jobs but it's not always easy given their skill set. And this is all if they get accepted.'

'There's criteria?' Penn asked.

'Absolutely. A witness has to give essential evidence in respect of a serious crime like murder; attempted murder; kidnap; serious sexual offences; or organised crime. There must be a fully documented and imminent threat to the life of the individual or the family, and they must be fully prepared to abide by agreed conditions.'

'Who makes the call?' Kim asked, trying to get a feel for the food chain.

'Investigating officers will be accountable for a decision to refer an individual for witness protection.'

'So who knows new identities?'

'A senior official in the Protected Persons Service; up to two probation officers; a police officer at commander level in the local area; and the assigned officer.'

'And who are the probation officers?' Kim asked.

'I'm sorry but I can't help you with that.'

'And the local commander in—'

'I'm sorry but I can't help you with that.'

Kim was about to ask what exactly she could help them with when her phone rang.

When she saw the name of the caller, she prayed she was getting an update on the findings of Keith Phipps.

'Keats?'

'Stone, I need you at Wren's Nest as quickly as your broomstick will carry you.'

'The housing estate?' she asked, ignoring the quip.

'The nature reserve, east side,' he said, ending the call.

All eyes were on her. Her own team knew what such a call from Keats meant.

Leanne looked from one to the other and then fixed her gaze on Kim.

'What's wrong. Is it another one?'

'I'm sorry but I can't help you with that,' Kim said, reaching for her jacket.

CHAPTER FIFTY-SEVEN

'You know, guv, there are days that I'm really glad you like me,' Bryant said, pulling out of the car park.

'Hey, I wouldn't go that far. I just dislike you less than a lot of other folks.'

'You do know that your instant dislike of her is a little irrational?'

'Not at all. I dislike most people before they've opened their mouths, so she had a fair opportunity to change my mind. Did you hear how she spoke to the guys?'

'I did.'

'And you felt her total lack of emotion when talking about families she's worked for in the past?'

'I did.'

'And you saw how unhelpful she was with certain questions?'

'I did.'

'And you still think I was harsh with her?'

'I think the main source of your anger is because she didn't share the secret of their identity.'

'She's a police officer, and in the game of criminal investigation, nothing trumps murder.'

'It was more than her job was worth.'

'Nothing trumps murder,' she repeated.

Bryant refused to budge. 'It's her job to keep their secret. Their lives depend on it.'

'Let's go ask Keith Phipps how that's working out for him so far. Oh, hang on, we can't cos he's dead.'

'You know, guv, there are days when I could say the earth was round and you'd disagree with me.'

'Guess what my answer is,' she challenged.

'Nothing trumps murder, I know, so I think I'll shut up and drive.'

CHAPTER FIFTY-EIGHT

Frost groaned as she tried to get out of bed. On the third attempt, she managed to push herself to a sitting position and couldn't wait to get out of the damn thing. She'd tossed and turned, moaned and groaned, trying to get her neck and shoulders into a comfortable position. Eventually, she'd hitched herself to a sitting position and fallen asleep, exhausted, for just a couple of hours.

She groaned some more as she made it to the bathroom and back again. She glanced at her clothes, but there was no way she was attempting to get dressed until she had to collect the hire car she'd arranged online last night.

Fitz wasn't expecting her at the office, and she had played down the shunt when he'd called her, following her brief text message. She had told him nothing of the call from Morley's people. If he was the man she thought he was, he would refuse to print any more articles on Trisha Morley to ensure her safety. And right now, she didn't want him to be the man she thought he was.

Whereas she could lie to everyone else, she couldn't as easily lie to herself. Yes, the accident had scared her. Yes, she'd wondered if she should continue; but just as she was scared, she was also now pissed off.

The truth was that she'd spent many years hating herself for backing off. Like many others, she'd been bullied mercilessly all her school life because of her deformity, and she had taken it. She had allowed the bullies to intimidate and frighten her. She had taken it silently and cried alone. She had despised herself for not standing up to them, and once she left school, she had vowed never to let anyone make her feel that way again.

For now, she would stay in her pyjamas and carry on with what she'd planned. Today her article was about the forensic evidence presented at trial. The pieces of Trisha that hadn't burned with the rest of her.

She placed cushions on the sofa and made a pot of coffee before switching on her laptop.

It was time to throw another bun.

CHAPTER FIFTY-NINE

Stacey couldn't quite work out the woman who was sitting at the spare desk, fiddling with something on her phone.

Not once had she shown any emotion when talking about the lives of the family she'd been protecting, or when confronted by the horrific photos of Keith Phipps on the board. Leanne had identified the body, so she knew how Keith had looked, but Stacey couldn't look at the pictures without feeling something and she hadn't even known the guy.

Stacey understood the woman was available to them as a go-between to the UKPPS. She just wasn't sure what she was supposed to do with her in the meantime.

She resolved to do nothing and pretend she wasn't even there. Penn had already donned his headphones and got stuck in.

She picked up the phone and dialled the contact number she'd been given by the boss for DI Lynes.

He answered on the fourth ring.

She introduced herself.

'I've been waiting for your call,' he stated, his voice giving no indication of how he felt about it. 'So you gonna give me any idea what's going on? Why we have to open up all our findings to you guys up in the Black Country?'

'I'm sorry but I have no idea. I've just been told to make contact and discuss protocols for information sharing and—'

'Yeah, yeah, that's what I thought you were gonna say,' he offered stiffly.

Stacey remembered what the boss had said about sensitivity.

'You know, I remember once when I was about ten years old, my mom arranged for a girl down the street to come over for a play date. I wasn't all that fussed cos I didn't really know the girl. Anyway, she came and brought nothing with her. She played with all my stuff, but I didn't get to play with hers. Gotta be honest, I felt a bit shafted by the whole thing.'

Silence met her ears before DI Lynes burst out laughing.

'Stacey Wood, I like you, and I sure like those ballet slippers you're wearing to tread gently. The privacy and disclosure documents have been signed by folks higher up our food chain, and my tech guy has developed a link to this one case only. It's a temporary link and if accessed by anyone other than you, it will go nowhere and the link will be destroyed. And it should be landing in your inbox about now.'

As promised it appeared.

'You'll be able to witness our investigation in real time, but if there's anything urgent I'll give you a call.'

Stacey was blown away by his co-operation.

'I'm sending a separate link later to the post-mortem. Again, it will only be accessed by one login.'

'Got it,' Stacey said, glancing at Penn.

'Now, is there anything else I can do to make your day easier, Stacey?'

She could hear the humour behind his words.

'No, sir, I think—'

'Hang on,' he said, covering his mouthpiece with his hand. She heard no detail from the muffled voices in the background.

'Well, Stacey, it would appear that you were wrong and there is more I can do for you at the beginning of this fine day. I have a positive identification on our victim. Does the name Dennis Burke mean anything to you?'

Stacey said the name aloud, staring in Leanne's direction.

The woman grabbed her phone and headed for the door.

CHAPTER SIXTY

Wren's Nest had the honour of being declared the UK's first national nature reserve for geology in 1956. It wasn't the area's only claim to fame. Kim remembered from school that the caves were mined for hundreds of years for valuable limestone, and the world's first industrial steam engine was built by the Victorians next to Wren's Nest to pump water from mines and tunnels.

Approaching from the east side as instructed, they travelled a single-track road that wound around a few bends and then opened up into a rough car park that clearly marked the beginning of a walking trail.

'What's with the metal fencing?' Kim asked as Bryant parked behind Keats's van.

'About one square mile of the site has been closed off for a couple of months, following some kind of rock slide during a school trip. No one hurt but they've closed it off for safety.'

'Clearly someone didn't get the memo,' Kim said, showing her ID to the guarding officer.

'About a hundred metres dead ahead,' he offered helpfully.

She and Bryant trudged the path in silence. She guessed both of them were wondering what the hell they were going to find. So far, they'd had a naked man roasted to death, a naked man tortured on a stretching mechanism and, judging by the bare leg she could see to the left of Keats, this victim wasn't wearing much either.

'What we got, Keats?' she asked, taking a pair of blue slippers from Bryant.

He stepped aside to reveal a sight that at first glance appeared quite comical.

The man lay staked to the ground at both ankles and wrists. A ceramic mixing bowl lay atop his stomach. A red circle of burned skin wound around the base of the bowl. A trail of blood had oozed from beneath the bowl and made a route over his hips to pool on the ground.

'I'll give you a minute to take it all in, because when I lift this bowl, you won't be able to look anywhere else.'

CHAPTER SIXTY-ONE

'Where's she gone?' Penn asked, removing his headphones.

Stacey shrugged and turned to look out the window.

'Oh, I see her down there,' she offered, spotting Leanne walking in circles with the phone glued to her ear.

'Do you think their family members know what they do?' he asked, pouring himself a coffee.

Stacey shrugged. In some ways, the life of the handler was similar to that of the witness. They couldn't be open and honest about what they did or who they worked with, probably had to make up back stories for themselves and tell lies to most people they met. Stacey couldn't imagine being in a position where she couldn't share the rigours of her day with Devon.

'Do you think that's why she's so cold?' Penn asked, watching Leanne out of the window. 'She's not part of a team; her work is secret so she can't share the biggest part of her life with anyone.'

Stacey stood and joined Penn at the window, watching her walk the car park.

'Why do you think she had to change her name five years ago?' Stacey asked.

'Maybe something to do with her new assignment being crime-family related. Taking every precaution and all that.'

Stacey idly wondered what lengths she would go to herself to keep doing her job.

Leanne turned and saw them both watching.

'Talking of which, I really don't think the Tyler family killed our guy,' Penn said, returning to his seat.

'Come on, they've got a good reason,' Stacey argued. 'If his testimony put those brothers away for a few years, they've got more reason than anybody to want to see him dead. It's not like they were gonna come out of prison, shake his hand and agree to forgive and forget.'

'Agreed, but it's all too showy. Too ostentatious.'

'But they would have wanted him to suffer.'

'Indeed they would; but if they'd found him, they would have been far more likely to bundle him into a van and take him back to their own area. Why go to the trouble of scoping out a place that's unfamiliar to them? Better to throw him in a vehicle and do it in a place they know well.'

Stacey could see his point, but it was too big a lead to write off on a hunch. The man had put members of a crime family behind bars.

She was about to argue her point further when Leanne entered the room.

'The guy in Somerset, Dennis Burke,' she said, taking her seat.

Both she and Penn looked at her expectantly.

'Yep, he's definitely one of ours.'

CHAPTER SIXTY-TWO

'What the fuck?' Kim asked as Keats removed the cake mixing bowl.

She leaned closer. 'Keats, is that…?'

'A rat,' he confirmed.

'Jesus Christ,' Bryant exclaimed.

Keats had been right about one thing.

As horrific as the sight was, she was unable to look away.

'Explain,' she said, pushing down the nausea.

'It's a medieval form of torture that was considered to be cheap and effective,' Keats answered. 'There are many variants but this is the most common, which is to restrain the victim face up and to place a rat on his naked stomach, covered by some kind of container, which would be gradually heated up. The rat has no other means of escape and would slowly tunnel through the abdomen, causing the victim a slow and agonising death.'

Kim tried to get her head around the wish to cause someone to suffer so horrifically, and who would have a strong enough stomach to watch?

She pulled herself back and focused on the scene. 'Burn marks?' she asked, pointing to the red circle around the open wound.

'Yes, I'd say from some kind of blow torch used to heat the bowl.'

'Even that would have been bloody painful,' she said, looking around.

'Found by Vera Lyndhurst over there,' he said, nodding towards a slight, middle-aged woman sitting on the ground, still sobbing quietly.

Bryant headed over to take details. Kim already suspected that Vera did not have the physical strength to overpower this man, but everyone had to be ruled out.

'She's a volunteer here at the reserve. There's a few of them from the community who check twice a day that there are no folks in the danger area.'

'So the last check was?'

'Five o'clock last night, and I'd say this began not long afterward. The poor fellow suffered for at least ten to twelve hours.'

'Bloody hell,' Kim said.

'Heck of a way to die,' Keats observed, shaking his head.

Kim took one last look over the body and paused as Bryant returned.

'Is that a scar?' she asked, pointing to a thin trail of white leading away from the bloody mess.

'Appendectomy, probably in childhood,' Keats confirmed.

She took out her phone just as it began to ring.

'Just the man, Penn, I need you to start checking mispers straight away.'

She gave him a description of the male, including the scar. She would save the gory details for later.

'Will do, boss, but I'm ringing to tell you that the guy down south is a witness as well.'

They had all suspected as much by the manner of death.

'Links to organised crime?' she asked hopefully. It would give them one clear route to follow. Now, if he too had pissed off the Tyler family in London, they could have this thing solved by teatime.

'Sorry, boss, not even close. He used to be—'

'Save it, Penn. We're on our way back,' she said, ending the call.

Three bodies in two days. It was time for her team to regroup.

CHAPTER SIXTY-THREE

Frost sat back; having read through the court transcripts of the investigation, she now understood the sequence of events.

On the third of May, Trisha had called Penny and told her that she and Nick had had a huge row. She'd threatened to leave him, and he'd sworn he would never let that happen. Trisha had cried and told Penny how scared she was but had insisted on no police involvement. They had ended the call with Trisha promising to ring Penny the following day.

Penny had waited until late afternoon before trying to call her sister. The phone had gone to voicemail. She'd left messages before resorting to calling Nick. Nick had stated that when he'd returned from a night out, his wife had been gone. He'd assumed she'd just gone to visit friends or family following an argument. Penny had hounded the police, who had believed Morley's lies for over a week before investigating further.

Financial records showed no activity on the bank account, and a search of the house had revealed that nothing was missing.

After being told by the phone network that Trisha's phone hadn't been used after the phone call with her sister, and that it hadn't travelled away from the home, the police had finally secured a search warrant of the extensive property, and on the second day they'd found what they were looking for.

At the southern border of an eight-acre field was an area of scorched earth and sodden ash. In the bush line was a discarded fuel can.

The ashes had been painstakingly collected and removed for analysis.

Although the weather and local wildlife had played havoc with the forensic collection, they had managed to sift enough to find remnants of clothing and jewellery, handbag and purse, and bones from the forearm and teeth that had both matched Trisha's DNA.

Morley had been arrested and had not spoken except through his lawyer ever since. He'd been charged with the murder of his wife two days later.

Frost couldn't help putting herself in Trisha's position. The constant fear she must have felt every day, the physical pain she endured.

Frost found herself wondering if she'd known that the violence was escalating to the point where she would lose her life.

She hobbled to the kitchen for a coffee refill, willing her muscles to loosen up. She'd started this week wanting only to give Trisha a voice, a whisper amongst the shouting from Nick's camp. She'd wanted to remind people that there was a victim, a woman who had suffered horrifically at this man's hand, but the injustice of the situation was growing more ferocious inside her. Trisha had been with her for every waking moment, and just the thought that the bastard responsible was most likely going to walk free and resume his life was now abhorrent to her.

She no longer wanted to report the outcome. She wanted to change it. She just didn't have the first clue how.

CHAPTER SIXTY-FOUR

'Nothing yet on victim three, boss,' Penn said as she walked in the door.

Kim nodded as she took her jacket and hung it up in her office. Bryant took the opportunity to update them on the crime scene they'd just visited.

Stacey's eyes were wide as she listened. Even Penn wore an expression of shock, but the statue at the spare desk showed no trace of emotion.

Kim couldn't help but wonder what had happened to her for her to either ignore or close off her emotional response.

'Okay, enough on that,' she said, pouring from the pot. It wasn't an image she wanted to revisit over and over again.

'Did you get photos?' Penn asked.

And sometimes she worried about Penn's emotional response more than others.

She raised one eyebrow in his direction before turning her attention to Stacey.

'What do we have on victim two in Somerset?'

She glanced at Stacey's screen, which linked directly to the case in Clevedon and was updating in real time.

'His name is Dennis Burke and lives about three miles from the crime scene. The team down there has informed his wife and teenage daughter and are now doing door-to-door enquiries and visiting his workplace at a sheet metal manufacturing plant. His post-mortem is due in about half an hour and Forensics are still at the scene.'

Kim nodded her understanding. Now she knew what Lynes was dealing with, she wanted to know what they were dealing with.

Kim turned her attention to Leanne. The woman stared back at her.

'If I look at you, you speak.'

'Sorry, I'm not as well trained as the rest of your team.'

Kim bit back any reply. It didn't do her team good to see her being petty. She continued to stare. Waiting.

'Dennis Burke was previously named Adam Hawthorne, a graphic designer from Manchester. Out one night with some old college friends, he got separated from his buddies and witnessed the gang rape and murder of a twenty-year-old girl. His testimony secured convictions against two of the four attackers.'

'Leaving two still free?' Kim asked.

Leanne nodded. 'He was placed in protection after his young daughter, who was eleven at the time, came home with a broken arm and a warning.'

Who the hell would use an eleven-year-old girl to send a message? Kim asked herself. Clearly people who were prepared to do a whole lot worse.

'Graphic designer to sheet metal worker?' Kim asked.

'As I've already explained, the programme can't match the lifestyle of an individual. It does what it can.'

Kim considered just how much Dennis Burke had lost for doing the right thing: his home; his extended family; his career. There was no doubt the system was broken.

'What are the chances of both Keith's and Dennis's enemies finding them in the same week and exacting their revenge with the exact same MO?' Kim asked, crossing her arms.

'I'd bet ten to one against,' Penn said.

'If they're not being punished for their individual reasons for being in the programme, what are they being tortured for?'

'Information,' Stacey offered.

Kim nodded. 'He has to believe they know something he wants.'

'But they don't,' Bryant offered quietly.

'We can't know…'

'Yeah, we can,' he said decisively while looking at the board. 'These people are not superhuman. They're not trained Navy SEALs conditioned to withstand torture. They're normal human beings being subjected to the most painful, horrifically slow deaths imaginable. If they had the answers, they'd give them.'

The room silenced. Bryant was right. The killer wasn't getting the answers he wanted.

'Okay, guys, given what we know now, Bryant and I are going back to the beginning. I want to take a good look at that psychologist's notes about—'

'They're gone,' Leanne said simply.

'Sorry?'

Doctors kept records.

'Destroyed. He called me after your visit. I advised him to shred them.'

Kim regarded her silently for a minute. 'Sorry, but I'm just wondering if there's anything else you can possibly do to obstruct this investigation.'

'It's what we do.'

Kim knew she had to get out of the room before she did or said something she'd live to regret.

If this was her boss's idea of co-operation and assistance, he could stick it where the sun didn't shine.

'Okay, Bryant, we'd best go see what the good doctor can remember without his notes. The rest of you, carry on with what you were doing and Leanne—'

'I don't work for you, so you don't get to tell me what to do.'

It was a good job, Kim thought, grabbing her jacket. Her instruction to the insufferable woman would have contained only two words, and one of those would have been off.

CHAPTER SIXTY-FIVE

'You know, it really is amazing what they do,' Penn said, dunking a biscuit in his coffee.

'How the hell can you watch and eat?' Stacey asked, shaking her head.

'Easily,' he said, popping the whole soggy mess into his mouth.

Watching the post-mortem remotely wasn't the same as being in the room. For one he wasn't surrounded by the smell of anti-septic mixed with decay. On the other hand, the post-mortem was being carried out at a teaching facility morgue, and the camera in the top right-hand corner of the room was giving him a bird's eye view of the whole process.

'Penn, if he's gonna use that saw again, can yer turn the sound down?' Stacey asked without looking up.

The sound quality from their end was superb, and he could hear every movement. It was one-way sound, so he couldn't ask any questions. A suited-up DI Lynes was doing a good job, although his female colleague had rested against the work surface a couple of times.

'Wanna take a look, Leanne?' he asked, glancing to his right.

'I'm good, thanks.'

Penn cursed the good manners his mother had instilled in him, which dictated that every now and again he felt compelled to acknowledge her presence in the room, even though she had not initiated conversation with either himself or Stacey once.

He turned back to the screen as the pathologist motioned for Lynes to come closer. He didn't hesitate.

'There are ligaments here that have simply snapped under the pressure,' she said, pointing to the exposed shoulder. Penn could see that the muscles which would normally resemble tightly wound string were limp and stretched.

'Both shoulders and elbows have been dislocated, and the wrists have been completely separated.'

'I cannot even describe to you how painful this would have been, both to most of the joints in his body but also the abdomen.'

'Cause of death?' Lynes asked, removing his mask.

'Heart attack. The physical trauma was too much for his body to take.'

'Might have been a welcome relief,' Lynes said, touching the victim lightly on the shoulder before stepping back.

'The team on the ground is getting the exact same results as us,' Stacey said, bringing Penn back into the room. She nodded towards her computer and the updates that were appearing on the police log in Somerset. 'Neighbours know very little about the family. Teenage daughter didn't mix very much.'

'Is it really worth it?' Penn asked, turning to Leanne. This was the second family that had been forced into secrecy and deceit for doing the right thing.

'It is to us,' Leanne answered simply. 'We get to put dangerous people away because some individuals are prepared to do their civic duty.'

'Okay, but how is he getting his information? How does he know where to find them? Could the system have been hacked?'

Leanne shook her head. 'There is no system to hack. It's all kept on stand-alone computers. There's no network link.'

'But he's getting it somewhere. There's no way we've got some random psychopath into torturing people, who has managed by sheer coincidence to find two people in the witness protection programme.'

Penn tried not to let his frustration show as Leanne returned her attention to her phone. He was starting to understand the boss's attitude towards the woman. She wasn't like a police officer at all and seemed to have no interest in trying to find the person responsible.

He turned back to the post-mortem, which appeared to be winding up, but his thoughts had turned in a new direction.

For information to get out, there had to be a fault with either the system or the people, and if the system wasn't broken, you had to look at the people.

'Hey, Stace, got a minute? I have an idea.'

CHAPTER SIXTY-SIX

'Looking very casual today, Doctor Crewson,' Kim noted as the psychologist opened the door.

'Admin day,' he explained before opening the door wider to let them in. Of course, he had nothing to hide from them anymore. He knew his records were in slivers in the bin.

'Ah, so what day is shredding day?' she asked.

'I'm sorry, Inspector,' he said, closing the door to a utility room and quietening a washing machine on spin cycle.

He continued through to his office. 'I don't know what you're talking about.'

'We know the truth about the Phipps family,' she said, sitting down.

'What truth?' he insisted.

Kim felt annoyance begin to creep up on her but pushed it down. He was just making sure.

'We know they were a protected family and that Matrix Enterprises has been paying the bill for their sessions. Sessions we hope you might be able to share with us, now we're in the loop.'

Damn, she couldn't help that one bit of animosity that was attaching itself to everyone who hadn't told them the truth.

'It's not an easy situation for anyone, Inspector. I was given one point of contact, and her advice was to—'

'Yes, we know, but now we're aware of the truth, we'd appreciate a bit more honesty. Anything you can tell us about the family, despite not having your notes.'

'Okay,' he said, reaching for his glasses, even though there was nothing to read. She wondered if the gesture transformed him into business mode.

'I was contacted five years ago by the UKPPS and asked if I'd treat a family that had been displaced to the Black Country through the witness scheme. Once I agreed, I met with Leanne King, who explained the secrecy and confidentiality. I was not given any details of their previous life – no names or places – and I was required to help them adjust to their new life.'

Even the doctor had been expected to work with one hand behind his back.

'Go on,' she urged.

'They came to see me as a family for a few months and then individually. At first, they were like aliens: shell-shocked, as though they'd been transplanted from another planet. Gradually, the tension began to ease out of them and their visits became less. Keith was the first to go. Once he got a job, I think he was determined to make a go of it. Diane continued for another year or so but dropping the visits to every few weeks. She struggled more than Keith, I think.'

'She was prescribed medication?' Kim asked.

He nodded. 'I recommended she seek it from the doctor. The anxiety and paranoia were becoming unmanageable. She was having full-blown panic attacks in the middle of the street.'

'Fear of retribution?' Kim asked.

'Yes, but it got worse instead of better as time went on. She'd got to the point that every person who laid eyes on her was connected to the Tyler family.'

'I thought you weren't given details.'

'Not by the police, but the family was free to give me any information they wanted. It would have been impossible to treat them otherwise.'

Kim could understand that, but she was also starting to see how difficult it was to control the secret. The police could implement measures but the onus was on the family to remain tight-lipped, and sometimes they just needed to talk.

'Eventually, Diane's visits trailed off, but she still made appointments for the boys as and when they needed them.'

Another hole to plug, Kim thought.

'And the boys?'

'The younger boy adapted much more quickly, but Tommy struggled the most out of all of them. He was still coming to see me until last week.'

'Why?'

'Tommy was eight when they moved. He was just making friends and finding his place in a social group. He was an outgoing, confident boy in his former life, part of every sporting team and the hardest hit by not being able to share. He wanted to belong to his peer group, but his school mates were all starting to discover the Internet and social media, and he wasn't allowed to do any of that. His parents wouldn't let him anywhere near the Web.' A shadow crossed his face. 'But I think he might have been accessing the Net somehow.'

'Yeah, that'd be about right,' Bryant said with a wry smile.

Kim glanced his way.

'Guv, he's a teenage lad, desperate to fit in with his buddies. We didn't have the Internet when I was fourteen but we did have Knock Door Run.'

'What?' Kim asked.

'It was a stupid game where you'd just knock on people's doors and hide, so there was no one there when they answered. Great fun for kids but really annoying for adults. My mum said she'd keep me in for a month if she caught me doing it.'

'And?'

'I snuck out and did it anyway.'

Well, if the boy had somehow set up a social media account, there was only one other place he could have done it.

He had to have done it at school.

CHAPTER SIXTY-SEVEN

'Okay, this is everything I can find,' Stacey said, planting the sheaf of papers to the right of her keyboard.

'In date order?' Penn asked, grabbing a marker pen and heading for the only clear whiteboard in the room.

'Yep,' she answered, not yet completely sure of what they were doing. Only that Penn had asked her to print off every article she could find on the UKPPS.

Leanne had disappeared about ten minutes earlier without a word to either of them.

'Okay,' Penn said, seeing the puzzlement on her face. 'We know that our guy is getting his information from somewhere, despite what Leanne says. If there's no technology leak, it has to be a person. Now, let's say you work for one of the most secretive bodies of law enforcement and you know you've passed on information that's sensitive or secret. What do you do?'

Stacey said nothing.

'That's a question, Stace.'

'Oh, okay.' She thought for a moment. 'Well, if I'd done that, I'd probably leave. I'd want to get away from—'

'Exactly,' Penn said, pointing as though she'd just won a prize. 'But it's not like we can just ring them up and get a corporate staff list.'

'So… what exactly are we doing again?' Stacey asked, patting the pile of paper.

'Get the first article and read it out to me,' he said.

She did as he asked and read the page-long article about budget increases with quotes from staff members. Once she'd finished, she looked up to where Penn had listed three names and their positions.

Douglas Kilkenny – Chief Inspector
Amelia Dixon – Accounts Executive
Henry Rusco – Logistics Executive

Aah, now she got it, and although it was a long road, she could see where his mind was going.

'Next,' he called out as she reached for the second article.

CHAPTER SIXTY-EIGHT

'So you think one of his buddies at school helped him get on the Net?' Bryant asked as they neared the school.

Yes, that had been her initial thought: that Tommy had been so desperate to belong, he'd defied his parents' instructions anyway. There was just one problem. According to everyone they'd spoken to, Tommy didn't have any friends.

'Stop the car,' she said as they turned into the school entrance.

'We can get closer to… oh, I see,' Bryant said, pulling in.

Just to the right of the school entrance, two figures appeared to be gesticulating heatedly at each other.

'Isn't that…?'

'The headmistress and the supply teacher.' He paused. 'Include a priest and we have the makings of a good joke.'

Kim ignored him as she continued to watch the body language.

Anna Lennox was doing most of the talking and pointing. Liam Docherty was occasionally chipping in and sometimes shaking his head.

Every time Anna took a step forward, Liam took a step back.

The headmistress was dressed only in her blouse and trousers, but Liam had his briefcase and a coat resting over his forearm. Was he coming or going? she wondered.

Both stopped speaking, as though some kind of impasse had been reached.

Anna glanced over at the car park, said one more thing and headed back into the building.

Liam hesitated for a full twenty seconds before heading over towards the cars.

Neither appeared to be aware they'd been playing to an audience.

'What was all that about?' Bryant asked, switching off the engine.

'Not sure, but I think we should go and find out. You go after her and I'll go after him.'

CHAPTER SIXTY-NINE

'Wait, wait, wait,' Stacey called out as Penn wrote down the seven names mentioned in a three-page news report on the UKPPS just a week earlier.

Penn stood back and looked at the board that was now full of names and positions.

'Second name down, Amelia Dixon, Accounts Executive, was in that position but isn't anymore.'

The name quoted in the most recent article had been Hilary Owens.

'Gotta be worth taking a closer look at Amelia Dixon,' Penn said as his office phone sounded a single ring, indicating it was an internal call.

'Yo, Jack,' he said, taking a gamble it was the desk sergeant. He just hoped it wasn't DCI Woodward.

'Got a lady down here. Wants to report her husband missing,' Jack said as Penn breathed a sigh of relief.

'Got any details?' he asked, not wanting to be pulled away unnecessarily from the potential new lead they'd just uncovered.

'Yeah, he's nothing like the description you gave me, which is why I'm calling you,' Jack offered sarcastically.

'Oh, Jack, you're too—'

'Look, I've got a houseful down here. She says he's late-thirties, reddish hair, average build, blue eyes…'

'And?'

'Yes, he had an appendectomy in his teens.'

'I'm on my way,' Penn said, ending the call.

CHAPTER SEVENTY

Kim aimed for the supply teacher as Bryant headed into the school.

'Everything okay?' she asked, taking Liam Docherty by surprise.

'Just a disagreement over priorities,' he explained, putting his belongings in the back seat of his Ford Focus.

'Can you just answer a couple of questions before you go?'

'Of course,' he said, leaning against the car.

'Tommy Phipps, was he good friends with any other boy in particular?' Kim asked. If they could confirm he had accounts on social media, they could check to see if he'd been compromised in any way or had put something out there that had somehow led the killer to them.

Liam shook his head. 'Not that I saw. It was a concern to us that Tommy didn't really mix with any of his classmates. We tried to include him—'

'So you don't know if anyone might have helped him set up a Facebook page or an Instagram account?'

He frowned. 'Would it have been so bad if they had? All boys his age are on social media.'

'We just need to know if Tommy spent time with anyone in particular?'

Liam crossed his arms across his chest. 'This is all very cloak and daggery. I'm sure if you explained the secrecy and the reason for the strange questions, I could assist you more.'

'We have plenty of assistance, thank you, so if you could just answer th—'

'There are no students I'm aware of that Tommy was particularly matey with. I think they'd all decided to leave him alone. We felt sorry for the lad, to be honest.'

'We?' Kim queried.

'Yeah, me and Jacob, my assistant. I mean, sometimes...' His words trailed away as something clicked in his head.

'Please continue,' Kim urged.

'Well, sometimes Jacob would call him over if he was alone at lunchtime, to show him some kind of new computer game, but I'm sure he wouldn't have overstepp—' He stopped speaking, as though he didn't want to get into any trouble.

'You can be sure of that, can you?'

He appeared flustered. 'Well, no, I wasn't always around, but I trust Jacob with th—'

'I think we need to talk to Jacob,' Kim said, glancing towards the school.

'He's not here,' Liam said, opening his car door. 'And that's what the head and I were arguing about. He's not answering his phone or called in. I want to go check on him and the head is worried about covering my class.'

'Have you seen him since our visit yesterday?' Kim asked, feeling a burn in her stomach. He sure had beat a hasty retreat once they'd turned up.

Liam shook his head.

'Okay, Mr Docherty, I appreciate your concern for your colleague, but I think it might be best if we try and track down Jacob Powell.'

'He hasn't done anything wrong,' the teacher protested.

Kim appreciated his loyalty, but that wasn't for him to say. She was about to answer when her phone rang.

'Excuse me,' she said, stepping away from the teacher.

'Go ahead, Penn.'

'Victim three, boss – we've got a positive ID.'

CHAPTER SEVENTY-ONE

I am disappointed that she didn't stay as long today. A light drizzle forced her from the bench earlier than normal.

She has no idea that she is my rock, that I get comfort from watching her absently throw crusts to the ducks. She comes, she sits, she stares and for some reason that simple constant in my life gives me the strength to go on.

I take the few short steps into the bathroom and pause. I look in the mirror and am again confronted with everything I have lost: my friends; family; stability; familiarity; and, in some ways, even myself.

The person who stares back at me is not the vision of myself I have in my mind. When I close my eyes my face is plumper; it has more colour. I am younger and without the dark circles beneath my eyes. My hair is longer, a different colour. Many days I have trouble imprinting the new me on top of the old one. It sounds ridiculous to say that I miss myself, but I do.

I take my toothbrush from the cup and lay it down on the sink, ready to receive the line of toothpaste I squeeze onto the bristles. Some spurts and hits the tap. I put the toothpaste back and turn the tap before picking up the brush. Every task has a rhythm, a process to be considered, a logic that I'd rarely considered before and yet provides me with comfort now. It is a reminder that I am alone and that I must find my own way to survive.

Was it worth it? I ask myself as I leave the bathroom.

My gaze rests on the space to the right of my bed.

Yes, absolutely it was.

CHAPTER SEVENTY-TWO

The house of Rhonda Mullins was a two-bed terrace in Hayley Green, just a couple of miles from Halesowen Town Centre, and Bryant pulled up in front of it no more than ten minutes after she'd received the call from Penn.

A conversation during which she had instructed Penn to head over to the address of Jacob Powell: the only information Bryant had been able to extricate from Anna Lennox. During their conversation, the woman had admitted that she'd received the emails from Stacey but that she'd been too busy to respond. Bryant suspected that she'd got wind of it being connected to the body found on Monday and was awaiting guidance on what she could and couldn't share.

During her own conversation, Liam Docherty had gone on to explain that the man was experiencing some family difficulties and that was why he'd had to leave so quickly the day before. Kim wasn't buying it. In her experience, the only people fleeing from the police were folks with something to hide, and she had to make sure that that something wasn't connected to the Phipps family.

Bryant parked behind the squad car of the officers dispatched to break the bad news. A photo shown to him by Mrs Mullins of the two of them on holiday in Blackpool just a couple of months ago had left Penn in no doubt that Dean Mullins was their man.

A male police officer answered the door to reveal a female police officer sitting next to a slight woman with red-rimmed eyes on the sofa. Although small, the property had been furnished in all shades of cream, giving a light, airy feel to the space that ran right through to a kitchen extension on the back.

Rhonda Mullins looked like a woman whose body had collapsed on itself. Her pale cheeks were hollow beneath a jet-black hair dye that added nothing to her complexion. Kim ensured that her grave expression didn't give the woman even a moment to hope there had been a mistake. Receiving the news twice was even harder.

'Mrs Mullins, I'm DI Stone and this is DS Bryant. We're here to talk about the death of your husband.'

Bryant opened his mouth.

'But may I first say how sorry we are for your loss,' she added.

'Th… Thank you,' the woman offered, as though unsure exactly what to do or say.

Kim nodded to the constable that she could remove herself from the sofa. She did so and Kim took her place.

'I understand that this must be a shock for you, but we need to ask you some questions about Dean.'

Rhonda nodded towards the police officer who was now at the door with her colleague. 'She said he'd been murdered. Is that true?'

'I'm afraid so, Mrs Mullins, and we need to know—' Kim stopped speaking as the memory of her first interview with Diane Phipps played through her mind. The evasion; the secrecy; the misdirection; the lies.

She leaned back and called to the officers on the door.

'Guys, can you give us a minute?'

They stepped outside and closed the front door behind them, leaving just the three of them in the room.

'Mrs Mullins, before we ask you any other questions, I need to ask one important one.' It was a gamble, as she couldn't risk letting the cat out of the bag unnecessarily – but she also couldn't work around another pack of lies.

'Go ahead,' she sniffed.

'Are you and your husband part of the witness protection scheme?'

Surprise registered on her face as she began to shake her head.

Fuck, she'd called it wrong and divulged the sensitivity of their enquiry.

'Mrs Mullins, I must ask that—'

'Sorry, Officer. I should be clearer. No, we're not in the scheme. At least not anymore.'

CHAPTER SEVENTY-THREE

'Not anymore?' Kim asked, sitting up straighter.

'We left. Dean couldn't hack it.'

'Why were you placed in the scheme?' Kim asked.

'Dean was an ex-gang member. He was part of The Deltas.'

Kim knew the gang well. It was a multi-racial gang that operated out of Hollytree Estate and was so named because of its Dudley postcode. She'd been responsible for putting one of their ring leaders, Kai Lord, behind bars for a good few years to come.

'Dean had been with them since he was thirteen years old. He was twenty-six when he decided he wanted out, but you know how that goes.'

In Kim's experience, there was only one way out of a gang like The Deltas and that was in a wooden box. They liked to brag that they had no ex-gang members.

'The only way out he could see was to use the information he had and offer it to police in exchange for protection.'

'And?'

'His knowledge got a few people put away for minor offences, but it got one guy sent down for attempted murder and kidnap. Apparently, that was enough to guarantee safe passage.'

Kim could hear the bitterness in her voice and decided to keep her talking. For now, she was distracted from the death of her husband and Kim didn't know what she might learn.

'What was the scheme like for you?'

'Fucking awful. We had no idea what we were getting into or how drastically our lives would change. You lot care only about a conviction.'

Kim tried not to react. Dean had been a man who had lived on the wrong side of the law for years but had used that same resource for his own benefit when it had suited him, and then had the gall to throw it away when it hadn't panned out how he'd expected.

'They took all our phones and stuff away and put us in a B&B while investigating. Once the trial was over, they handed us a Lidl map and told us to choose an area we wanted to live. Dean had been to Blackpool once, so we chose there. Police said they'd try and create an equivalent lifestyle and that was bollocks. Every answer to any question is delayed until after the trial,' she said, using her fingers to frame the last three words.

'We had thirty minutes to gather our stuff. I mean, even bailiffs give you an hour. And if folks think all police officers are polite and helpful, they can think again. Those in plain clothes get away with murder. They can treat you however they like and you can't tell a soul.'

'Were you mistreated by…?'

'Forget it,' she said, waving the question away.

'What happened next?' Kim asked. She was guessing the officers involved had been less than enthusiastic about providing protection for a man that had flouted the law for years.

'Eventually, we were taken in a van to a safe house in Shropshire, with nothing more than cows and sheep and a daily allowance. We didn't know that was when they were getting rid of all our paperwork. Killing us off, deleting our lives. We could have died and no one would have known. When your life is dead, where do you go for help?

'You then get to choose a new name, but how can you behave normally in society? You're given no back story so anything you invent you've got to stick to, all of you.'

She shook her head. 'One time we went round for a cuppa with the neighbours, simple enough, you'd think. Just a quick polite coffee, but there's always questions. Harmless ones like "So where did you get married?", and we both answered at the same time with different responses. You can't make friends in case you slip up. We were bloody miserable.'

'Couldn't you request a move?' Bryant asked.

'To where? You just take the exact same problems with you. You get paranoid that everyone is a threat. You view every question as suspicious. You just can't remember every detail of your new identity, places, people, memories – cos they never happened. It's like watching a TV box set and trying to remember everything that happened to who, on what day. It's bad enough for adults, never mind kids. Our daughter couldn't mix; she was constantly tempted to tell her best friend the truth. You can't build any kind of relationship through fear you're gonna fuck up. You even hesitate before signing your own name cos it's not your name, but that's not even the worst of it.'

She'd painted a pretty grim picture of it so far, so Kim wondered what the worst of it actually was.

'You can't tell your family where you're going. For their sake, you have to cut off completely. You worry about them; they definitely worry about you. You cause all this by doing the right thing.'

For your own reasons, Kim couldn't help but think.

'But you had support, help to adapt and adjust?' Bryant asked.

'Oh yeah,' she said, rolling her eyes. 'We had a psychologist who told us to do breathing exercises to alleviate the stress, and our protection officer up north was as clueless as we were. And protection? A light wind or a deep breath would have blown him over.'

'So you left?' Kim asked.

Her expression changed as she was brought back to the present, back to her current nightmare. A tear spilled over and rolled down her cheek.

'Dean knew how unhappy me and Lexi were. He knew the risks in coming back, but he insisted. He knew he was the one in danger, and he was right.'

Kim chose not to clarify. She knew beyond a shadow of a doubt this was not the work of anyone from Hollytree.

She was about to ask if Dean had remarked on anything suspicious during the last few days when her phone rang.

She excused herself and walked into the hallway.

Before she answered, she heard Bryant asking the exact questions that had been in her mind.

'Penn,' she said.

'Boss, about the information leak. It might be nothing, but there's someone we think you should see.'

CHAPTER SEVENTY-FOUR

It was almost three when Penn pulled up in front of an end terrace on a small housing estate in Blackheath, Rowley Regis. There was no car parked outside the house, and he got the immediate impression that Jacob Powell was not at home.

Nevertheless, he parked the car and approached the front door. The old-fashioned black-and-white bell sounded in the hallway. He waited. No response. He rang again and then tried to look through the letterbox.

Beyond the front door, he could see a couple of pairs of shoes and a thick winter cardigan. He moved to the right, cupped his eyes and tried to see beyond the net curtain, but the denseness of the lace was like an impenetrable wall that probably held in as much warmth as the glass.

Penn considered for a moment. He could understand the boss wishing to speak to Jacob Powell, but they didn't suspect the man was in any danger. Nor did they have any evidence linking him to a crime. Summoning the big key and smashing down the man's door wasn't really an option. Now, if there was a way to get in without causing any damage, that would be different.

He stood back to see if there was any open window, but the place appeared to be locked and secure.

'Jesus Christ,' he cried, stepping back as a hefty black cat appeared on the inside windowsill. Penn would swear the feline was glaring at him suspiciously.

He tried again to look beyond the net curtain, through the space which had been made by the cat, but each time he got closer to the window, the cat moved in reaction to his proximity and obscured his view.

'Cheers, Kitty,' he said before an idea occurred to him. He leaned down again at the letterbox, pushed it open and took a good sniff.

'Aha, maybe,' he said to himself as he vaulted over the waist-high fence at the side of the house.

He smiled as he reached the back door.

Gotta be worth a shot, he surmised as he judged the distance of the cat flap to the lock halfway up the door.

Most people left their key in the back door and just locked and unlocked it.

He lowered himself to the floor and pushed away the image of the black kitty clawing his hand to shreds as soon as it popped out the other side.

He slowly pushed his hand through the opening and moved his body as close to the door as he could manage. The right side of his face was pushed up against the frame. Without being able to see, he felt around in the general direction of the lock. The tip of his fingers touched on a light metal ring. Just another inch or two. He pushed himself further, his cheekbones hard against the wood, and gave one almighty stretch, getting his thumb and forefinger around the end of the key. Now he'd got hold, he knew he couldn't turn it but had to try to pull it out. He kept his grip as horizontal as he could and pulled as a pain shot through his stretched shoulder.

He gasped with relief when the key slipped out of the lock in his hand.

He retracted his arm, stood and shook the dirt from his trousers before putting the key in the lock. He knocked the door one more time before turning the lock. For all he knew, Jacob Powell had been on a 24-hour bender and was sleeping heavily upstairs.

Still no answer, so he turned the key and stepped in.

His heart jumped as the black cat darted past his legs and ran out the door.

Penn called out again but his voice echoed around the house. The policeman in him took a good long sniff of the air. There was no scent of lingering bodies. Despite the man being a cat owner, there was no discernible smell at all.

His gaze took in the kitchen, where he found nothing out of the ordinary. For a man living alone, it looked reasonably in order.

To be sure, he moved the toaster to the right. Yeah, Jacob lived alone.

Whenever he had cleaned the kitchen down at home, he had wiped every surface and his mother would always come in and move the toaster.

'Men clean what they see. Women clean what they can't see,' she would always say with a smile, he remembered fondly.

Both he and Jasper missed her terribly, but they were getting by, just one day at a time. But he did now recall that he hadn't moved the toaster for weeks.

He stepped out of the kitchen and into the lounge, which looked out onto the road.

At eye level, everything appeared reasonably clean and tidy, if a little dated – until his gaze landed on the rug in the middle of the room, where he saw a hammer beside an Apple Mac that had been smashed to smithereens.

CHAPTER SEVENTY-FIVE

The home of Amelia Dixon lay on the outskirts of Stratford-upon-Avon, the birthplace of William Shakespeare, and looked to be a three- to four-bed semi, with a small gravel driveway. A property that was around £300,000 in the Black Country easily sold for half a million on Alcester Road.

Although Kim admired the process-of-elimination detective work Penn and Stacey had done, she wondered if the one-hour drive from the Black Country would yield any better results than the smashed-up computer Penn had just called her about.

She had instructed him to call Mitch and get the experts at Ridgepoint to have a look. She didn't doubt Stacey's ability to interrogate the laptop, providing it was all in one piece, but trying to put it back together first was another matter entirely.

'You do know this woman could have left for any number of reasons?' Bryant asked, parking the car and voicing her own misgivings; but it was a lead, of sorts, and needed to be ruled out.

Kim knocked the door and got her ID ready. Amelia Dixon certainly wasn't expecting a late-afternoon call from police officers.

The woman who answered the door was in her early fifties and wore her hair in an auburn bob that curled around her face and ended at jaw level. The telltale signs of grey peeped out from the side parting.

'Ms Dixon?'

She nodded.

Kim held up her ID. 'May we come in for a minute?'

She didn't move. 'What's this about?'

'It's in relation to your former employment, Ms Dixon,' Kim said, hoping that would be enough to get them through the door.

It did, and she opened the door reticently.

The first thing Kim noted was the overwhelming smell of dog. It was a smell she was used to in a lesser quantity; keeping her own home stink free proved a challenge, made worse after a walk in the rain, but this was way stronger.

The woman stepped aside and held the door open for her and Bryant to enter a hallway that, although spacious, was a little dingy. The paintwork was scuffed, and the wallpaper was starting to peel in the corners. The space held a distinctive smell that Kim knew well.

One of the reasons for that smell came bounding towards them.

'Sorry, that's Lucky, my eldest,' Ms Dixon said, as though talking about a child.

Kim stroked the head of the cream Labrador.

The woman opened the door into a small lounge where a further five dogs of varying size and shapes came hurtling towards the door.

'Kitchen,' she said, stepping aside then closing the door behind them. 'My rescues,' she explained, and Kim couldn't help but warm to her slightly. She appreciated anyone who could find it in their hearts to give a rescue dog a home, let alone six of them.

'May we?' Kim asked, pointing to the sofa.

'Go ahead if you don't mind dog hairs on your clothes. That's Bertie's spot, and he moults.'

Kim sat. If the worst thing she got on her clothes today was dog hair, life wouldn't be so bad.

'Nice photo,' Bryant said, pointing to the mantelpiece.

Kim noted the framed picture at one end of the fireplace and a candle in the middle.

'Yes, that's Lucky, who you met at the door. My husband used to walk her along the river every day.'

'I'm sorry for—'

'Oh no. Don't be. He's not dead. He had a midlife crisis two years ago and decided to refresh everything in his life. Twenty-three years and nothing to show for it. But that's history so—'

'We're here about your former employment with Matrix Enterprises.'

'I'm sorry but I can't really discuss that.'

'We know what it is, Ms Dixon. We know that the company is the financial institution that supports the witness protection programme.'

'Okay,' she said cautiously but offering nothing.

'You left your job recently?'

'Is that a crime, Officer?' she asked with a smile, but the tension had crept into her face.

'Not at all, Ms Dixon, but we're just curious about the timing in connection with a case we're investigating.'

'I'm really not sure how I can help you, Officer. I dealt with money. I paid bills. I set up direct debits. I had no particulars on people. I saw no names.'

That would explain why she had made no link to the murders in the news and her own role at Matrix Enterprises.

'So why did you leave?' she pushed. Kim could understand that the woman wouldn't have had access to the vital information of names and reasons, but she still didn't like the coincidental timing of the murders and this woman leaving her job. She'd be happy to have a decent reason for her leaving a job she'd been in for more than ten years.

'I needed some time out. I'd been through a lot with my marriage break-up, and it was just time for a change.'

Kim thought that was one of the weakest excuses she'd ever heard. She'd have preferred a reason she could believe.

'Now, if you don't mind, Poppy needs a bath,' she said, standing.

Kim followed suit. She had no more reason to push. She had no evidence linking the woman before her to any part of the investigation, but there was a sense of suspicion in her stomach. Bryant's open expression told her he didn't agree and was ready to leave.

She headed for the front door and glanced again at the peeling wallpaper.

She turned before her palm met the door handle.

'I'm sorry, Ms Dixon, but quite honestly I don't believe you.'

Amelia Dixon bowed her head and burst into tears.

CHAPTER SEVENTY-SIX

Kim sat back down and waited for the woman to get herself together.

All the signs told her Amelia had not reacted well to the breakdown of her marriage. She'd surrounded herself with dogs, probably seeking company. She'd allowed jobs her husband had most likely done to deteriorate. A photo, probably of the two of them, had been removed from the mantelpiece and never replaced.

She suspected Amelia had enjoyed being a married woman and ached to get her old life back. Unsure, newly single, wounded, hurt, confused and, above all else, lonely. One of the easiest emotions to exploit.

'It was an email that started it. A polite, self-effacing, humorous email asking if I was the Amelia Dixon from Littletown High School, in Staffordshire, that he was trying to track down.'

Kim managed to stifle the groan as the woman tapped her own head lightly.

'I know it's on a level with "I have a huge investment waiting for you in Nigeria, Kenya, Libya if you'll just send your bank details", but there was something just so authentic about it.'

She took a breath. 'I replied, explaining that Dixon was my married name and that I wasn't the girl he was looking for. He replied, saying that was a shame, as she'd been his high school sweetheart and after losing his wife to cancer he was hoping to reconnect.'

It was getting harder for Kim to keep the groan in her mouth.

'Anyway, we fell into easy conversation back and forth. We talked about our partners and sympathised with each other. We'd email a few times each week. I was comfortable. He wasn't asking me for anything, and I was enjoying the contact. I really felt that he understood me.'

'So…' Kim prompted.

'One night, I realised it had been a few days since I'd sent him a message and he hadn't replied. I was concerned, so sent a quick message to check on him. He immediately replied, saying he was about to check on me, as I hadn't replied to his message. I searched and I hadn't received it.

'He explained he'd had the same problem with AOL and had installed a program on his own computer that ensured no emails got lost. He already told me he worked in IT.'

Of course he had, Kim thought. It was called priming.

'He said if I told him my IP address and password, he could install it remotely overnight so as not to inconvenience me.'

She cringed as she said the words.

'So he had access to your computer and contents all night?'

Amelia nodded with shame at her own naïveté.

'I woke up to the blue screen of death. I couldn't access my emails, so I tried on my phone. I couldn't log in to my account. It had been closed.'

Damn it, there was no way to try and trace the sender through her. She could only hope that Penn was having more luck. Although, Kim realised, that was not her biggest problem at the minute.

'And you didn't tell anyone what had happened?'

She shook her head. 'I assumed he was after bank details or passwords, so I cancelled everything even though nothing had been touched.'

'And you left your job?'

'Yes, I just wanted to run away from the whole situation.'

And now to the real problem.

'What sensitive information would he have been able to access on your laptop?'

'Nothing that would identify any particular witnesses.'

'There must have been something or he wouldn't have been trying so hard,' Kim reasoned.

Amelia began to wring her hands, and Kim was racking her brains. She was trying to remember everything she'd been told.

'So you were responsible for paying all the bills and invoices?' She nodded.

'Were these lists of payments itemised on a spreadsheet?'

'Yes, but there were no names of witnesses or—'

'Did you pay the rents?' Kim asked as a horrific thought occurred to her.

The nodding of the head started slowly.

'Fuck,' Kim said out loud.

Their killer knew where every person in the witness protection scheme lived.

CHAPTER SEVENTY-SEVEN

'It's not looking good,' Penn said, putting down the phone a minute after Stacey had ended her call too.

She knew that Mitch had headed to Jacob's house to collect the computer, to take it over to Ridgepoint House, before returning to Wren's Nest to do a final sweep of Dean Mullins's crime scene.

'Apparently, Mitch's best computer guy laughed his head off when he emptied the laptop guts on his desk, so I'm thinking we're not gonna get a lot from that.'

'Neighbours have anything to say?' Stacey asked. Her colleague had knocked a few doors while waiting for Mitch to turn up at the property. Apparently, he'd made time to feed the cat as well.

'Kept himself to himself, which is pretty much par for the course in this investigation, wasn't unpleasant but didn't engage in nice long chats either. You got anything?'

Stacey shook her head. 'Nothing yet. Mrs Lennox still ay happy to divulge anything further until we issue her with a court order for the information.'

'But she already gave Bryant Jacob's address,' Penn queried.

'Well, maybe we should send Bryant back to get Jacob's whole file, because she's not willing to give it to me.'

Penn sat back and regarded her. 'You know, Stace, when you make sergeant, as you most definitely will, you're gonna have to learn different ways of talking to people.'

'Oh, please continue,' Stacey said, crossing her arms.

'I'm not criticising or being condescending, but I heard how you spoke to Lynes. You trod gently and got the desired result. You also spoke the exact same way to Anna Lennox. With some folks, you just gotta be a bit firmer is all, and as I can see you're not responding well to my friendly advice, I'm gonna take this opportunity to wind my neck in.'

Stacey chuckled. Not once had she been able to stay annoyed at Penn. He was far too self-aware.

'You seriously think I'm not firm enough?' she asked, unfolding her arms.

'All I'm saying is horses for courses. Some people need a bit more of a push, but it's okay if you can't—'

'Oh, it's like that, is it?' Stacey asked, picking up the phone. The gauntlet had been thrown.

Penn headed to the coffee machine while she waited for an answer.

'Mrs Lennox again, please. It's DC Wood from Halesowen CID.'

Stacey tapped her fingers on the desk while she waited.

'Officer?' Anna Lennox greeted her with a question in her voice, obviously surprised to hear from her again so soon.

'Mrs Lennox, I reflected after the end of our conversation and I'd like to make sure you understand just how serious this situation is.'

'You told me people died. I understand the seriousness of the situation perfectly well.'

'Given that you do, would you not consider giving us complete access to your staff files?'

'Constable, I'm sure I made myself clear a few moments ago. I offered your colleague Jacob's address so that his safety could be checked. As soon as I have check—'

'You also understand that we are trying to prevent any further deaths, and your co-operation would—'

'Please don't try to put that responsibility onto me. I have protocols to follow and guidance I must seek before opening my personnel files without proof of any wrongdoing.'

Stacey could feel the frustration growing inside her. Not least because this was not a stance she was comfortable with. But Penn was right. She had to learn how to toughen up some time.

'Mrs Lennox, I must insist that you allow us access to the file of Jacob Powell as a matter of urgency,' she said, inserting a metal rod into her words.

The woman was silent for just a few seconds. Stacey waited with bated breath. Had the strategy worked?

'The answer is no, Officer, and if you attempt to bully me again, I will be making a formal complaint against you.'

The call ended and silence echoed in her ear.

That had been her first minor test as sergeant.

And hadn't that gone well?

CHAPTER SEVENTY-EIGHT

Frost didn't exactly relish the prospect of going back home.

She'd collected the hire car and then popped to Tesco, in Cradley Heath, to pick up a few bits and pieces and drink a cuppa in the café. She didn't enjoy working from home, even though she loved her little house in Quarry Bank. It was her own little sanctuary after a day amongst people and noise, but without the chaos of the day, it was just a quiet place to be.

She'd removed the neck collar issued by the hospital early afternoon and then taken a long bath, which had helped ease the aching in her bones. She'd spent the rest of the day reading forensic examination reports offered as evidence at Nick Morley's first trial, and then progressed to piecing together the investigation. In truth, after the initial delay in finding the remains of Trisha Morley, the officers hadn't put a foot wrong. The ulna and the radius bones from the forearm had been in good condition and the teeth – two molars and a central incisor – had all been quickly identified as Trisha's. Nick Morley had been arrested the same day.

Frost was only sorry there hadn't been more of Trisha Morley to bury.

Her article had been submitted to Fitz, who had made a couple of small changes before authorising it. After which she'd headed out to collect the hire car.

She sipped the last of her coffee as the barista came from behind the counter and began collecting used cups.

She took out her phone and clicked on her earlier article and was both surprised and gratified to see over three hundred comments. She scrolled through them and couldn't help the smile that pricked at her mouth. After weeding out the trolling comments, she was pleased to see the tide was turning in public opinion just within the scope of her articles. On Monday, the first article had received far fewer comments and had been fifty-fifty in opinion as to whether Nick Morley had killed his wife or if some random stranger had wandered onto his property and committed the crime.

But now the comments were a good ninety per cent against the barrister, and with one article left for tomorrow, Frost was happy with the result. If nothing else, she had got Trisha's name out there. She had reminded the public that a woman had lost her life. She had taken the spotlight away from Saint Nick and his cronies.

She couldn't say it had left her unscathed. She knew she was a pesky fly in their ointment, a shadow being cast on the halo they were shining around Morley's head. She knew she had poked a bear and that bear had retaliated last night at the traffic lights. But she also knew she wouldn't be bullied into backing off.

'Okay, enough,' she whispered to herself, grabbing her bag. The supermarket café had totally emptied, and the staff were mopping the floor. It was time to go home.

She had to admit that the short trip out had exhausted her. She guessed her body was still reacting to the shunt, but her mind was wired. Just seeing those comments. It might be a drop in the ocean, but it was a drop nonetheless.

She paid quickly for her woeful basket of groceries and headed out to the car.

For a moment, she'd forgotten that she wasn't looking for her beloved Audi and instead was driving a Toyota Corolla.

She threw the carrier in the back of the car, any thoughts of a late tea already forgotten. She wanted to get home and get started on the article for tomorrow, where she would cover the trial.

She also resolved that she'd reply to Fitz's last text message, checking on her, as soon as she walked in the door.

The journey from Tesco to her home was barely a mile, but it was long enough. The Toyota felt like more car than she needed compared to her own Audi, which she'd learned today was going to be off the road for at least two weeks.

'Bastards,' she whispered to herself as she parked the car. She was probably as pissed off at not having her car as she was about the fact she'd been hurt.

Priorities, she thought as she slid the key into the door lock.

The door began to open before she turned the key.

As she pushed lightly on the glass panel, her heart dropped into her stomach.

The door widened to reveal the whole of her living room. Her voice was barely a whisper as she asked:

'What the fuck has happened here?'

CHAPTER SEVENTY-NINE

'Nope, you're not having another one,' Kim said as Barney crawled along the floor towards where she sat on the sheet in the garage. Damn dog knew she'd only handed him a small carrot once he'd come in from the back garden. Trust her to get a dog that understood portion control.

'Maybe later,' she said, ruffling his head.

His tail swished the floor once before he lowered his jowls onto his front paws and closed his eyes.

'Tough day, eh, mate?' she asked, thinking about her own day.

The majority of the journey back from Stratford-upon-Avon had been spent on the phone, initially to Woody to explain what they'd learned from Amelia, and then ten minutes later a call had come from Superintendent Wexford, wanting to confirm what he'd already been told by Woody.

She'd wondered what action might be taken against Amelia, but Kim wasn't sure what crime she'd actually committed. She hadn't knowingly taken sensitive information and handed it over. She'd been duped. Slowly and cleverly.

She supposed Amelia wasn't the priority for UKPPS right now. Their attention and resources were directed at how to deal with the fact that every address housing a member of the witness protection programme was in the hands of a crazed killer. Except he wasn't, she corrected herself. He was methodical, intelligent, creative and strategic. There was nothing about him that was crazed.

'What does he want?' she said out loud.

Barney opened his eyes, realised there were no words in the sentence of interest to him and closed them again.

So far they had nothing to link Jacob Powell to the murders, except his strange behaviour and a busted-up laptop found by Penn at his address. She was hoping the techies could pull something from his laptop carcass to link the man to Amelia Dixon. It was a long shot, she knew.

She decided it was time for a fresh coffee and stood, shaking some life into her behind, which had turned numb.

'Really?' she asked as her phone began to ring, as though it had been waiting for her to stand up.

She switched off the iPod before reaching for the phone. The screen was illuminated with a number she knew well.

'Stone,' she answered.

'It's Jack, from the front desk.'

The second part hadn't been necessary. They'd been working together for years, but she was unsure of his reason for calling. After-hours calls normally came from the control room.

'Just handing over, marm, and I noticed you'd put an alert on the property of Tracy Frost, who lives at—'

'Yes, Jack, I know where she lives.'

'Received a call about an hour ago. Her house has been ransacked. Officers were dispatched immediately but, seeing your name on the alert, I thought you'd want to know.'

'Any injuries?'

'None reported.'

'Okay, Jack, thanks for letting me know,' she said, ending the call.

Shunted in her car yesterday, her home broken into today – it looked like Nick Morley's cronies were trying to scare Frost good and proper.

She sensed the arrival of that distant voice, prompting her to assist Frost in some way. She fought it back with the knowledge that the woman hadn't been hurt, and she was sure the officers present were handling it appropriately.

She emptied out the old coffee from her cup and refilled it. Barney sidled up and stood before her.

'What?'

He sat and stared.

'What do you want me to do? I can't stand the sight of the woman.'

He moved forward.

'She's in safe hands. The folks there will look after her.'

He tipped his head.

'Listen, buddy, I can't go sticking my nose into everyone's problems. She took it upon herself to run with this story.'

And you started it by taking her to see Penny Colgan in the first place, said a small voice inside her head.

Regardless.

'There's nothing I can do,' she said, turning away from his accusing stare.

She counted to ten and turned back. He hadn't moved an inch.

'Damn it, Barney, you drive a hard bargain.'

She sighed heavily. She knew when she was beat.

'Okay, come on – we're going for a short ride.'

CHAPTER EIGHTY

'Happy now?' Kim asked, parking a few metres away from Frost's house.

It was almost ten and it had taken only minutes to reach the home of the reporter, who was leaning against a squad car with a jacket draped around her shoulders.

Frost eyed her questioningly. 'Bloody hell, Stone. What you doing here? I ain't dead.'

'Just passing, saw the commotion and wondered who you'd pissed off today.'

'Same folks as yesterday by the looks of it,' she said, trying to control a shudder that ran through her body.

'May I?' Kim asked, approaching the front door.

'Yeah, carry on. There's a couple of officers in there, but Forensics won't be out until tomorrow.'

Kim glanced inside before entering, her eyes trying to form a clear path she could take without disturbing anything further.

She tiptoed in and took a quick look. The place had been decimated. Possessions had been thrown from every drawer, and what could be smashed had been.

Smashed but not taken, she thought, glancing at the fifty-inch TV lying face down in a pool of its own glass. The cushions on the sofa had been slashed and thrown around the room.

Kim didn't need to go any further.

She turned to Frost. 'Rest of the house?'

'Same.'

'Anything taken?'

Frost shook her head. 'Not that I can see.'

No, Kim expected not. This had nothing to do with personal possessions; contrary to popular belief, burglars left barely any mess. They got in, took what they wanted and got out as quickly as possible. As a PC she'd attended burglaries where the victim had remained unaware for hours.

There was no question this was a hate attack, intended to induce fear. And when the officers had finished, what was Frost supposed to do then? Sit amongst the debris of her home as though nothing had happened?

She glanced back at the car where Barney awaited her return. How was she supposed to explain to him that she'd left Frost trembling out on the pavement?

Before she even realised what she was doing, the words were out of her mouth.

'Go pack a bag, Frost. Right now, because you're coming with me.'

CHAPTER EIGHTY-ONE

'Bloody hell, Stone, didn't realise you had a dog,' Frost said, looking through the window of her Golf. 'Who the heck would give you control of a living, breathing thing?'

Kim unlocked the doors. 'He's not keen on strangers, so don't frighten—'

'Hello, boy,' Frost said as Barney lurched towards her, wagging his tail. His seat belt prevented him reaching her.

She sat in the front passenger seat and turned. 'Hello there, lovely boy. Who's a little cutie pie?' she asked in a googly voice.

Kim raised one eyebrow as she put the key in the ignition. 'Frost, stop that, it's freaking me out.'

'But he's so gorgeous,' Frost said as Barney licked her hand. 'Look, he likes me. He knows I'm a nice person.'

'He chases his own tail for hours every day thinking it's a toy, so forgive me if I don't trust his judgement,' she said, pulling away from the kerb.

'Err… so where are you actually taking me? And why do I feel this is gonna end with the words "and she was never seen again"?'

'My house,' Kim answered.

'You have a home?' Frost asked, genuinely surprised.

'No, I sleep in a skip every night. Of course I have a home.'

'My mistake. I thought you had some kind of charging station in your office.'

'You feeling a bit less shaky, cos you seem to have found your mouth again.'

'Well, come on. This is a bit surreal, isn't it? I have an overnight bag, and I'm going to your house. And we don't even like each other.'

'Yeah, tragic, isn't it?'

'So why?' Frost asked pointedly.

Kim wasn't even sure herself. All she knew was that when she'd seen Frost leaning against that car, draped in a jacket that was doing nothing to stop the shivering or put the colour back into her face, the thought of her having to go back in there, or find somewhere to stay and allow her mind to fester on what had happened hadn't sat well with her.

'Someone's gotta keep you out of trouble,' she answered.

'You're still weird,' Frost said.

'And you're still a bitch. Both facts are unlikely to change just cos you're kipping in my spare room for the night,' Kim said.

Frost burst out laughing. 'Oh, jeez, I needed that. It's good to know that your act of kindness isn't going to change anything between us.'

'It won't,' Kim assured her, pulling up onto her own drive.

'Hmm, nice but not what I was expecting. I mean, it's just a house.'

'As opposed to what?'

Frost shrugged as Kim leaned over and undid Barney's seat belt.

'Okay, spare room is up the stairs and second on the left,' Kim said, opening the front door.

The second that Frost was inside her house, Kim wondered if she'd made a huge mistake. Her only visitor was normally Bryant, who she threw out if he stayed longer than an hour.

'Happy now?' she asked Barney as she passed him a carrot. He took it to his chewing rug in the middle of the lounge, which she took as a yes.

She emptied the coffee pot and prepared a fresh brew. It was one night. She could put up with a visitor for one night. The house was plenty big enough, and she could console herself with the fact that she'd done the right thing. And now she understood her own reasoning. Frost was trying to do the right thing.

'So how long you lived here?' Frost asked, walking around Barney who was hoovering up chunks of carrot. Kim noted that Frost's limp was more pronounced when she wasn't wearing high heels. Right now, her feet were encased in thick woollen socks, and she was a good two inches shorter than Kim.

'Ten years or so,' she answered.

'You are kidding?' Frost asked, looking around.

Kim followed her gaze from behind the breakfast bar. She had a decent sofa that Barney appreciated more than she did. There was a TV in the far corner for which she'd lost the remote. There were a couple of scatter cushions and a small coffee table. She wasn't big on material things, and her one prized possession, the single photo she had of herself and Mikey, was safely treasured on her bedside cabinet.

'Talk about taking Marie Kondo's advice to the extreme.'

'Who?'

'Decluttering expert,' Frost said, taking a seat on one of the bar stools.

'Oh,' Kim said, holding up a mug as a question.

'White with one sugar please,' Frost said, and then smiled ruefully. 'How strange that only the other day I said it'd be nice to chat over coffee some time. I'm still not sure of your motives for—'

'Frost,' Kim said, turning towards her. 'Was there a time when you had my entire childhood history in a file in the boot of your car, which you chose to return to me unread?'

Frost nodded before taking a sip of the coffee Kim had slid towards her.

'Well, let's just leave it at that then, eh?'

Kim grabbed her coffee and opened the door to the garage.

'Ooh, what's in there?' Frost asked, following her, cupping her own drink.

Kim stood aside.

'Oh,' Frost said, spying the bike parts on the king-size sheet. Kim didn't mind the disappointed reaction. Few people saw the beauty in bike parts that she did.

'It's just rubbish.'

But she drew the line at that.

'Frost, shut your mouth and go back to the—'

'I mean, what exactly is it?' Frost asked, ignoring her instruction and walking around the sheet.

'It's the beginning of the restoration of a Vincent Black Shadow.'

'And that's what you do to relax, restore old bikes?'

'Yep,' Kim said, lowering herself to the ground. There was no point in switching on the iPod if Frost wasn't going to bugger off.

'Why?'

Kim thought about all the reasons she did it. The fact that the process took her back to the happiest three years of her life, when she'd spent hours with her foster father, Keith, while Erica had cooked in the next room, listening to her collection of classical music.

She thought about the fact that the finished product, when auctioned, paid anonymously for the communication equipment for a teenage girl with muscular dystrophy.

'It helps me think,' she answered, choosing to share none of these reasons with Frost.

'So you gonna leave the angry bear to sleep now or what?' Kim asked, steering the conversation away from herself. If Morley's cronies were behind the ransacking of her home, that was her second warning.

'Am I bollocks!' Frost said, leaning against the countertop. 'There's no point starting a bun fight if you don't bake enough dough.'

Kim raised an eyebrow at the analogy.

'Tomorrow's article is about the trial, for the good it will do.'

'I've read your articles,' Kim admitted. 'They're not bad, and you've certainly put the name of Trisha Morley on more people's lips.'

'It's not enough,' Frost said, pacing the room.

'What exactly are you hoping for?'

'A conviction. I want him to pay for what he's done.'

'Careful, Frost, you're talking like an investigator,' Kim warned. 'It's what we all want. The idea of that bastard walking free sickens every officer who came into contact with him or the case. You've done more than anyone outside of the force. You've given the victim an identity,' Kim said. 'And you've paid personally for it.'

Frost shrugged away her words. 'But I still know that regardless of anything I've written, the bastard is going to get away with it.'

'You can't be sure of—'

'Oh, come on, Stone. Don't humour me. The frustrating part of the whole thing is that the jury was just dying to convict him the first time around, but the defence made such a thing about Trisha never reporting her injuries or asking for help. No sane person would look at her list of injuries and be convinced that she was that accident prone. If she'd have said only once to someone, somewhere that Nick had beaten her, I think the jury would have felt vindicated in offering a guilty verdict. Instead, they were blinded by the picture of Trisha living in a nice big house, buying nice clothes and jewellery, going on fancy holidays and—'

'Hmm…' Kim interrupted.

'You're gonna have to translate that hmm… Stone, I don't know you well enough.'

'I'm not the most experienced at this, but don't folks act the same when they're away?'

Frost stopped pacing. 'You think he might have continued to beat her on holiday?'

'A leopard doesn't change his spots if you put him in a different cage.'

'And you think Trisha Morley might have told the truth to a foreign doctor?'

Kim shrugged. 'You never know. Maybe she felt safe enough to tell the truth to someone if she was miles away.'

'Shit, you're right. Messing with this stuff does help you think better. You got a computer I can use?'

Frost's own laptop was in a hundred pieces back at her home.

'By the side of the sofa.'

Frost rushed out and there was peace again.

She glanced at Barney. 'There we go. That's how w—'

She stopped speaking as her phone began to ring.

It was Mitch at almost eleven o'clock.

Shit.

'Stone,' she answered.

'Inspector, I'm at the site of our last victim and I need you here. Now.'

CHAPTER EIGHTY-TWO

Kim pulled up at the cordon at Wren's Nest to find it buzzing with activity. Even Keats's van was back in place. What the hell was going on? Last she'd heard from Penn, Mitch had been on his way to do a final inspection and close the site down.

As she headed along the path, illuminated by officers with torches, she spared a thought for her dog left in the hands of Frost, who had been instructed that she would face a slow and painful death if anything happened to Barney in her absence. The reporter's assurances that he would be fine with Aunty Frost had done little to quell her trepidation.

'What the hell, Mitch?' she asked, reaching the now cleared site where Dean Mullins's naked body had lain with a rat embedded in his stomach.

'Follow me,' he said gravely, treading a path that now looked well worn.

'You wanna give me any kind of clue?' she asked, following closely.

'You'll see for yourself in a minute.'

Kim could make out activity in the distance between the tree branches, but what the hell could Mitch have found so far from the crime scene?

His pace quickened as the collective torch beams threw more light their way.

'Mitch, I swear, if you don't give me some kind of clue I'm gonna—'

He stepped out of the way as they reached the area.
Keats glanced her way before stepping to the side.
She looked down to the ground and then back at Keats.
'You have to be fucking kidding me?'

CHAPTER EIGHTY-THREE

Three separate circles of torchlight were trained on the body of a female in her mid-thirties.

Lying on the ground, face up, a wooden door had been placed over her body from her ankle to her neck, lengthways. Upon the door lay heavy rocks, stacked and placed along the whole length of the door. The woman's arms were stretched above her head and staked into the ground.

'It's another form of stoning,' Mitch said as the area lit up further with a camera flash. 'It's a slower, more painful method than being buried in the ground with your head exposed. As horrific as that is, a few good shots and you're gone. There's no fast way out of this one. The stones are added one at a time, slowly, gradually breaking bones and squashing vital organs in the—'

'Can we get them off her?' Kim asked, feeling her chest tightening, as though those rocks were upon her torso. She knew the woman was dead, but she wanted the weight removed.

Mitch looked to the photographer, who took one more shot and then nodded.

Kim stepped forward and removed the first rock.

'Inspector,' Mitch protested.

'You have my DNA, Mitch, you can rule me out.'

'Not that. There are plenty of us here to—'

'I'm good thanks, now where do you want them?'

Mitch shook his head and pointed to a sheet of clear plastic a few metres away. 'Make lines from left to right, so we know the order they were removed.'

She nodded her understanding. Every rock would be inspected for evidence, and Mitch needed to know where they'd been within the pile.

He was right, she acknowledged, as half a dozen pairs of hands began to move the rocks.

She wasn't surprised when Keats joined in too. They disagreed on many things but agreed on most things when it came to victim care. Within minutes, the number of stones in the line was greater than the pile on the door holding down the body. Kim felt her breathing ease a little more with every stone that was removed.

Once the stones were off, Kim stepped aside as the forensic techs gently lifted and removed the door. Immediately, she was surprised at how little trauma was evident on the outside of the body. She couldn't even imagine the damage within.

The woman was dressed simply in light jeans and a sweatshirt. A pair of trainers covered plain black socks, and there was no jewellery that Kim could see. She also noted the absence of any handbag. She suspected the personal possessions had been taken like all the other victims. Probably done to slow them down but, given that no one was who they appeared to be, it was like starting from scratch even once they had a name.

Both she and Mitch stepped aside as Keats commenced his initial inspection.

'What do you reckon to the weight?' Kim asked, nodding towards the stones.

'At least a ton, maybe a ton and a half. It's like having a skip full of dirt lowered onto you very slowly. Your guy has some patience, I'll say that,' Mitch observed as Keats took the liver probe from his dubious-looking tool kit.

Never a part of the process Kim relished, she did appreciate it gave them a good indication of time of death.

Her mind had hung on to something Mitch had said about patience.

She sniffed the air. 'Hey, Mitch, you smell that?' she asked as Keats shook his head and checked his probe.

'What?' Mitch asked. 'I can't smell anything.'

'Exactly,' she said. 'I made the assumption you'd stumbled upon an earlier crime scene but…' She took a few steps away, looking in the direction of the first body that had been found in the area.

'What are you thinking?' Mitch asked, following her.

'The absence of the smell,' she said as the answer became clear to her. 'Mitch, he was doing these two at the same time.'

Mitch looked at the distance between the two points and considered before nodding his agreement.

'Given the state of both bodies, I think you could be right.'

Kim paused for a moment, trying to process the fact that their murderer had walked back and forth between the two people he was torturing, leaving one in horrific pain to go inflict more on the other. How did a person have all that thinking time and carry on anyway?

She shuddered and turned back to the body, where Keats was extracting the liver probe for the second time.

'Stop making a meal out of it, Keats. This ain't your first rodeo,' she called out.

He ignored her and didn't even look her way.

She approached him. 'What's wrong?'

'Time of death.'

'Yeah, I'm not expecting it to the minute,' she said, frowning at his pensive expression.

'Twelve hours,' he said and waited for the penny to drop.

It didn't take long.

'Fuck, fuck, fuck,' she growled, understanding the reason for his distress.

As they'd all pored over victim number three earlier that day, victim four had still been alive.

CHAPTER EIGHTY-FOUR

The news was no more palatable when Kim delivered it to her team the following morning, and her words were met with stunned silence as they all tried to digest what she'd said.

In the few hours they'd been away, the investigation had claimed a fourth victim along with the knowledge she could have been saved. All three members of Kim's team were staring at the photo she'd placed on the board amongst the others.

The silence of her team matched the stunned mood present the night before at the crime scene, broken only by Keats's half-hearted and not really truthful reassurances to Mitch that even if they'd found her, it was unlikely she could have been saved. The words had fallen on deaf ears because they all knew one thing to be true: where there was life, there was hope. Mitch would always wonder what would have happened if he'd set his perimeter forty metres further out, or if he'd inspected the area earlier.

Mitch had done nothing wrong. Establishing a crime scene perimeter was not an exact science, especially outdoors. The priorities would have been to protect the immediate area in which the crime had taken place, all places where the killer had interaction with the victim, and routes in and out of that area. The path from the car park to the scene of Dean Mullins's death had been placed within the boundary, but there was no reason to suspect that the killer had moved beyond the crime scene further into the woods. But no amount of reassurance would appease the forensic technician.

As they'd left the crime scene, they'd all known there was a possibility they could have had one less victim. And it was that thought that had stayed with her all night.

As she'd retrieved her dog from the foot of the spare bed where Frost had snored lightly, as she'd taken him on a 3 a.m. walk around the park and as she'd dozed lightly on the sofa for a couple of hours, her only thought had been the vision of all of them at the crime scene of Dean Mullins. When only a quarter mile away lay a woman fighting for her life, unable to move, to call out, even to speak but with a heartbeat and a pulse.

She stole a glance at Bryant who had been right there with her.

A muscle in his jawline was doing gymnastics, and he refused to meet her gaze.

'We gotta get him, guys, before he gets the chance to hurt anyone else.'

It was that conviction that had catapulted her from the sofa and into the shower before 5 a.m. And after leaving a note with instructions for Frost about Barney, she had left him sleeping on the sofa and hurried into work.

'Do we know who she is?' Stacey asked, still looking at the photo on the board.

Kim shook her head. 'Fully clothed but no identification.'

'Any mileage in the fact that the three male victims were stripped naked but the female wasn't?' Penn asked, tapping a pen on his lower lip.

'Not sure; the removal of the clothing thing might be functional,' she said, thinking of Keith's burned body and the rat in Dean's stomach.

'But the guy on the rack didn't need to be naked,' Penn offered.

'Look into it, but I want you back on tracking that van we saw going into the trading estate, and Stace, I want you to circulate a photo of Jacob Powell to uniforms so—'

'Can't do it, boss. Don't have one,' Stacey said, opening her hands.

'Excuse me?' Kim asked. It was a pretty basic request.

'No presence on social media, Mrs Lennox still isn't playing ball, and even the school website doesn't include photos.'

'Jesus Christ,' she growled. She turned to Bryant. 'You got the best look at him. Give the local teams a description.'

'Will do but my description is gonna fit just about any guy with a beard, as well as a couple of women I know, but I'm happy to do it,' he said, picking up the phone.

Kim turned back to Stacey. 'Okay, get on to the phone records of all our victims. Did any of them know each other or is there any number that made contact with them all? One of you stay on top of the techies about Jacob Powell's computer. I know it's a long—'

Kim stopped speaking as Leanne appeared at the door.

'Thanks for joining us,' Kim said impatiently. She was either here to help or not, but to keep coming and going was helping no one.

'Listen, if you're not gonna get here at the right—'

'What the fuck is that?' Leanne asked, staring at the white-board.

Kim followed her gaze. 'Our fourth victim, found late last night.'

'Is she dead?' Leanne asked, turning towards her. Kim was shocked to see the colour had drained from her face.

Kim nodded as Leanne reached for the edge of the desk.

'You know her?' Kim asked.

'Of course I fucking know her. She's a protection officer, just like me.'

CHAPTER EIGHTY-FIVE

'We met around ten years ago in training. Her name is Sarah Lessiter. She was a couple of years younger than me and didn't handle certain aspects of the training programme all that well.'

'Go on,' Kim said as she heard Stacey start to tap lightly in the background. Now they had a name, they would very soon have an address.

'At first, you're given all the training on systems, the protocols, the reasons, the legalities. It's classroom based and you absorb every bit of information. You're taught memory exercises so that you don't have to write anything down. You role-play scenarios of different situations. You're taught physical moves and holds beyond the normal police force criteria. They do all kinds of psychometric tests on you, to see if you have the right temperament for the job. The first part is all about the process, about what might happen, preparing you for eventualities and emergencies, explaining the secrets you have to keep from family and friends. You can't tell a soul who you're protecting.'

'Go on,' Kim urged. It was the longest she'd heard Leanne speak. Perhaps they might finally learn something.

'Over the course of the training, recruits fall away. I started in a group of fifteen and by the final test there were four of us left. Sarah was one of the four, and it was the final exercise she struggled with.'

'Which was?' Kim asked.

'Empathy test. Without warning, you're put into a car and taken to an unknown place, a town maybe fifty miles or so away. No one speaks or explains properly what's going on. You're taken to a room and left for hours. Then they take your phone, smash it and tell you that you can contact no one.'

'But it's not real.'

'It bloody well feels it. You're then taken to a bed and breakfast and left there. You can't contact anyone, and you can't tell anyone who you are. Instant fail. By day three, I was really starting to panic about my mum worrying. An elderly lady started talking to me at breakfast one morning, and I was too nervous to speak to her in case she was a plant and I failed. It doesn't take long for the paranoia to set in. I found out later that she was nothing to do with the training, but the man sitting behind me, eating his scrambled eggs, was listening to every word. After six days, I was pulled out, given a new phone and taken back to my home. On the way, it was explained to me that no one would like me very much if I chose to do this job.'

'And that didn't faze you?' Kim asked.

Leanne shook her head. 'I'm not all that likeable anyway, so it was no great shakes.'

Kim hid her smile of amusement. She liked people who were self-aware.

'My trainer explained that in the eyes of criminals, we're the people who look after the grasses. To other police officers, we're nothing more than babysitters, and to the witness themselves we become the only remaining symbol of a system that upended their lives. Everyone else fades out of the picture, leaving only the protection officer. As their frustration grows and their full understanding of their new situation becomes real, there's only us left in the picture, and there's still a lot to do.'

'Like what?' Kim asked on behalf of everyone else that was listening to every word.

Leanne took a deep breath. 'It's not just the physical aspect of keeping them safe. There are many red flags that alert people that someone is in the programme. Not so important for folks who aren't interested but dead giveaways to people who are looking.'

'Like what?' Penn asked, turning to give Leanne his full attention.

'They get their back story wrong. They tell the same person something different because they can't remember what they said the first time. They're adult orphans with no siblings. They have few or no visitors. They look wrong, like their names don't suit them. They have an accent that doesn't match the back story they've fabricated. They have shibboleths.'

'What now?' Penn asked.

'Pronunciations or colloquialisms that are unique to an area that you haven't worked into your history. It's like saying "Yow am" and then trying to claim you've spent no time in the Black Country. Mannerisms count too; city people talk faster. Other signs are job knowledge if you've invented a weak or inflated CV. You stand out if you're too cautious. People's favourite subject is normally themselves, so if you've known someone for a while and still divulged nothing it looks odd. No wedding photos, no albums, no social media history and that's especially problematic with adolescents who struggle to remember the constructed history at the best of times.'

Even Stacey was listening intently now.

'You work hard with the family to invent a history rich enough in detail but not complicated enough to trip them up.'

'But surely once the information is in there?' Penn said, tapping his head.

Leanne turned his way. 'Make up a brief history in your mind. Be whoever you want to be.'

'Okay.'

'Which school did you go to?'

'Edge View in Bromsgrove.'

'Who was your best friend?'

'Curtis Dobbs.'

'Who was your favourite teacher?'

'Mrs Johnson.'

'My cousin actually went to Edge View in Bromsgrove same time as you: Samantha Finch, did you know her?'

'No, I don't…'

'Tall girl, long blonde hair, good at maths. I'm sure she was in Mrs Johnson's class as well.'

'Oh, hang on. Yes, I remember her now,' Penn said, trying to keep up. 'I think we had a couple of lessons together.'

'Hang on, no, it wasn't Edge View she went to, it was Valley View.'

'Oh, I must be remembering someone else.'

'Is there anything you told me that was true?' Leanne asked.

'The name of my school, as the question came quickly.'

'Yeah, questions do that. Even innocent ones can take you by surprise, but as a witness you've just given me a true fact which is a starting point. I know where you went to school. In the hands of the right person that's enough.'

'But I didn't have time to—'

'Who was your best friend?'

'Curtis Dodds.'

'Not Curtis Dobbs like you told me a minute ago?'

Penn smiled in defeat.

'You gave me three pieces of information, but because they weren't all true, the false ones aren't ingrained in your memory. Three basic pieces of info, so imagine having to remember a whole past life.'

'Jeez,' Penn said, scratching his head.

'You said something about Sarah struggling with the last part of the training,' Kim said, bringing her back to their victim.

'Yeah, her mother was ill at the time and she almost caved, but she managed to stick it out.'

'How do you know?' Kim asked, raising one eyebrow.

'Sorry?' Leanne said, but Kim knew the woman had already sussed where she was going.

'Given the secretive nature of your work and the vulnerability of your witnesses, I would have thought that contact between protection officers was strictly forbidden. So how do you know she struggled? Did you keep in touch?'

Leanne hesitated before nodding. 'We kept in touch for a while, offered each other support. Shared problems; but we never divulged details of our families, I swear.'

'Were you in touch recently?'

Leanne shook her head. 'Not for a few years.'

'Why not?'

Leanne shrugged. 'Just stopped calling each other.'

'When?'

'About five years ago.'

'Around the time you left your last family?'

Leanne coloured. 'Maybe.'

'Why?'

'Can't tell you that.'

'Is that when you changed your name?'

'Maybe.'

'Why?' Kim pushed.

'Can't tell you that.'

'For fuck's sake, Leanne, will you just—'

'I've told you enough,' she said, standing. 'I know nothing more that can help you find this psycho lunatic, so I'll bid you all farewell,' she said, glancing once more at the whiteboard.

'Leanne, just wait a—'

'Sorry, but no. This shit just got way too real.'

CHAPTER EIGHTY-SIX

'Thank the lord for that,' Frost said after ending the call from the police. She could return to her home around midday.

'But I might just take you with me,' she said, rubbing Barney's head as he snoozed on the sofa beside her.

Frost had no idea what time the inspector had returned during the night, but she was aware that Barney had been with her then he hadn't and then he had again.

It was only now that she considered the drive of the woman she loved to taunt. Called out late at night, back home to sort her dog out and then gone again before Frost had risen at 7.30 a.m.

She'd followed the curt instructions on the note to the letter, as she got the impression that interfering with Barney's well-being was something she would do at her own peril.

In truth, the woman had surprised her by turning up at her home the night before, and although she would never admit it, there had been a reassurance in her presence. Even if Stone had only come to gloat, it was a familiar face amongst the chaos.

But she hadn't gloated, and Frost had seen that closed, set expression she'd adopted after seeing the state of her house. She knew the expression well, as it was the one that shaped her face in all their dealings with each other.

Last night she had appreciated Stone's no-nonsense, take-charge manner and her insistence at removing her from the scene. As she'd stood by the car, she'd been overwhelmed by the rage, the feeling of being violated and the sheer neck that she would be bullied into backing off. She'd tried not to think of the officers now trudging through her home, compounding the feelings of vulnerability. The nausea had never been far from her stomach, and she was grateful to have been removed from the situation.

But after a good night's sleep and some distance, she was ready to get back to both her home and her story.

Yes, Stone had warned her, again, of the dangers of what she was doing, but she also knew that those same warnings would not deter the woman giving her the advice. Someone, somewhere had to give Trisha Morley a voice and, despite warning her off, the inspector had offered her another avenue to explore. She had never considered what might have happened between the couple while they'd been out of the country.

Following the prompt from Stone last night, she'd been able to log in remotely to her work intranet and had searched the scanned court documents for any references to injuries sustained outside the UK, and she had found nothing. There was nothing in her notebook either, so it was either an avenue the CPS hadn't explored or they had come away empty.

She checked her watch. It was just after nine and now an acceptable time to try and find out.

Penny Colgan answered on the second ring.

'Hey, Penny, sorry to call so early.'

'It's no problem. Just dropped the kids off at school. How are you?'

Frost appreciated the warmth in her voice, although this response was taking some getting used to. She was more used to people hanging up on her once they knew who she was and oftentimes before.

'Listen, I've been thinking about something and I need your help.'

'Shoot,' she said as Frost heard the car door shut.

'Trisha and Nick travelled quite a bit, didn't they?'

'Oh yeah, travelled the world. Always going to different loca-tions. Nick liked to brag about where they'd been: Vegas; Niagara Falls; the Barrier Reef, in Australia; Great Wall of China. I lost count of the countries they visited. Why?'

Frost felt her heart drop a little. It had seemed like a good idea but trying to track down medical records in all of these countries could take months.

'Was there anywhere in particular Trisha liked to go?'

'No, it was a different continent every time.'

Frost felt the deflation of a good idea being popped before her very eyes.

'Wait a minute. There was this one place.'

'Go on,' Frost urged, trying to stop all the air from coming out of the balloon.

'In Italy. Trisha loved Italy. They went before they were married. Did all the usual sights and tours of Rome, Venice, Milan, but they happened upon a small town near Lake Como. I can't remember the name of the place even though she told—'

'Hang on one sec,' Frost said, typing in a search of towns on Lake Como. She immediately saw that the lake was fifty-six square miles and was studded with villages and towns, so if Penny couldn't remember the name, her search would end right now.

She didn't bother to call out the town of Como, as Penny would have remembered that.

'Was it Bellagio?'

'No.'

'Tremezzina?'

'No.'

'Nesso?'

'No.'

'Menaggio?'

'No.'

'Varenna?'

Hesitation. 'Yes, that's the one. Trisha fell in love with the area.'

Frost put in a Google search for Varenna and hit the top article. The place was a municipality in the Province of Lecco, just short of forty miles north of Milan and covered an area of approximately four square miles.

'They went back a couple of times, I think,' Penny continued. 'Same village, same guesthouse that had a view of some monastery or villa or something.'

'Villa Monastero?' Frost asked excitedly as she continued reading the Wikipedia article. It was a Cistercian convent founded in the twelfth century, which was now a museum, botanical gardens and convention centre.

'Yeah, that sounds right. I remember one time Nick booked a trip for her birthday and then cancelled it when he found out she'd met me for a coffee.'

Frost felt her hackles rise at the casual cruelty the man had employed to keep Trisha under control.

'Sorry but I can't remember anything else.'

'You've been a great help, Penny. Thanks for your time,' Frost said, ending the call. It was a starting point, and maybe all was not lost after all.

She put a basic search into Google for guest houses in the area she'd been given.

Maybe this place she loved had provided Trisha with the confidence to say something to someone. Maybe she'd felt comfortable enough to open up in a place that was familiar to her yet distant enough from her daily life.

Well, judging by her Internet search she had twenty-two opportunities to explore.

She called the number of the first guest house on the list.

It was answered almost immediately.

'Excuse me but does your property have a view of the Villa Monastero?'

CHAPTER EIGHTY-SEVEN

'You reckon we're a dumping ground or what?' Bryant asked as they headed towards Kidderminster.

'For what?' she asked, although she suspected she knew what he was talking about.

She'd spoken to Woody first thing and explained that she needed the details of the family Sarah had been protecting, and he'd managed to give her both that and Sarah's home address at the same time. They were heading towards Sarah's witness family, to give her relatives a chance to digest the news.

'Cos I was reading last night,' he continued, 'and apparently there are dumping grounds in America; many of theirs relocate to Maine, though their system is very different to ours.'

'Go on,' Kim said, happy to let him talk. It had been a long night and for some reason her mind had stuck on Leanne since she'd stormed out of the squad room.

'Well, in the US it's called WITSEC and offers protection to 18,000 federal witnesses, which costs the government ten billion dollars annually.'

'Bloody hell. Why so much?'

'From what I read, they allow some to have breast implants, facelifts and even dental work. They're given around sixty thousand dollars before having to find work, and trials involving WITSEC have an eighty-nine per cent conviction rate.'

'Not bad,' Kim acknowledged.

'They also have a clearing house for recent inductees, which can house up to six families. They're all locked in separate rooms; apparently, less than five per cent of relocated witnesses are completely free of any wrongdoing themselves.'

'And they're getting free cosmetic surgery?'

'Oh yeah, and have you seen Maine with its beaches and lobsters? It ain't the Black Country, I can tell you.'

'Do they have a waiting list?' she asked.

'Yeah, the queue is a mile long, and I'm sure you know I'm just filling the air in the car with rubbish until you tell me what's on your mind.'

'It's Leanne. There's more going on there than we know. She's still keeping secrets, even though folks are dying all around her.'

'It's kind of her job to keep secrets though, isn't it?'

'I'm not talking about other people's secrets. I'm talking about her own. Do you see how her face closes up every time we mention the people she protected before?'

'To be fair, I don't see any change in her expression whatever we mention,' Bryant said.

He had a point. The change in her was subtle, but Kim had learned to study micro expressions and notice things in people's behaviour. And there was something that Leanne didn't want them to know, Kim thought as Bryant pulled into Cedarwood Drive.

'Ooh, different,' he said, looking for number six. The road was a cul-de-sac, with about twelve detached houses arching around a small green with a planted area and a couple of benches.

A BMW 5 Series was parked on the drive of number six, with a gaping space beside it, as though another car had just left or hadn't yet returned.

'Well, witness protection ain't paying for this,' Bryant said, pointing out the obvious difference between this and other properties they'd visited.

The door was opened by a smartly dressed woman in her mid-forties before they'd even had chance to knock. Their only information was the name of the witness being protected.

'Mona Atkins?' Kim asked.

The woman nodded, her expression a mix of irritation and impatience.

'Which one of you is my new protection officer?' she asked, looking from one to the other.

'Neither,' Kim said, holding up her identification. 'We're CID, investigating the murder of Sarah Lessiter.'

'What's that got to do with me?'

The woman hadn't missed a beat, and her expression hadn't changed at all. It was evident there had been no emotional connection between the two women.

'We need to ask you a few questions. Do you mind if we come in?' Kim asked, trying to study the woman's features. There was something slightly familiar about the cool blue eyes and the full lips. It was like trying to place an actress you'd seen in a film.

'If you must but be quick. I don't want your visit being mentioned to my husband. Now what do you need to know?' she asked, standing in the hallway and clearly the point past which they were not going to get beyond.

Leanne had said something about some people in the programme who didn't even divulge their past to new spouses. Whether necessary for safety or not, it was a level of deceit that Kim could barely comprehend.

'It'll be bad enough explaining another "old friend",' she said, using her fingers to frame the words.

For a moment, Kim forgot they were here because a woman had been murdered, so caught up was she in this woman's inconvenience at having to explain the presence of a new protection officer in her life.

'So what do you want? I have to leave for work. Call centres don't run themselves.'

'It might be an idea to call in late,' Kim said, trying to keep the chill out of her voice.

'Are you people trying to ruin my life?' she asked, adding a little melodrama to the mix. 'You turn up here, at my home, looking like police officers and now you want me to arouse suspicion by turning up late for work?'

'I'm sure non-witnesses are sometimes late too,' Kim offered.

'And I'm sure they have the luxury of being able to tell the truth as well,' she shot back. Her face was beginning to colour. 'You have no idea of the sacrifice and hard work it's taken for me to construct another life, to make people look only at the parts of me I want them to see. Fifteen years I've been living this life that you don't even have the courtesy to treat with respect.'

The mention of the number of years had the effect of a screen being removed and with it went any sliver of sympathy Kim might have felt.

Mona Atkins had the same initials as Melanie Abbot. The blonde curly hair had been tamed into a sleek helmet and toned down to a light brown. The woman before her bore very little resemblance to the photo of the nineteen-year-old girl who had helped her boyfriend conceal the murder of an eight-year-old boy. The public outcry against this woman had equalled if not exceeded the rage against her boyfriend, who had committed suicide before the trial. She had faced the public anger alone. Eventually found guilty of perverting the course of justice, she'd served three or four years and been released with a new identity before her twenty-fifth birthday.

'I assume the two of you weren't close,' Kim said, returning to the reason for their visit. Whether Mona chose to ring in late or not, Kim wasn't leaving until she'd asked her questions.

Mona's eyebrows drew together. 'Why would we be close? She was doing a job. Providing a service. I was no closer to her than I am to the bin man.'

Kim realised she didn't need to rely on what Mona had done in the past to fuel her dislike. There was plenty to focus on in the present.

In her experience, shared secrets drew people together, especially if she had chosen to share nothing of her past with her husband. But not here.

Perhaps sensing her displeasure, the woman offered a qualifier, as though trying to retract her coldness towards the death.

'Admittedly, she was better than the last one, okay. She knew her job and only bothered me when necessary. I didn't always take her advice, but it was well meaning and—'

'What kind of advice? Was there a specific threat against you?'

Mona shook her head and glanced again at her watch.

'Look, they do spot checks on you. They tail you for a day and watch your every move. I suppose it's kind of like an audit to make sure you're still taking the necessary precautions, that you haven't become complacent. Then they advise you, tell you that you're not varying your route to certain places enough or that you didn't lock your door or spent too long talking to a stranger or that you walked along a road that was deserted or not covered by CCTV. It's like a regular risk assessment. She knew her stuff but wasn't intrusive.'

'Had she mentioned anything to you about strange occurrences, being followed or…'

'Am I at risk, Officer?' she asked plainly. Any thought for Sarah had been replaced by all thoughts for herself.

'That's actually what we're trying to find out,' Kim snapped.

Mona's expression changed, as though she wasn't used to being snapped at. She was clearly the queen of the world she'd constructed. Kim was struck by the fact that she viewed herself as an asset, much like a celebrity would do. She was the focus of the protection and the minions should remember that rather than the fact these people were being paid to keep her alive.

'I think you should leave,' Mona said, opening the door.

Kim realised that she knew nothing more than when she'd walked in the door.

But there was something she'd said earlier that came back to Kim.

'You said Sarah was better than the last one. What did you mean?'

Mona sighed with impatience.

'There are officers that are more forceful than others. As I said before, Sarah carried out her audits and offered advice and suggestions. The last one threatened me with expulsion if I didn't remove a couple of harmless photos from my social media account.'

In this age of facial recognition, Kim could understand the officer's concern. Just one piece of information or data and the whole thing could unravel.

'I was wearing a hat and glasses so there was no real issue, but I was very rudely reminded of the rules.'

Kim understood the frustration in trying to keep someone safe when they cared less about doing it for themselves.

'And this officer reprimanded you?' Kim said, understanding why that particular officer was now in the past.

'Oh, yes, but she soon understood you don't mess—'

'She?' Kim asked.

'Oh yes, the one before Sarah was a class A bitch. No, I didn't like Leanne at all.'

CHAPTER EIGHTY-EIGHT

'Starting to feel a bit like a maze, this one?' Stacey said as an email pinged her inbox.

She'd asked DI Lynes for the phone records of Dennis Burke, and he'd sent them through straight away.

'I kind of get her though,' Penn said, staring over her head.

'Who?'

'Leanne. She's a bit hostile and stand-offish, but I get why she's got that hard shell. Living and working in secret all the time. I suppose you build a wall cos you're not really a part of any team.'

'You like her?' Stacey asked, raising an eyebrow.

'Nah, nothing like that. She scares me, but it does make you grateful for the team you've got.'

'Aww… thanks, Penn, cos I'm assuming you mean me.'

'Yeah, course I mean you, Stace,' he said, smirking. He turned back to his computer. 'But bloody hell, this is a nightmare.'

'Wassup, homey?' she asked, printing off the second set of phone records. Every time she did it, she thought about the trees; but some things didn't compute in her brain unless she could see them in black and white.

'This bloody van.'

'Go on,' she said, reaching for the printout. She switched her screen back to the real-time investigation in Somerset.

'What about it?'

'I thought I had a lead on that van, until one guy remembered it was his brother-in-law bringing in some breakfast sandwiches and a coffee.'

'So you can definitely rule that one out,' Stacey said, looking for a bright side to his predicament.

'Yep, only another forty-nine to go,' he said miserably.

'You know what I'd do?' Stacey asked.

'Resign and take up whittling?'

'Not my first choice. I'd just run them all again, even the ones you've got explanations for.'

'Why? I've already run the ones unaccounted for through the DVLA, so why would I run the ones I've ruled out as being there on legitimate business?' he asked, looking at his full list of vehicles that had entered the trading estate.

'Because people make mistakes, like matey boy who'd forgotten about his breakfast delivery. For example, how many white Transit vans you got on your list?'

'Altogether, fifty-three,' he said doing a quick count.

'How many are confirmed as being there on business?'

'Forty-one.'

'So you're telling me that forty-one small businesses were able to confirm the registration numbers of the white Transit van that visited them. In full?'

She could see that the mist of despair was clearing in his mind.

'You dow think that even one of those people was too busy to talk to you and decided to just confirm the third or fourth one you threw at them to get yer off the phone?'

'You know, Stace, you might just have—'

He stopped speaking and began tapping as her phone began to ring.

'DC Wood,' she answered, wondering for the hundredth time how it would sound replacing the C with an S.

'Hi, it's Percy.'

Stacey opened her mouth to seek more information, but he was good enough to help her out.

'Percy Poole from Ridgepoint.'

'Ah, Percy. Hi,' she answered, hoping he was ringing because he had something.

She unconsciously crossed the fingers on her left hand for luck.

'Right, I can't tell you much. The computer was pretty toasted, but we were able to get a look at the deleted information files.'

'Go on,' Stacey said. This was more than they could have hoped for.

'There's a block of emails, deleted, about eighty messages back and forth, all binned in one dump a couple of weeks ago. I can't get to the content, but I can tell you the recipient's name was Amelia Dixon.'

'Percy, you are an absolute angel,' Stacey said, ending the call.

'Well, Penn, looks like our teaching assistant did have something to hide after all. Jacob Powell was the man corresponding with our ex-Matrix employee.'

He finally looked up and then back at the screen.

'And he also owns a white Transit van.'

CHAPTER EIGHTY-NINE

'I'd have liked to have been a fly on the wall for a spat between those two,' Bryant observed once they were back in the car.

'Oh yeah, talk about a rock and a hard place,' she agreed. 'They're both pretty hostile and—'

Bryant smirked. 'Oh, the irony.'

'Bryant, it's way too early in the day for—'

She stopped speaking as her phone rang.

She put it on loudspeaker as Bryant drove them towards the home of Sarah Lessiter.

'Penn,' she said.

'We've got a link from Jacob Powell to Amelia Dixon, boss,' Penn said. 'He sent the emails and he has a white Transit van that entered the Hayes Trading Estate on Saturday afternoon and left at 7 a.m. Monday morning.'

'Bloody hell,' Bryant said as she felt that familiar stirring in her stomach.

'Okay, get the warrant and get over to his house and take the place apart.'

'Already on it, boss,' he said. 'Registration number has been added to Bryant's earlier description and recirculated.'

'Good job,' she said as Bryant pulled up at the home of Sarah Lessiter.

She wanted to get back to the station and follow up this lead of the teaching assistant. She wanted every pair of eyes and hands trying to find him.

She was doubtful of what she was going to learn from Sarah's family when they were already closing in on their killer.

CHAPTER NINETY

Stacey sat back and stretched her blurry eyes wide as Penn went tearing out the door, clutching the search warrant in his hand.

Even though she was now alone, she could feel the excitement of the investigation moving up a gear. Good old police detective work had uncovered solid links between the teaching assistant and stolen information from Amelia Dixon. But in her mind the evidence wasn't strong enough. All they could prove was that Jacob and Amelia had corresponded by email and that Amelia's computer had gone kaput. Convenient circumstantial evidence that would not convince a jury that, even if true, had led to four horrific deaths.

They needed more links between killer and victims, they needed forensic evidence to tie him to each and every murder, or they needed a confession.

But a confession was not going to happen until they found him. Hopefully, Penn was going to find a link at the man's home, and she would try to find the connections between him and the victims.

She re-stretched her eyes once more and went back to the phone records laid out on her desk.

She had now collated all the phone records for the victims for the twenty-four hours before their murders. She had more data but it made sense to work outwards from the last time the phones were used.

Four sheets lay before her, placed in order that the bodies had been found. Keith Phipps, Dennis Burke, Dean Mullins and Sarah Lessiter.

She looked over them all first, just a cursory glance, allowing her brain time to pick out anything obvious. She pushed all thoughts from her head and just gazed at each piece of paper in turn. She was reminded of those 3D Magic Eye posters, where you had to force your eyes to relax before your brain could do the work of showing you the actual image.

She scrunched up her eyes as they passed from one sheet to the next and stopped as a number near the bottom of Sarah's sheet jumped out at her.

'What the devil are you doing there?' she asked, tapping the page.

CHAPTER NINETY-ONE

The first thing Kim noticed about Sarah Lessiter's home was the level of security. Sited on the top corner of the property was a pan-tilt-zoom camera that covered the front and around the side. The sensor told her it was motion activated. As she stepped into the brick porch of the old Victorian end terrace, she saw another camera in the top left pointed down at the spot where they stood. There wasn't anybody getting in her house without her getting a good look at them first.

The door was opened by a PC who nodded towards an ornate archway that led into the lounge.

Kim was relieved that for once she was not the one delivering the news.

The PC sitting on the sofa tapped the man's arm, stood and joined her colleague at the door.

'Mr Lessiter, may I say how sorry we are for your loss,' she said, taking a seat.

Dale Lessiter raised a pale face with reddened eyes up towards her.

In that one glance, she felt the full force of his grief.

A brief look around had told her there were no children or pets; there were no toys or photos of anything other than the couple appearing to be laughing and happy in a number of different locations.

The lounge held one of the largest televisions she'd ever seen, and the reclining sofas were aimed towards it. Sound bars and speakers were placed strategically around the room. It was a space fashioned for adults and told Kim just how Sarah had enjoyed unwinding after a long day at work.

'Is there anyone we can call?'

He shook his head. 'There's just Sarah's mum, but I can't call her yet, not yet. She'll need me to be strong and right now...'

He allowed the words to trail away, and Kim understood that right now he couldn't be any support to anyone else.

Kim idly wondered at their circle of friends. Did they keep to themselves due to the nature of Sarah's job? Some couples existed with friends and colleagues on both sides as well as shared acquaintances, filling their spare time with the company of others. And then there were couples who existed on their own island with few friends. She suspected the Lessiters were the latter. Her sympathy for the partner left behind just went up a gear.

'The officer...' he whispered, nodding towards the door, 'said she was murdered. Is that true?'

Kim nodded.

He shook his head. 'We always knew there was danger involved but this. I mean we never really...'

'How much did you know about your wife's work, Mr Lessiter?' she asked gently.

'Not much. Only her job but never the families she worked with; I understood that and— Is that what this is about? Has someone found the people she was protecting?'

'I'm sorry, Mr Lessiter, but—'

He waved away her response. It wasn't important. It wasn't going to bring her back.

'And how was Sarah with her work?' Kim asked.

'She had good and bad days like everyone else. Some days she came home pissed off and annoyed if people refused to listen to her, if they didn't take their own safety seriously. Last few months have been a bit hard on her, I think.'

Remembering her previous meeting with Mona Atkins, Kim could certainly understand why.

'She loved her job, Inspector. She did everything she was supposed to: she kept secrets; she changed her routes; she left the house in the middle of the night when needed and—'

'For what?' Kim asked.

'If the families heard a noise or they received a crank call, anything that caused them concern; Sarah was their only link to their old life.'

'And had anything like that happened recently?' Kim asked.

He shook his head. 'Not for weeks now.'

'Was there anything at all that Sarah mentioned that was out of the ordinary, anything that concerned her?'

He began to shake his head and then stopped. 'No, it's probably nothing.'

'We'll take it,' Kim said.

'She said something about a man calling out at her as she got off the train a couple of days ago. She ignored him and gave him the slip. It rattled her a bit.'

'Why?' Kim asked.

'Dunno. Apparently, he thought her name was Karen.'

CHAPTER NINETY-TWO

Kim returned Stacey's call once they were back in the car.

'Sarah tried to ring Leanne, boss, two days ago. Leanne didn't take the call, and I don't think Sarah left a message.'

Sarah had known Leanne as Karen back when they were training. The coincidence of someone calling out that particular name had led her to try and warn her old friend.

'Okay, Stace, thanks,' she said, ending the call.

'You think this is about that Mona woman we just visited?' Bryant asked.

Kim shook her head. 'Mona knew Leanne by her new name. This person was asking after the name she had before.'

'Why did she change it?'

'She wouldn't say. Any time we've asked her about previous witnesses, she's closed up completely.'

Kim tapped her fingers on the dashboard as a few things began to clear in her mind.

'You'd tell, wouldn't you?' she asked absently.

'Tell what?'

'Anything you knew given the torture our victims have suffered.'

'I'd like to think I could hold out for a while, but yeah I'd probably cave.'

'So obviously our victims didn't have the information he was after but… oh shit,' she said, taking out her phone.

Woody answered almost immediately.

'Sir, I need to speak with Superintendent Wexford. It's urgent.'

'Stone, you're going to have to give me something better than that.'

'I think our guy is murdering people for one reason. It's to find one person. I think he wants Leanne. He's after someone called Karen, but none of our victims would have known her as that, except one. Sarah Lessiter knew her as both. Leanne needs to be warned as soon as possible, but I also need to speak with the superintendent.'

'For what reason?'

'I need to know who she looked after as Karen.'

CHAPTER NINETY-THREE

Penn watched as the officers used the Enforcer to break down the door. This time, the visit was official and protocols needed to be followed. In addition, he'd posted the back-door key through the front letterbox and knew there was no other way in.

'Clear,' the officer shouted as the door crashed against the wall. The cat scarpered past their legs and headed straight into the garden next door.

Penn listened at the doorway for a second but there was no sound. Jacob Powell was definitely not home.

He ventured into the hallway, seeing the same things in the same place, almost.

There was something different that he couldn't place.

He waved behind him, beckoning the officers to begin the search. Two headed straight upstairs, one into the lounge and one through to the kitchen.

He followed the officer to the kitchen and that was when he saw the key back in the lock of the door. The millimetre of milk in the cat feeding bowl confirmed it. The dishes had been empty. He had put half a tin of cat food in the bowl but hadn't found any milk.

No call had been made to the police that his house had been entered and property taken. There had been no report received from this address of any kind.

There was no doubt that Jacob knew they were on to him, so why come back at all? What had prompted his sudden need to return?

He glanced outside and saw it.

In the middle of the grass was a small fire pit, formed of house bricks.

He stepped outside and moved closer; the acrid smell of plastic burning was still present in the air. He leaned down and took a good look at the part-burned debris, which appeared to be a mixture of all kinds of materials. He spotted the burned leather remnants of a wallet; a blackened and melted card that may have been a driving licence; pages of A4 paper that had been burned together.

He knew he couldn't touch it and took out his phone to call Mitch. He suspected he was looking at the personal possessions of the victims removed to slow down identification; as if identifying these victims hadn't been difficult enough.

He walked around the pit as he pressed Mitch's name on the phone.

There was a small amount of wording visible on the top of one of the burned pieces of paper.

He leaned down and read what he could see and was able to make out the words.

'Common mistakes… Witness protection.'

He straightened as he waited for Mitch to answer his call.

There was no doubt in his mind that the teaching assistant was their killer.

CHAPTER NINETY-FOUR

'Cross your paws for me, Barney,' Frost said to the dog lying at her feet.

In between calling and sending emails, she had followed Stone's instructions to the letter.

She'd let him out around ten and then given him a carrot at eleven. And she'd done it on the dot too. Knowing Stone, she had some secret camera hidden away watching her. She suspected that a voice would have sounded from somewhere with a timely reminder had she been a minute late.

She'd probably given him more tickles than necessary, but it was kind of automatic when he nestled beside her that her hand would find its way into his thick, soft fur.

'Your buddy will be here for you soon. Does she send you with a packed lunch, an overnight bag? No, you just go as you are, eh?'

Frost silently remonstrated with herself. She'd never been one for talking to herself, but with Barney around she couldn't seem to help it.

She gave him another tickle, and although it hadn't been twenty-four hours, she was going to miss him when she returned home later today.

'Maybe she won't notice if I take you home with me, eh?'

Although Frost reckoned that one single action would be enough to get her killed, and even though Stone had not adopted any of Barney's warm and fuzzy traits, she clearly loved the dog very much.

'Make it come, Barney,' she said, tapping the screen, as though it would make the email magically drop into her inbox.

It was on her ninth call that she'd found a guest house owner who had remembered a pretty, blonde English lady with sad eyes who sat on the veranda every morning with a cup of tea.

An emailed photo and a second call had confirmed the lady in question to be Trisha Morley.

Frost had managed to get the dates they'd visited over the last five years, which she had known would give her a starting point with the local hospitals.

And just as she'd been weighing up the enormity of the task ahead, the woman had offered something trivial that probably meant nothing to her but meant a whole lot more to Frost. She'd remarked that on their last visit, Trisha had never even said goodbye as she normally did. Instead, she'd gone straight to the car and her husband had checked them out.

As she'd thanked the woman and hung up, Frost had already slotted that piece into place. Would Trisha really have wanted to present herself if she'd been injured and covered in bruises?

She'd checked Trisha's medical records, and the dates had coincided with Trish having to have her arm re-set two days after their return.

It had narrowed the dates down and enabled her to be more specific with the information she was requesting. Her third call had been to the Bellano Hospital, where after half an hour of holding for a fluent, English-speaking nurse, Frost had explained what she was seeking.

The nurse had confirmed Trisha's attendance at the hospital, and Frost had punched the air with her free hand.

The nurse, Antonella, had refused her request for the medical records, until Frost had explained the situation fully and had sent her the news reports of Trisha's murder, by email, as they spoke.

Frost had detected a change in her manner. Antonella had revealed that Trisha had been dropped off at the hospital by her husband and been collected by him two hours later.

Frost prayed that not having Nick standing over her shoulder might have prompted Trisha to confide the real reason for her injuries. When she'd pressed Antonella on the possibility, the nurse had explained that she would reveal nothing further until she had sought permission to share the public records, and if granted, she would send them along.

Frost had ended the call knowing there was nothing more she could do but wait.

The sound of the key in the lock startled her. Not so much Barney, who was already waiting at the door with a wagging tail.

Briefly, Frost felt a pang of jealousy. He had been her loyal companion for hours but was now prepared to abandon her at the drop of a hat.

'You must be the reporter,' the elderly man offered with a smile.

She nodded as he fixed the lead to Barney's collar.

'I'm Charlie. Kim sent me a text, warning me there was a strange woman in her house.'

Frost laughed at his devilish smile and realised how strange it was to hear someone call the police officer by her first name. To some people, she was Inspector, others marm, boss or guv, and Frost found herself wondering to how many people was she known simply as Kim.

'Okay, I won't keep you. We've got squirrels to terrorise, haven't we, boy?' Charlie said, leading him out the front door.

Instantly, the house felt empty without the dog, she realised, as her email dinged a new message.

Her stomach lurched as she saw it was from Bellano Hospital. And there were attachments. They had sent the report.

She copied the narrative into Google translate and began to read.

CHAPTER NINETY-FIVE

Kim entered Mary Stevens Park, in Stourbridge, alone, exactly as she'd been instructed. The information Superintendent Wexford was about to share was meant for her ears only.

She spotted the man sitting on the first bench, with a Jack Russell on a retractable lead. Two things struck her. Wearing his uniform, the man was imposing, authoritative. Everyone at West Midlands Police knew who he was. Right now, sitting here on a bench, he was a man pausing while walking his dog.

'Nice dog,' she said, taking a seat beside him.

The lead whirred as it retracted when the small dog left the patch of grass that had been the centre of his world and came towards her.

She tickled him behind the ears. Many people offered their hand for a dog to smell their scent. Kim had learned that such a gesture was pointless, as the dog would have smelled her as soon as she entered the park.

'Didn't have you down as a dog person, Stone.'

'Ditto, sir.'

'Before we proceed, we are contacting Leanne to make her aware of the danger.'

She nodded. His job not hers, although Kim had tried to make a quick call to her as they'd travelled away from Sarah Lessiter's home. She hadn't received an answer but she hadn't expected one. She'd left a message despite the fact they couldn't stand the sight of each other. The woman had rushed out of the office almost five hours ago, taking her secrets with her. Secrets Kim hoped she was going to learn right now.

'I know I don't have to remind you of the sensitivity and secrecy of—'

'You're right, sir, you don't.'

'Let me preface this by stating that Leanne is a very good protection officer. She has nerves of steel and takes her work very seriously. She is one of our best.'

Kim nodded her understanding. She wasn't interviewing the woman for a job.

'Leanne, or Karen as she was back then, was assigned to Boy X,' he said, as though that was enough.

Kim frowned and shook her head.

'Nineteen years ago, the canal tunnel murder in Wakefield.'

She nodded as the memories came back to her.

Boy X had been a thirteen-year-old boy who had abducted a girl aged seven from a play centre. He had raped, tortured and mutilated the little girl, who had eventually died of blood loss from her wounds.

'A little girl named Emily.'

'Let me finish. It was dubbed the most horrific murder Wakefield had ever seen. The injuries sustained to that poor little girl were enough to make grown men cry, and it did. Officers wept openly at the damage inflicted on her body. There were burn marks; joint dislocations; skin peeled from her flesh; insects and rodents had feasted on her. Two of the attending officers left the force within a month, and a third eventually had a full-on nervous breakdown.'

It was a state Kim could empathise with. No crime scene could be rewound.

'Boy X was caught within twenty-four hours of the body being found. He bragged about it to his friend, who didn't believe him until he showed him the pink sock missing from her body.

Terrified by what he'd heard, the friend told his mother, who called the police immediately.'

The superintendent took a deep breath.

'Although he was tried as an adult, Boy X never saw the inside of a real prison. Well, not then anyway. He was incarcerated in a youth offenders facility, where he learned certain lessons slowly.'

'What kind of lessons?' Kim asked.

'That you don't tell the truth about being beaten up by other kids. In fact, you just get it worse. My understanding is that in his first seven months, he was beaten nine times and the officers were hardly rushing to get in front of him.'

Kim realised that her empathy muscle appeared to have taken the day off.

Wexford continued. 'He was free before his eighteenth birthday. There was no question he had to be admitted to the witness protection programme under the conditions of a select few, most of whom you know about. Obviously, the public outcry against him was a threat to his life. He was placed in the West Midlands, and he got a job. Eventually he married but divulged nothing of his past to his wife. Leanne took over his protection eight years ago when his protection officer retired.

'There was friction immediately. He'd had the same PO for years, had reached the point where he treated the officer as staff. Gerald was nearing retirement and wasn't as attentive as he might have been. He wanted to charter a smooth sailing lane to his retirement date.'

Kim could imagine the shock Boy X had felt in getting Leanne, and not one ounce of her felt sorry for him.

'They clashed. He requested another officer, we refused and they ambled along for about nine months, until Leanne did her first audit.' He paused. 'Officers are required to carry out—'

'I know,' Kim interrupted. Mona had told her already.

'Leanne did the usual: followed him to work, lunchtime, etc., and all was good until he left work early. He drove fifteen miles out of his way to a primary school in Stourport. He sat in his car for twenty minutes watching and photographing little girls.'

'Shit,' Kim said.

'Exactly. It was enough for her to seize his computer. The images she found were sickening, beyond anything we've seen before. Always involving little girls and always involving violence.'

'What happened?'

'He was imprisoned for the offence of possessing indecent images.'

'For how long?'

'Three years.'

'Jesus, is that…?'

'He served two,' Wexford said. 'And you're right. It's no time at all. Unfortunately, the law makes the distinction between possessing and making an indecent image. And although every photo he held was a category A image, which are the most severe and cover images of children in pain, the maximum sentence is three years.'

'It's not enough. Not even close.'

'Agreed, but he served his time and was given a new identity when he was released. Leanne was assigned a new family.'

'She changed her name?'

He nodded. 'It was the safest way to sever any connection with Boy X.'

'And Boy X is still in the programme, even though he broke the law and should be behind bars for the rest of his life?'

'Yes, he is, and I for one am glad of the fact he's in the programme.'

'You can't seriously defend—'

'I defend nothing,' he snapped. 'He is a twisted, soulless, depraved man with sickening fantasies worse than any nightmare

I could conjure up. But under what other circumstance could we, the police, legally watch his every move, search his computer and basically invade his privacy whenever we want to?'

As a free citizen, even a convicted criminal, he would have much more liberty, Kim realised.

'Because there is no mistake that Boy X would reoffend,' Wexford continued. 'So yes, it costs thousands upon thousands to keep the piece of shit protected, but we don't do it for him. We do it to protect the public from him.'

Kim had to admit that she'd never thought of it like that before.

'And his identity?'

'Is something you don't need to know. He has been moved and, as ever, we will protect his—' He stopped speaking as his phone rang.

He answered it and listened as all kinds of thoughts began to go round in Kim's head. She didn't like Leanne one little bit but she knew how to do her job.

'Keep me informed,' he said, ending the call with a frown.

Kim's senses were alerted to an anxiety in the man that hadn't been present before.

'What?'

'Leanne can't be reached. Her car is at her house, and her home has been ransacked,' he said, standing.

'Fuck,' Kim said, saying nothing more as she sprinted back to Bryant, waiting at the entrance to the park.

It looked like the bastard had already got her.

And he'd probably now had her for hours.

CHAPTER NINETY-SIX

Despite what she'd been told to do, Stacey really didn't want to read anything more about Emily Harris. The sickness in her stomach and the involuntary tear that occasionally slid over her cheek were already too much for her to bear.

The name had brought up more than twenty-four million search results. It was a case she remembered vaguely from her mother watching the news reports before giving her an extra bedtime hug. She'd heard the name a few times since on a particular anniversary, and more recently there'd been a twenty-year vigil held at the place she'd been found. Her family had not attended.

For Stacey, it wasn't just the pain the poor little girl had endured that placed the brick of despair in her stomach. It was the fear. The little girl had come from a decent enough background and had probably not known the emotion too well, but from the moment Boy X had laid a finger on her flesh, it would have been the emotion that stayed with her until the moment she died. And although the injuries were beyond anything Stacey had ever read, it was that single thought that wouldn't leave her alone. No child should feel that pain, and no child should feel that fear, she thought as her eyes filled with tears once more.

She made no effort to stop them falling or to wipe them away. Her emotions were real and valid and she would hide them from no one.

Slowly but surely she began to understand the reason for the vague feeling of unease she'd had all week.

She was about to explore it more when her phone rang.

'DC Wood,' she answered.

'PC Silvester here. I'm letting you know that from the description you gave us of Jacob Powell, we think we've found your man.'

'Where?' she asked urgently.

She listened to his answer and the only words that came out of her mouth were, 'Oh shit.'

CHAPTER NINETY-SEVEN

Frost mounted the stairs to the offices of Winston Associates with confidence.

She'd returned home for as long as it had taken her to shower, change, apply make-up and find the highest pair of heels she owned.

The double glass doors opened as she approached. She strode through purposefully.

'Mr Daryl Winston please,' she said to the heavily made-up receptionist.

'And you are?'

'Tracy Frost, reporter at the *Dudley Star*.'

The friendly smile turned down a notch to cordial.

'You have an appointment?' she asked doubtfully. Obviously, Daryl Winston didn't take meetings with reporters from the local daily. She was pretty sure he'd take this one.

Frost shook her head as the woman's face relaxed, ready for the no-appointments speech.

'He'll want to see me,' Frost added, saving her the trouble.

Hesitation.

'Just tell him I have a doctor's report I'm sure he'd like to see.'

More hesitation.

Frost shrugged. 'Okay, it's no skin—'

'One second,' she said, picking up the phone.

Frost stepped away to offer her a little privacy.

'He'll be down in a second,' the woman said, failing to hide her own surprise.

She'd barely finished perusing their selection of life-sized posters, celebrating their award-winning campaigns, when a door to her left swung open.

But she'd had long enough for one particular poster to catch her attention.

'Ms Frost,' said the man standing in the open doorway.

His smile and manner were cool and professional as he offered his hand.

'Daryl Winston, pleased to meet you.'

The man who had called her after she'd been rear-ended.

She pointedly ignored the hand by swapping the folder she was carrying to her right hand.

There was little doubt in her mind that either he or someone in this building had arranged both her car accident and the ransacking of her house. She was shaking no one's hand.

'Please come through.'

She followed him into a short corridor with glass partitions separating rooms of various sizes.

He stepped into the first and the smallest.

The room followed the theme from the reception, with posters lit by warm wall lights.

A round table was surrounded by four chairs.

He took a seat. She followed and laid her folder on the desk.

'You have something to show me?'

There was no pretence about which one of their clients her visit was in relation to.

'I do indeed,' she said, laying a hand on the folder. She met his enquiring gaze.

'I didn't realise that the Korma Crisp was one of yours,' she said, referring to the poster that had caught her attention in the reception.

He frowned slightly, fully aware she was not here to discuss a crisp campaign.

'It was disgusting,' Frost said. 'I tried them and they were foul.'

He shrugged as though that detail was unimportant.

'Our campaign increased their market share by seven per cent, which in that particular industry is—'

'But it was quite a basic strategy, wasn't it? You simply blitzed advertising channels, telling people how tasty they were. You aimed your posters, billboards, social media, radio and TV at mid-teens who always want to be cool by trying the next new thing.'

'That target market is quite easily persuaded.'

'And how about the target market for Nick Morley? Are they as easily manipulated if you shout loud enough and for long enough that he's a good person? Exactly the same strategy. Are you hoping for as dramatic a turnaround in that same strategy applied to a murder case?'

He tapped his fingers lightly on the table and waited.

'Because this isn't about market share or sales figures or projections. This is about a man who killed his wife.'

'He is innocent until proven guilty, Ms Frost, as you—'

'And he will be proven guilty, Mr Winston, despite your attempts to steamroll anyone who gets in your way.'

He was unperturbed by her words and remained cool.

'I'm not sure what you're accusing us of, Ms Frost, but we were retained by Mr Morley and his legal team for image management alone. We feel that the campaign has been largely successful and that Mr Morley's reputation had been suitably restored to ensure he receives a fair trial when—'

'Have you read the reports or seen the injuries?'

'We don't need to. We understand that Mrs Morley was a clumsy individual who never once implicated her husband in the—'

'Open the file, Mr Winston,' she said, pushing it towards him.

He gave her a half-smile as he turned over the front cover. The expression died on his face as his gaze rested on the first photo.

A barely recognisable Trisha Morley stared back at him. A bulging black eye had swollen the right side of her face. Bruising covered two-thirds of her facial skin; dried blood had congealed at the bottom of her nostril; and her bottom lip had been split in the middle.

'Just how clumsy does one have to be to sustain these injuries, Mr Winston?'

She could tell by his expression that he wanted to look away but couldn't.

'There are more photos in that folder, just a selection for your perusal, and feel free to share them with everyone who worked on the campaign. Those are your very own copies.'

'I don't remember seeing these photos at the first—'

'They weren't presented but rest assured they will be. Any information I've gathered is now in the hands of the Crown Prosecution Service.'

She paused for a minute as he continued to leaf through the photo selection. He turned the pages slowly, and she noted there was little colour left in his face.

'Imagine if this was your sister, or your daughter, Mr Winston,' she offered, just to drive her point home. 'Though what I'd really like to draw your attention to is the final page in the folder.'

With relief, he turned quickly past the last couple of images to the doctor's report at the end.

That was okay with her. She'd arranged the photos knowing which images would stick in his mind, because they were the same ones that had stuck in hers.

'You'll see the section I've underlined, highlighted and circled with stars, where Trisha Morley states to the doctor that her husband beat her and threw her down the stairs.'

Due to her decoration of the text, the statement was difficult to miss.

She took a deep breath. 'It is unlikely that I will ever prove who was behind the attacks on me, even though they are dirty and dangerous actions to take against anyone.'

He opened his mouth to respond, but Frost continued.

'This is all going to come out and your positive campaign is going to make you look ridiculous. We all back the wrong horse sometimes, but to keep on backing the same horse once you know it's done is just stupid.

'You have the chance to back away from this before the trial, distance yourself and limit the damage. In doing so, you lay the ground for a fair fight in court. A decision made on the evidence alone.'

He pushed the file towards her.

'Please take that with you.'

'Are you sure you don't want to share—?'

'No, thank you. A statement will be issued within the hour.'

She took the folder and allowed the triumph to ease the tension in her shoulders.

These people had warned her to back off and now she was doing the same to them.

And it had worked.

She stood and headed for the door.

She paused and turned, needing to make one final point before she left.

'And just for future campaigns, Mr Winston, Trisha Morley was not a bag of crisps.'

CHAPTER NINETY-EIGHT

'He's gonna fucking jump,' Kim said, staring up at the Stambermill Viaduct.

They had raced to the imposing structure in Stourbridge the second they'd received the call from Stacey that someone matching the description of Jacob Powell had been spotted walking along the viaduct.

Constructed in 1850, the viaduct was 173 metres long and bridged the River Stour. Passenger trains no longer used the line, so that was one less thing to think about, but the odd freight train still came thundering through.

Birmingham Street from the Stourbridge ring road had been closed right through to St John's Road and Hungary Hill. Despite the traffic build-up, Bryant had managed to get them there in seven minutes, during which time Jacob Powell appeared to have stepped over the railing and was standing on a two-feet-wide ledge.

'It's definitely him,' Bryant said, and Kim believed him. He'd got a better look at the guy as he'd rushed away from the school. She had barely noticed the man in the classroom as Liam had introduced them.

'Where are we at?' she asked the incident commander just beyond the inner cordon.

'Negotiator is on the way. Around ten minutes out,' he said, checking his watch.

'May we—?'

'Not a chance,' he said with finality. 'One of our guys made it to the approach bridge and he stepped over onto the ledge. Ain't nobody going near him until the negotiator arrives.'

Kim got it but she needed to speak to him.

She needed to assure him that everything was going to be okay. It wasn't, but she wanted this man to see the inside of a courtroom for what he'd done, and it was the only way to find out what he'd done with Leanne.

The calculations were forming in her mind and turning into numbers she didn't like. Leanne had left the station before nine that morning and it was now after four o'clock. If it was Leanne he'd been after all along, she was probably dead. If Jacob had wanted her for information on Boy X, Leanne no longer knew where he was and was probably dead, the logical voice in her mind said.

And yet, he'd made a mistake and left Sarah Lessiter alive. Could he have done the same thing with Leanne?

She moved away from the crowd to get a better look.

The movement must have caught his eye, as he looked her way. Their gazes met and although she couldn't read his expression, she knew he was looking right at her.

He hesitated for just a couple of seconds before he stepped forward and fell to his death.

CHAPTER NINETY-NINE

It was almost five when Kim strode into the squad room.

She hadn't hung around once Jacob Powell had hit the ground. As horrific as the situation was, he was no longer her priority.

'Okay, guys,' she said without removing her coat. 'Our one single focus right now is on finding Leanne. There's a chance she could still be alive.'

She saw the doubts in the eyes of her colleagues and she understood it. Jacob had left three dead bodies behind; leaving Sarah had been a mistake due to her breathing being so weak beneath the wall of rocks. She wondered if he'd be foolish to make the same mistake again.

'Unlikely, boss,' Penn said, voicing the doubt for all of them. 'You can be sure?'

'He must be sure she's dead. It's the only thing that explains why he just threw himself off a bridge. He's reached the end of the road. He got Leanne, the only person who could tell him where Boy X was, and she didn't know. He's been moved, so it doesn't matter how much he tortured her, she didn't know where he's been moved to. It left Jacob with nowhere left to go. He knew we were on to him, so his choices were death or life in prison.'

Kim completely accepted his logical argument. But while there was even the smallest chance that Leanne was still alive, she wasn't going to quit.

'Thanks, Penn, but on this occasion I'm gonna be the optimist in the team. Now, think people, what's his link to th—?'

'It's his cousin, boss,' Stacey said, reading from her screen.

'What?' she, Bryant and Penn asked together.

'Jacob Powell is the cousin of little Emily Harris, the girl tortured by Boy X. There's no mention of him in later news reports about the family, anniversary catch-ups or talking-head pieces when a new documentary has been made, but I've just found an earlier piece about Emily's aunt Kitty suing to get her own child back from the little girl's mother after a prison stint.'

'Go on,' Kim said.

'The child was misnamed as Jacob Harris, which is why his real name hasn't shown up on any of our searches. Emily's mother, Rosie, took care of Jacob off and on while he was a baby due to her sister's drug habit. She sued to become his legal guardian when Jacob turned one. Nothing happened for years until Rosie's sister got clean and tried to get Jacob back when he was seven. She never even stayed clean long enough to make it to court. Jacob was eleven years old when Emily, his cousin, was murdered by Boy X.'

'But she would have felt more like his sister,' Kim observed, understanding how it felt to be the older sibling. She'd been Mikey's older sister by only minutes, but the urge to protect him had never lessened during the six years they had together.

'Okay,' she said, pulling herself back to the present. Knowing why he had wanted Leanne so badly didn't help them find her right now. 'We have the motive. We know Jacob Powell wanted revenge for what happened to Emily, but what we need to focus on now is location. Where would Jacob have taken her?'

'I've requested the data for Leanne's phone,' Stacey interjected. 'I've explained the urgency, so I'm hopeful we'll get something through soon.'

Forensics were currently tearing Leanne's house apart, though Kim already knew that any DNA found would belong to Jacob Powell. There was nothing there that would help her one little bit.

'It's through,' Stacey called out.

They all congregated behind Stacey's chair.

Stacey opened the document and quickly looked at what had been sent.

'Fantastic,' she said as her fingers flew over the keyboard.

'What?' Kim asked.

The printer kicked into life, but the wall of people prevented Stacey from reaching it.

'Err… guys,' she said.

They all moved to the side.

Stacey offered Kim the top sheet of paper.

'Okay, this is her activity log,' Stacey said, looking at the screen. 'She left here around 8.30 a.m., yeah?'

'Yep,' Penn answered.

'Well, she made a call before she'd even left the car park.'

'To who?' Bryant asked.

'Doesn't matter,' Stacey said. 'We already know she was alive and kicking at that time.'

Kim knew Stacey didn't mean to sound dismissive. Her brain had kicked in to full-on analytical mode.

Kim watched as she scanned the call log and moved to the next sheet.

'Her signal bounced off the mast at Romsley. An hour later she made a call which bounced off the mast at Dunstall Hill.'

'Closer to her home in Wolverhampton,' Penn observed.

'Easy enough but now it gets…' Stacey's words trailed away as she continued to read. 'You called her, boss?'

'And left a message,' Kim answered.

'You were the last activity on her phone.'

Kim shook her head. That couldn't be right. She knew that Wexford and his team had been trying to reach her after that.

'Nope. You were the last. No more pings from anything. Battery could have been removed after your call to her.'

'Where was it?' Kim asked urgently.

'Mobile phone mast at Wombourne.'

That was about five miles away from Leanne's home. And if that was the last place Leanne had been with her battery in her phone, then that's where they'd start the search.

'Come on, Bryant,' she said, heading for the door.

On the way out, it occurred to her that she'd never been in this position before.

She had the motive, the killer and all she needed to find right now was the victim.

CHAPTER ONE HUNDRED

'Okay, what the hell are we supposed to do now?' Stacey asked as the boss and Bryant sped out of the room.

'We're supposed to follow the logic of his previous murders and try to identify where he might have taken her,' Penn said, wheeling his chair around so they were both looking at the same screen.

Stacey loaded Google Earth and zoomed to the last location that Leanne's phone had registered a signal to the tower.

'Jeez, Penn, how do we…?'

'Okay,' he said, looking at the board. 'Let's look at the locations he's used. He found an abandoned building to roast Keith Phipps. It was far enough away that no one would hear the screams but big enough that the smoke from the fire wouldn't be a problem. He found a deserted spot in Somerset to stretch Dennis Burke. He found a similar spot to torture Dean Mullins with the rat, which was close to where he could access the loose rocks to torture Sarah.'

'You know, there are easier ways,' Stacey said, sitting back.

'Go on,' Penn said, standing up.

'Well, we thought he was using these sick forms of torture for pleasure at first, and now we know they were used for extracting information. But why so elaborate?' she asked as Penn started to pace the room. 'He could have used just one location to do the same thing to all of them. Why the big show of— Penn, what the hell are you doing?'

'I'm being him,' he said, walking the space between the two sets of desks and turning. He was gathering speed. 'I've killed people. I've watched people die horrific deaths to get the information I want. No one has given it to me. The more I think about what was done to Emily, the more the rage is filling my body. No one is telling me where Karen is. She's the only one who can tell me where he is.'

Stacey watched as his pace turned frantic. The words were coming faster.

'If I can just find Karen, I'll know where he is. Finally, I have Karen. I need to know. I have her now. She's going to tell me. Everything I've done has led to this. I'm so close I can feel it. She's the only thing that stands between me and finding the person who did those horrific things to my little cousin and—'

'Penn,' Stacey called out, unsure what he was trying to achieve.

Penn stopped pacing and stared at her.

'He won't have taken her far, Stace. His impatience and excitement would have been driving him to get it done. He'd finally got Karen, the key to everything, in his possession and he would've wanted to start work on her immediately. We should concentrate on locations close to the last point of contact. Now, if we had some idea of what he might have had planned for—'

'Hang on one minute,' Stacey said as Penn retook his seat beside her.

She clicked back on the article she'd read about the injuries inflicted on Emily's body by Boy X.

Burning – Check

Dislocation – Check

Rodent Activity – Check

Hit with a brick – Check

That left only one form of torture beyond the sexual assault.

'Penn, I think there's a chance that Jacob Powell has skinned Leanne alive.'

CHAPTER ONE HUNDRED ONE

It was almost seven when Bryant pulled into the car park of a McDonald's in the general area of where Leanne's phone had last pinged the tower.

'Guv, I'm not sure how we're gonna—'

'Well, let's all go and have a drink and wait for someone to find her body then, shall we?' she snapped.

'I was gonna say I'm not sure how we'll cover the whole area between the two of us, but feel free to snap my head off.'

'Sorry, I'm just—' She stopped speaking as her phone rang.

'Okay, Stace, give us something,' she said, putting the phone on speaker. Kim knew that mobile phone providers used approximately 23,000 base stations around the country which, with any luck, would narrow their search area considerably.

'Right, that ping covers a three-mile radius from the base station. We don't think he would have taken her too far. He'd have been eager to—'

'Okay, got it. So where do we go?'

'That's the problem, boss. We think for this one he could have chosen to do it inside or out.'

'What are you talking about?' Kim asked.

'We think he was replicating things that were done to Emily. Besides the rape, the only thing left is slicing skin from her—'

'Okay, Stace,' Kim said, feeling the hairs prickle on the back of her neck. Right now, she didn't need to picture the horror Leanne had been through.

'Okay, we've got Halfpenny Green.'

Kim knew the area well. A small airport and a village surrounded by green belt. She could see how the expanse of open space around the airport might be appealing; however, the place was in use and he would have risked being seen.

'Next.'

'We've got Seisdon Quarry, which was closed down a couple of years ago. It's remote and deserted.'

'Any more?' Kim asked, waiting for something to strike her.

'The last one is an abandoned private recycling plant in Wombourne, if he wanted to do it inside.'

'Tell me more.'

'It's on Botterham Lane, off the Bridgnorth Road. There's a fishery not too far and a trading estate just across the canal from—'

'That's the one,' Kim said. 'Get as many officers as you can to check the others and anything else you might find, but we're gonna head to Wombourne.'

Bryant had already started the car before she'd finished speaking.

Kim knew they were searching for a needle in a haystack, but age-old processes had not let her down yet. The process of elimination followed by the application of logic were tools necessary for any police officer's tool bag. Jacob had abducted Leanne during the day, so he needed somewhere he wouldn't be seen; the industrial estate opposite would mask any sound.

Everything he'd done so far had a link back to his cousin, and she had to believe that the proximity to the canal was symbolic for him too.

She firmly believed they were heading in the right direction.

She was just terrified of what she would find when she got there.

CHAPTER ONE HUNDRED TWO

'Okay, teams dispatched to the other two locations,' Stacey said, putting down the phone. She could feel her hand trembling slightly with the rush of adrenaline.

'I'm gonna look at other possibilities a bit further out. In case she's not there. What you doing?'

'Plotting a route from Leanne's house to the recycling centre. I'm hoping to catch the van on a traffic camera, to confirm we've sent the boss to the right place.'

'Good idea,' Stacey said.

She knew they could have torn off to the other locations, but their time was better spent here, lending operational support. And she wanted to cover both their arses in case they'd called it wrong on the proximity. If the boss turned up nothing at the recycling plant, she wanted to be able to offer other ideas.

'Got him,' Penn shouted, making Stacey jump, reigniting the adrenaline rush that had been calming down.

'Jesus, Penn, calm—'

'Passed a traffic cam on Vicarage Road at 9.45 this morning.'

'And he threw himself off the bridge at around four, so he had a good few hours to torture her.'

'Let's stick with the good news, Stace, that it looks like the boss is heading in the right direction, eh?' he said without looking up. 'Now, I'm gonna plot a route from the recycling centre to the aqueduct and see if we can find out what time he left.'

'Anything I can help with?' Stacey asked as her desk phone rang.

'Hey, Jack,' she answered.

'DC Wood, could you come down to reception? I've got a lady here who would like a word.'

'I'm a bit busy at the minute,' she said. Surely he knew they were dispatching teams all over the immediate area.

'Yeah, but she insists. Wants to talk about Jacob Powell.'

'Who is she?'

'Head teacher of some school or another who thinks she's a famous singer.'

She put down the phone and headed out of the office, past Penn, who was looking more troubled than she would have liked.

CHAPTER ONE HUNDRED THREE

'Penn thinks we're on the right track,' Kim said, ending the call.

By her reckoning they were about two miles out, and inadvertently her fingers had crossed in her lap.

Every ounce of logic told her that the woman was dead; but if he could make one mistake in leaving Sarah alive, he could do it again. *If there's any chance you're alive, Leanne, hang on for just a little bit longer*, she prayed.

It was fair to say that the two of them hadn't hit it off, and although no one, not even Bryant, had remarked on the similarities between them, it was a fact Kim was coming to realise. Yes, she blamed the woman for not letting them in on the secret in time to save lives, but would she herself have done anything differently?

It was a question she still hadn't answered by the time Bryant turned into Botterham Lane.

The privately owned recycling plant didn't look as she'd imagined it. She'd pictured a dilapidated building, worn from age and use.

'Outgrew itself, guv,' Bryant said, reading her thoughts. 'Moved to a bigger plant in Oldbury.'

'Park here,' she said, seeing an opening in the fence between two battered and dented skips.

'I can probably drive around and get us closer to—'

'Takes too long. We'll walk from here,' she said, getting out of the car.

Bryant followed her through the gap in the fencing and stood by her side as she appraised the building that appeared to be around an acre in size. The external grounds she could see appeared as though they had been left halfway through a shift. A couple of wheelie trolleys had been parked beside cubes of mulched paper.

'Okay, you go left and I'll go right,' she instructed.

'Sshh…' he said, putting his fingers to his lips.

'Why? We're either gonna find her or not, but at least we know where our murderer is, so feel free to make as much noise as you like.'

He nodded his understanding as he headed off to the west side of the building.

She headed east, to a small entrance door beside a double roller shutter.

The torch on her phone didn't pick up a can that clattered along the ground.

Her heart jumped into her mouth before she remembered there was no one here to fear.

CHAPTER ONE HUNDRED FOUR

'Miss Lennox?' Stacey asked, showing her identification.

'It's Mrs. Not all principals are dried-up old spinsters.'

Stacey looked for humour in her words and found none.

Stacey opened her mouth, but Anna Lennox didn't appear to be in the mood to listen.

'Despite your bullying antics, Officer, I have brought you Jacob Powell's file as soon as I received authorisation from the board to share his details.'

'Mrs Lennox, I apologise for my overzealousness, but when we're working a major investigation—'

'An apology isn't really an apology if it includes a but,' Anna said, holding the plain manila folder towards her. 'I've copied everything in his file. I have to ask if this has any connection to an online news article that mentions "a staff member from Ormiston Forge" that was involved in a police incident in Stourbridge earlier today.'

Stacey nodded but said nothing. She really needed to be back at her desk, supporting the boss. There was nothing more to learn here. The file was useless to her now she knew Jacob Powell's relationship to Emily Harris.

'Is he… dead?' she asked, swallowing before the final word.

'I'm sorry. I can't really tell you more until family members have been informed.'

'I understand. Can you just tell me if it's Liam? He suffers sometimes from bouts of—'

'No,' Stacey said, shaking her head. 'Your supply teacher is perfectly safe, as far as I know.'

Stacey felt something form in her stomach as the woman frowned.

'I think there's been some kind of mistake.'

Stacey said nothing and let the woman speak.

When she'd finished, Stacey sprinted to the front desk and picked up the phone.

'Pass yer phone, Jack,' she cried.

He did, and she dialled Penn's internal number with trembling fingers.

'Penn, we've got a problem.'

'Well, make that two cos that Transit van never came back.'

CHAPTER ONE HUNDRED FIVE

Kim froze as the door opened in front of her.

Emergency lighting illuminated the macabre sight of Leanne King lying half-naked and semi-conscious on a stationary conveyor belt that rose up into the air like an escalator.

Her arms had been stretched around each edge of the belt and tied underneath.

Her top half was clothed, but her lower half was naked except for a pair of plain black panties.

The figure bent over her hadn't heard Kim enter, and it took her less than a second to realise their mistake.

Liam Docherty was Jacob Powell.

Her mind catapulted back to the first meeting at the school. Anna Lennox hadn't introduced them. The teacher had come into the office at the school and introduced himself and then introduced his teaching assistant once they reached the classroom. He had swapped their names so that they had been looking for the wrong person. He must have known he was close to finding Leanne and that the confusion would buy him enough time to find her and get Boy X's location. The absence of an identity photograph had further compounded the mistake.

Kim felt the tension dry her mouth.

She used her undetected advantage to survey the scene and almost winced at the damage inflicted on Leanne's legs.

In at least twenty places Kim could see rectangles of flesh where the skin had been torn open. In his hand Jacob held a metal comb with teeth filed to very sharp points, as though imitating an animal claw.

He took the comb and gouged the skin, dragging it down and splitting the flesh. He then moved the comb a fraction to the left and did it again, tearing the upper layer of flesh from her skin.

Suddenly Leanne's eyes snapped open and filled with pain. A muffled scream sounded against the gag and had it been allowed to go free, Kim was sure it would have been the worse sound she'd ever heard.

Leanne began thrashing her head from side to side. The suffering in her eyes made Kim want to throw up.

Leanne's head stopped moving for just a second as her gaze landed on Kim.

A whole multitude of emotions passed through her eyes: hope, despair, relief until her face once again contorted with agony.

By Kim's reckoning she'd been subjected to this for around nine hours, and Kim wasn't sure how much more she could endure.

She had to make it stop, but there was no way she could rush him. He was more than thirty feet away. He could kill Leanne with that claw in a second.

'You're wasting your time,' Kim called out loudly, keeping her voice strong and even.

He turned her way, mild surprise shaping his features although he appeared unperturbed.

He placed the bloodstained claw close to Leanne's throat. 'If you take one step forward, I'll kill her,' he said calmly, and Kim had no doubt that he would. Four people had died horrifically in this man's quest for revenge.

He wiped the bloody claw on his jeans and turned his body slightly so that he could continue what he was doing and keep Kim in his peripheral view.

Her presence had not unnerved him one little bit. His hand was steady as he prepared to start clawing at a brand-new area of flesh. Kim had come across few people so totally detached from the pain they were causing, and he was doing it right in front of a police officer without even the slightest tremble. Her arrival had not changed his demeanour or interrupted his plans, she thought as he paused and lifted the gag from Leanne's mouth.

'Are you ready to tell me the truth?'

'I don't know where—'

Her words were cut off as he stuffed the gag back into her mouth.

'Still playing hard to get. No problem, I can do this all night,' he said, teasing the claw against her skin so she knew what was coming.

Leanne's eyes lit up with fear. Her head again thrashed in protest at the pain she knew was to come. She'd been suffering this for what must have felt like an eternity. Kim thought of all she'd done in those nine hours while Leanne had been here, suffering this torture.

'She really doesn't know where Boy X is,' Kim said again. She had to get his attention away from the claw and Leanne's flesh.

The claw headed towards the skin.

'Jacob, I have some sense of what you're going through,' she called out.

'Yeah, I'm gonna fall for that one. Don't empathise with me, Inspector. It won't change anything.'

'My twin brother,' she said, trying to stop him dragging the claw over the flesh. 'Tortured and murdered when he was six years old. Nothing I could do to stop it.'

Something in her voice caused him to pause. She continued.

'We know Emily was your cousin, but I'm guessing she felt more like your little sister. I've read about her, Jacob. What he did to her was horrific. It was unlike anything I've ever dealt with.'

'Do you have any idea how those pictures go over in your mind? How they play over and over again and there's nothing you can do to stop them?'

'You shouldn't have known,' Kim said. He'd been barely more than a child himself. There was much she shouldn't have known.

'They tried to keep it away from me, tried to shield me, but it was everywhere: on the news; in the papers; people talking; kids taunting. I got to know everything. The pictures in my head every waking minute. And the nightmares.'

He shook his head and looked back at Leanne's leg.

'Yeah, the nightmares are the worst,' she agreed. 'I still get 'em,' she said honestly. 'And you wanna know the worst ones?' she asked, watching his hand carefully. 'They're the ones where in your dream it's not real or that there's a chance you can change things, alter the outcome, there's hope that it never happened, that it was a dream within a dream. You know one of the cruellest dreams I ever had was that my brother was still alive and that no one had told me. I didn't care about why no one had told me or why they'd kept it secret. I wasn't angry. I was just happy to have him back. Until I woke up.'

His expression told her he'd had similar dreams. They were the worst; the cruellest tricks that the resting mind could play.

'Jacob, I understand why you did the things you did,' she said, switching from the truth to total lie. She would never understand the torture he'd inflicted on people who hadn't committed the crime against Emily. These people had not been responsible for the nightmares that haunted him.

'We understand that you befriended Amelia Dixon to get access to her financial records. We know you got access to the property records of witnesses. You even got old payroll information and you were looking for someone named Karen.'

And that name change had saved Leanne's life. Until now.

She had been right under his nose, had even collected the boys from school the day that Keith Phipps had been murdered. It didn't escape her attention that it was also an error in names that had misdirected her and her team.

'He's still alive. Don't you understand how that eats away at my insides? Every day he lives a life where he's protected, coddled. I know he didn't serve any real prison time. It was in all the papers. He's never paid for what he did to Emily. You tell me how that's fair?'

'I can't, Jacob, because it isn't. The person who caused my brother's death is still alive too, but I have to hope she's never known a minute's peace since.'

He frowned, as though wanting to know more. She had distracted him slightly from his own story by sharing some of hers.

'But he'll do it again. I have to stop him. He'll never change.'

Kim suspected he was right on that score.

'You're wrong, Jacob,' she said. 'There are people, good people, making sure it doesn't happen again.'

A small tear escaped from the corner of Leanne's eye. She'd got the message.

Jacob shook his head.

'I can't be sure. I have to finish what I started, and she is my last obstacle. I think she knows where he is.'

He pulled at the claw, and Kim saw the straight lines of tearing flesh. Agony contorted Leanne's face, and Kim knew she had to do anything she could to get Jacob and his claw away from her.

'Jacob, I swear to you that she doesn't know the location of Boy X. He's been moved for his own protection. She doesn't know where he's been taken.' She paused. 'But I do,' she said, before turning and heading out of the room.

CHAPTER ONE HUNDRED SIX

Kim's only thought as she ran was the prayer that he would follow her. She had to hope that the logic of what she'd said would dawn on him and that his focus would be drawn away from Leanne and redirected at her.

The sound of the heavy metal door opening behind her confirmed that it had.

Never before had she found herself running away from a murderer.

She had to think quickly. She couldn't call out to Bryant. There was no way he'd hear her, and she had to stay one step ahead of Jacob.

She decided to keep travelling anticlockwise around the building. Bryant should be coming in the opposite direction: if they met, they could overpower Jacob together, because she was willing to bet that he'd brought his despicable claw with him.

Okay, evasion until help came, she decided, stepping around the corner of the building.

'Fuck,' she said under her breath as a wall-mounted security light illuminated the whole area, telling Jacob exactly where she was.

'Come on, Bryant,' she said as she began to run.

She could hear the footsteps gaining behind her. She'd thought outside was the better option, but now she wasn't so sure. She had no idea where they were. If there were more motion-activated lights, they were going to keep giving away her location.

The decision was taken out of her hands as she reached a ten-foot-high metal fence that prevented her journey around the perimeter of the building.

Damn, she'd only managed a quarter of the way; Bryant was nowhere in sight.

She could still hear Jacob behind her and, although he was gaining, he hadn't yet caught her. The sensor lights she was illuminating were providing a clear path of light for him to follow.

She slipped as quietly as she could back into the building through an identical metal door to the other side.

As she stepped into the building, the emergency lights flashed on, revealing a similar setup on this side of the building as the one she'd originally walked into.

A horizontal sorting conveyor inclined to an elevated metal viewing platform, before turning like a roller-coaster ride to run in front of hoppers where the waste fell.

Kim had to think. Her aim was to keep Jacob away from Leanne for long enough, so that Bryant would reach her and call for help. Once her gag was removed, Leanne would be able to tell Bryant she had not been alone, and her colleague would be on his way to assist.

That was the plan anyway, she thought as she looked for somewhere to hide. It was all about time and delay, and although she'd put a minute or two between them, she knew he was after her and she didn't fancy that claw ripping at her flesh.

The door opened. Jacob stood ten feet away from her. The hesitation had cost her the small advantage she'd had.

'Where is he?' Jacob growled, brandishing the claw at her.

Kim was tempted to admit she didn't know, but she couldn't risk him returning to Leanne. She had no way of knowing if Bryant had reached her yet.

She jumped up onto the horizontal conveyor belt and began to scale the ascending section, using the ridge between the belt and the belt guide as a foothold. A protruding screw caught in the hem of her trousers. She yanked her foot and heard the fabric tear. Jacob's hand grabbed at her foot and touched the heel of her boot. She kicked backwards, not daring to take the time to look behind.

Where the hell was Bryant and backup?

'You will fucking tell me where he is,' Jacob said, scaling the belt behind her.

Kim ignored the fear rising in her stomach. The man just feet away from her had murdered four people in the most horrific ways imaginable.

Jacob managed to grab the back of her jacket as she clambered onto the top platform. She lurched forward to disengage his hand and stopped short of a section of missing handrail. She grabbed the last piece of railing to prevent herself from falling from the thirty-foot height. She stumbled backwards to avoid the drop.

Jacob grabbed her arms and pinned her against the railing with his body. His right fist thundered into the side of her head.

'Where the fuck is he? You have to tell me.'

She shook her head to clear her vision as the pain vibrated around her head. Both his hands were on her, leaving her powerless to move. The claw was the only weapon between them and he had possession of it.

'Give me the claw and I'll tell you,' she said.

'You want this?' he asked, reaching into his jacket pocket and pushing her further against the railing, so that the bar was digging into the small of her back. She prayed it would continue to support her weight.

His hand raised, and the claw moved towards her face.

'Oh, I'll give it to you and then you'll tell me where he is.'

She shook her head away as she leaned further backwards, trying to bend herself away from the weapon.

She took quick advantage of the fact that only one hand was holding her wrists. She broke free and reached out, grabbing his hand. She pressed hard, turning the claw into his palm, then squeezed with every ounce of strength she possessed. He cried out as the blood from the claw started to ooze from his hand. He let go of her wrist to clutch his own hand and stumbled backwards, his face contorted with pain.

Too late, Kim saw his left foot move back and pause in mid-air before he fell backwards through the section of missing safety rail.

There was a sickening thud as his body hit the ground.

Kim's legs began to tremble. She collapsed onto the cold metal platform. She didn't trust herself not to fall through the gap right after him. She took a few breaths to steady her heart rate.

She glanced down at his inert form as the door crashed open and Bryant entered with four police officers.

The officers moved forward around her colleague, who had stopped in his tracks and was looking her way.

His reddened face and heavy breathing told her he'd got there as quickly as he could.

She held up her hand to signal she was all good.

A knowing smile tugged at his lips that said, 'Of course you are.'

The figure on the ground groaned and relief flooded her body. She allowed herself to fully relax.

She didn't want him dead. She wanted him to face justice for his crimes, and she looked forward to seeing this man in court.

CHAPTER ONE HUNDRED SEVEN

I look out of the window as I always do at this time. She is there on the bench, my constant, my familiarity. My link to the person I was before. My heart twists and turns inside my chest. The ache to go to her, to tell her everything, is stronger today than ever. It's a physical pain that starts in my stomach and grabs at my heart. I want to feel her arms around me. I want her to tell me everything will be okay. I want her to reassure me that I did the right thing. But I can't.

A woman approaches from the left. She is wearing impossibly high heels which give her a clumsy gait, as though she might topple over at any minute.

I don't know her but I know she's a reporter for the Dudley Star. *I've been reading her articles all week.*

She has been writing about me.

Somehow, she has turned the tide of public opinion. There is talk of new evidence, of a new witness. A public statement from the PR firm distancing themselves from my murder.

I shudder as the memories overwhelm me again. My right arm rubs at my left shoulder. Involuntarily, the hand slides down, seeking its mirror image. My tongue darts around my mouth, in and out of gaps. Parts of my body seem to be constantly searching for parts that are no longer there. They were removed and burned along with my clothes in the back garden of my home.

The teeth were easier than I'd thought, and as the blood had poured from my mouth, I opened wide and let it drip to the ground. As I closed my eyes and pulled hard on the pliers, the pain had shot from the nerves around the whole of my body. I had thought it would be preparation for what was to come next. I was wrong. Nothing could prepare me for the pain as I made the first slice across my flesh.

The tourniquet was tied tightly above my elbow. I waited almost an hour until I had no feeling in my lower arm, all the way to the tips of my fingers. I picked up the knife and tried to remember everything I'd learned.

I'd watched the final scenes of 127 Hours a hundred times, living those moments alongside Aron Ralston as he cut off the arm that was trapped by a boulder. By the third viewing, the emotion had left me and my viewing was analytical, studious. I no longer thought about the man behind the pain but only of the process.

I read articles and medical reports about cutting across the joint to avoid the bone. I learned that chopping at the elbow meant dealing with only one artery instead of two. I learned the value of a properly applied tourniquet to limit blood loss. I read up on the four major nerves that would retract into the muscle if I got it right. I read personal accounts of others who had severed their own limbs to survive. And that was exactly what I was doing.

My right hand shook as I held the knife above my elbow. Did I have the strength to go through with it? Could I take the pain? Was there any other way? But from the second I did the home pregnancy test, I knew that I had to escape Nick somehow. I knew the violence wouldn't stop, even if he knew his child was growing inside me. I knew there was no way he'd ever let me go, and our child would have bound me to him for ever.

I considered every possibility, before reaching the conclusion that he would find me unless he thought I was dead. And then I began to think of the girls he would meet after me, even if I did manage to disappear. There was no doubt in my mind that he would eventually kill someone.

It had to be final, for him and for me.

As I fought with my fear, Nick's rage-filled face swam before my eyes. It was the face that saw no reason. It was the face of the man that couldn't stop hitting and kicking me, despite the blood pouring from my injuries. It was the face of a man that I knew would somehow kill me or our child, but most likely both.

It was that one, single thought that propelled the knife towards the target, and for once I was grateful for the remoteness of the house. My scream had the power to travel for miles. The numbness had been temporary and all feeling returned as I made the second cut. From that point I knew there was no going back. The only way was forward.

I thought about Doug Goodale, a lobster fisherman who used a knife to cut off his elbow after getting it caught in a winch.

I thought about Bill Jeracki, who used a bait knife to cut his own leg off at the knee to free himself from a boulder.

I knew it could be done. I just had to stay strong and focused.

In saving my child I lost my mother, my sister and the rest of my family.

I ache daily for the pain I've caused them, that I am responsible for their grief, but it was the only way.

I return to the present and watch as my mum turns and hugs the reporter beside her on the bench. The woman is uncomfortable but accepts the embrace.

My mum is smiling and crying at the same time. A tear escapes and rolls over my cheek. I want more than anything to take away her pain, but I can't: not until Nick is safely behind bars.

Maybe then I can find a way to let her know that I'm alive, that despite everything, I'm happy.

But for now, I reach into the cot and scoop up my child. I hold him close to my chest, kissing his feathery head.

I take him to the window and make him a silent promise.

One day he will meet his family.

CHAPTER ONE HUNDRED EIGHT

Kim glanced out of her window of the Bowl at her team working at varying speeds with the promise of an afternoon off ahead of them. And by God how they deserved it.

Penn had promised Jasper a mammoth baking session to make up for the long hours he'd worked this week. Bryant had arranged to take Jenny for a surprise weekend away. Only Stacey seemed to be lagging behind with occasional glances her way.

Due to his injuries, Jacob wouldn't be fit for questioning for a few days, but with police officers guarding his room and two broken legs, he wasn't going anywhere.

Kim turned away from her team and looked out of the window. Despite the things he'd done, Kim couldn't bring herself to hate Jacob Powell. She was confident that justice would prevail and that Jacob would never see the outside world again, but damn it, she understood his motivation. The pictures that had warped his mind of the suffering his cousin had endured were horrific. That in itself was bad enough to live with, but compounding the rage and inability to do anything about it had been the knowledge that the person responsible had suffered very little for what he'd done and was now even protected by the same people who had worked so hard to put him away.

Kim knew there was no room for him to offer an insanity plea. Each crime had taken intricate and diligent planning and faultless execution. His job as a supply teacher had enabled him to move around locations with the freedom of not being tied to one school.

A conversation with Anna Lennox had cleared up that it was Liam Docherty who had hastily left the school that day, resurfacing only to throw himself from the Stambermill Viaduct. Liam was prone to bouts of depression, but what no one knew, not even Anna, was that he'd made an anonymous complaint to the school board about Jacob's seemingly unhealthy interest in one of his students: Tommy Phipps.

Kim surmised that when he'd seen them at the school, he'd assumed it was something to do with that and had fled.

Anna had also revealed that the argument she'd been having with Jacob outside the school had been about his unreliability. Leaving classes he'd been booked for and not turning up for others. Outside of work he'd been a very busy man.

Kim couldn't help but wonder what might have been the outcome if Jacob had known that Leanne was the woman he'd been looking for when she collected the boys from school that day.

At that point, Leanne had still known the location of Boy X because he hadn't yet been moved. Would she have cracked and told him? Would Sarah Lessiter still be alive? Would Dennis Burke have escaped the rack? Would Dean Mullins have avoided the rat torture? Would two other lives have been better than three?

It wasn't for Kim to dwell on the quality of lives taken or spared, but one thing she did know was that Leanne King had done her job and she had done it well.

It was fair to say the two of them were never going to be friends, but Kim couldn't ignore a grudging respect for the woman who worked as part of no team doing a job that she couldn't really talk about. In some ways, she was in no better position than the people she protected. Only she did it by choice.

Her earlier enquires to the hospital had told her Leanne had already been transferred elsewhere. The force had moved her for her own protection. She knew that despite everything, Leanne would heal and move on to another family that needed her protection.

'Boss?' Penn said from the doorway, disturbing her thoughts.

'Yep, if you're done, get lost,' she said with a nod towards the door.

He grabbed his coat and two carrier bags of cooking supplies from underneath his desk.

Her thoughts returned to the week they'd all had and inevitably the image of Frost popped into her mind.

Few people surprised her, but Frost certainly had over the last few days. Meeting the family of Trisha Morley had ignited a passion in the woman and unleashed her investigative skills in the right direction.

She'd heard that Ariane Debegorski had come forward to testify, strengthening the case against the man, but the real nugget had been the medical report from the Italian hospital. A key defence of Nick Morley's last trial had been his wife's failure to report. But the bloodhound had found it.

She reached for her phone and pressed the reporter's number.

'Hey, Stone,' Frost answered. 'How's my favourite boy doing? Is he missing his aunty?'

'You've been easily replaced by a lizard chew toy I gave him after you'd gone. He's struggling to tell the difference.'

Frost burst out laughing.

'Look, Frost,' she said, realising that the two of them were never going to graduate to first name terms.

'There's no need, Stone. I know you're calling me to tell me I did a great job and that you're pleased that on this occasion I used my powers to do good and that you're impressed with my tenacity and—'

'Actually, Frost, I'm ringing to say you left a pair of dirty knickers in my laundry basket, and I ain't touching 'em with a full-on Hazmat suit.'

Silence.

'Yeah, you were closer the first time, but let's not get carried away.'

'Seriously, you really are ringing me for that?' she asked, shocked.

'Well, I'm quick enough to ring you when you've pissed me off, so…'

'You know, Stone, I'd never admit it in public, but you're not as bad as everyone—'

'Yes, I am, as I'm sure you'll remember the next time you come hassling me at a crime scene. But for now, let's just say you did a bloody good job. Now bugger off cos I've got work to do.'

Kim could hear the reporter chuckling as she ended the call.

Bryant appeared at the door. 'Guv, I'm all done.'

'Okay, off you go and don't forget to take your bucket and spade.'

'Err… it's the Cotswolds, guv. Not sure there's much call for it.'

She smiled as he turned and headed for the door.

Leaving only Stacey, who was once again looking her way.

Kim headed into the squad room.

'Okay, Stace, out with it,' she said, hitching herself onto Bryant's desk. The constable should have been finished an hour ago. She'd hung back for a reason.

Kim tried not to react to the pensive expression on her face as she took a deep breath.

'Boss, I don't want it,' she blurted out.

'Stace, what are you…?'

'The promotion, boss. I dow want it. I'm not ready for it and I don't want it.'

Relief washed over her, not because Stacey didn't want promotion but that her problem could so easily be fixed. But what she did want was an explanation.

'Go on.'

'Boss, my life has changed a lot over the last few months. I'm a married woman, you know,' she said with a smile as the tension began to ease out of her face. 'Devon and I are just starting out. It's scary and exciting and right now I don't know what I want career wise. I might want to think about kids and stuff, making a family. I don't want to get caught up in career stuff until I know what I want, and being part of another team while I'm still working stuff out is—'

'Stace, you can't let that stop you from advancing,' Kim said gently, knowing Stacey had done the sums on the DI-to-DS ratio.

'Boss, I ay naïve enough to think this team will stay together for ever. Dawson's death taught me that nothing is guaranteed, but right now, for me, it's the right place to be.'

'Stace, I think—'

'Boss, please let me finish,' Stacey said firmly. Kim realised that the woman needed to have her say.

'I am dead proud of the fact that you think I'm ready for the rank. Your faith in me is appreciated and I hate to disappoint you but—'

'Stace, you—'

'Boss, let me finish. I'm not ready to lead people. I'm not ready to be an example for others to follow. If something makes me angry, I want to shout. If something upsets me, I want to cry. I want the freedom to be me. I ain't yet grown that inner strength to hide my feelings for the good of others. I know you're gonna say I'm ready, and in some ways you might be right, but I don't want it. Not yet.'

'May I speak now?' Kim asked with a smile.

'Sorry, boss, I just—'

'No need,' Kim said, holding up her hand. 'It is part of my job to develop my team. In ability and skill, you are more than ready for the next step in your career, but I will not try and push you into something you're not ready to do. I just want you to know that when the time comes, you have my total support. Okay?'

Stacey's eyes reddened as her body appeared to deflate with relief.

Kim guessed that this had not been an easy conversation for the constable.

'I don't think it'd hurt to get you out a bit more, so I'm not gonna stop pushing you to improve and challenge yourself.'

'Good to know, boss,' she said, nodding her agreement.

'But just one more thing, Stace. You've never disappointed me. If anything, you've impressed me more by standing up for what you want.'

Stacey nodded gratefully.

'Now get out and go and enjoy your long weekend. You're a married woman, you know.'

Stacey laughed as she gathered her things together and headed for the door.

Kim returned to the Bowl and allowed herself one selfish moment of pleasure that she wasn't losing Stacey quite yet. Whether the constable knew it or not, she was an integral part of the team.

She was still smiling when her phone began to ring.

She didn't recognise the number but pressed to answer and then hit the speaker symbol.

A loud automated voice boomed out, filling the empty room.

'You have a call from someone at Drake Hall Prison. Would you like to take the call? Press one for Yes and two for No.'

Kim's heart flipped before dropping to her stomach. There was only one person she knew at Drake Hall Prison.

Doctor Alexandra Thorne.

Her finger paused above the numbers one and two on her keypad.

She hesitated for just a second before she made her choice.

A LETTER FROM ANGELA

First of all, I want to say a huge thank you for choosing to read *Twisted Lies*, the fourteenth instalment of the Kim Stone series, and to many of you for sticking with Kim Stone and her team since the very beginning.

If you enjoyed it, I would be for ever grateful if you'd write a review. I'd love to hear what you think, and it can also help other readers discover one of my books for the first time. Or maybe you can recommend it to your friends and family… And if you'd like to keep up-to-date with all my latest releases, just sign up at the website link below.

www.bookouture.com/angela-marsons

For many years I've wanted to explore the subject of witness protection. The notion that someone's entire past could be erased fascinated me, not to mention the psychological effects of having to cut ties permanently with family, friends and all things familiar.

I wanted to explore all the reasons for a person being placed in the programme, but it wasn't until I began researching the subject that I began to understand reasons why people would actually leave the programme.

Something I wasn't prepared for was to learn about the impact on the protection officers and the secrecy and deceit they need to employ to enable them to do their job.

Understandably, it isn't easy (and nor should it be) to research the mechanics of the process, and much of what I learned came from personal accounts of being in or having left the programme.

As with every book I write, I learn something new about the subject I'm researching and this book was no exception.

I'd love to hear from you – so please get in touch on my Facebook or Goodreads page, Twitter or through my website.

Thank you so much for your support – it is hugely appreciated.
Angela Marsons

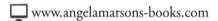 www.angelamarsons-books.com

 angelamarsonsauthor

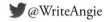 @WriteAngie

ACKNOWLEDGEMENTS

As ever my first and foremost thanks go to my partner, Julie. She meets the challenge of each new book with enthusiasm and passion as though it is the first. She never tires of the meetings, tantrums, guidance and encouragement needed to get through each one of these journeys. There is no doubt that these stories would not get written without her.

Thank you to my mum and dad who continue to spread the word proudly to anyone who will listen. And to my sister, Lyn, her husband, Clive, and my nephews, Matthew and Christopher, for their support too.

Thank you to Amanda and Steve Nicol who support us in so many ways, and to Kyle Nicol for book spotting my books everywhere he goes.

I would like to thank the growing team at Bookouture for their continued enthusiasm for Kim Stone and her stories, and special thanks to my editor, Claire Bord, who manages to make the editing process for every book not only painless but enjoyable too. Her passion for the books is relentless and inspires me to write the best books I can.

To Kim Nash (Mama Bear) who works tirelessly to promote our books and protect us from the world. To Noelle Holten who has limitless enthusiasm and passion for our work, and Sarah Hardy who also champions our books at every opportunity.

A special thanks must go to Janette Currie who has copyedited the Kim Stone books from the very beginning. Her knowledge of the stories has ensured a continuity for which I'm extremely grateful. Also need a special mention for Henry Steadman who is responsible for the fabulous book covers, which I absolutely love.

Thank you to the fantastic Kim Slater who has been an incredible support and friend to me for many years now, who, despite writing outstanding novels herself, always finds time for a chat. Massive thanks to Emma Tallon who keeps me going with funny stories and endless support. Also to the fabulous Renita D'Silva and Caroline Mitchell, both writers that I follow and read voraciously and without whom this journey would be impossible. Huge thanks to the growing family of Bookouture authors who continue to amuse, encourage and inspire me on a daily basis.

A special thanks to Nigel Adams, Fire Investigator and blogger extraordinaire, who offered his time and expertise to assist with some much-needed research.

Huge thanks to Sarah Lessiter who was the highest bidder to be named as a character in this book and donated a generous amount of money to a charity very close to my heart.

My eternal gratitude goes to all the wonderful bloggers and reviewers who have taken the time to get to know Kim Stone and follow her story. These wonderful people shout loudly and share generously, not because it is their job but because it is their passion. I will never tire of thanking this community for their support of both myself and my books. Thank you all so much.

Massive thanks to all my fabulous readers, especially the ones who have taken time out of their busy day to visit me on my website, Facebook page, Goodreads or Twitter.

Made in United States
North Haven, CT
11 November 2021